DEADLY MOTIVE

A DCI REECE THRILLER

LIAM HANSON

CRIME PRINTS

Published by CRIME PRINTS

An Imprint of Liam Hanson Media

ISBN-13: 979-8497365962

For my parents, who made me what I am today.

Current books in the series:

DEADLY MOTIVE

COLD GROUND

KILLING TIME

CHASING SHADOWS

DEVIL'S BREAD

DEADLY MOTIVE

Chapter 1

'WHAT'S IT DOING?' FISHY wiped a handful of lank, greasy hair from his face and spat on the rain-sodden ground. He raised the hood of his parka against the prevailing wind, pulled on its frayed drawstring, and squeezed his face out of the hole at the front of it. 'They're looking for us. I know they are.'

Onion pressed his back against the outer wall of the old factory building and watched the patrol car turn for another slow circuit of the industrial estate. 'They don't know we're here,' he whispered. 'Just killing time before going home to their wives and kids.'

The whites of Fishy's eyes bulged in their sockets. An untreated thyroid disorder mostly to blame. 'How can you tell?'

Onion was used to having to explain most things to his *slower* friend. Questions and answers often repeated before Fishy finally got it. He leaned into him and said: 'They'd have stopped and come this way if they were onto us. And they didn't, did they?'

Fishy stamped warmth into his numb feet, craning his neck until the patrol car was out of sight. 'This thing is making me nervous,' he said, fiddling with the parka's side-pocket.

A serious look of warning passed between them. 'Leave it alone then.'

Fishy tutted and set about sulking, which was something he was very good at. 'Why can't we chuck it in the river and go to the pub instead?'

Onion's patience was running out, and fast. 'Because we're gonna sell it.' He led the way through a gap in the chain-link fence, steering Fishy by the sleeve of his coat. 'So it won't be going in any sodding river. You got that?'

Fishy pulled his arm free. 'Billy said to get rid of it.'

Onion twisted at the waist and gripped the parka by both of its shoulders. 'We'll tell Billy it went for a swim.' He nodded. Smiled. Nodded again. 'All's good. You got that?'

'I thought you said we were gonna sell it?'

Onion massaged his eyeballs and tried one last time. 'Only you and me will know we sold it.' He waited for the penny to drop, but couldn't be sure it had. 'Billy will think it's gone for good. That it's sat there at the bottom of the sea. Our secret,' he said, tapping his nose.

'I like secrets.' Fishy found another place to spit. 'I said I like secrets.'

'I heard you the first time.'

'And Billy won't have Denny kill us, because he'll think we've done exactly what he told us to do.' Fishy's face split with a wide grin. 'You're clever.'

Onion patted the parka's material back into shape. 'Yeah, well. One of us has to be.'

They crossed a cracked concrete pad that swept around the rear of the building, taking care not to attract the attention of the mechanic working in the garage opposite. There was music coming from a radio and the repetitive sound of metal striking against metal. The grease-monkey would have heard nothing above the noise he was making.

Fishy fiddled with the ties of his hood. 'It's raining again.'

'It'll be dry inside,' Onion said, speeding him along with a gentle prod. 'Think how much tobacco you can get with the fifty quid Billy owes us for this.'

Fishy did the maths. Twice. Using both hands and all ten fingers. 'That's twenty quid each, right?'

'Not a penny less.' Onion wedged the sharp end of a squat crowbar into a crack between the door and its rusted frame. He hesitated and got up off his muddy knee.

'What's wrong?' Fishy nudged him out of the way. 'Let me see.'

Onion pointed with the length of steel. 'It's open already.'

When their eyes met, it was Fishy who spoke first: 'Someone's been in there. They could still be in there.'

Onion shook his head. 'Kids, that's all. And long gone by now.'

Learning difficulties aside, Fishy was blessed with an innate warning radar for all things not quite right, and just now, it was lit up like a Christmas tree. 'It ain't kids.'

'Not scared, are you?' Onion teased. 'Come on.'

The inside of the place was cavernous and unbearably cold. Like a deep underground tomb, it sucked every bit of warmth from their bodies, feet first. It smelled of damp, neglect, and something else that neither of them could put a name to.

'This place is evil.' Fishy kept his voice low. 'I can tell.'

Onion elbowed him in the ribs. 'I warned you about that nonsense. Cut it out.'

'It ain't nonsense. My nan reads tea leaves and knows everything that's gonna happen to people before it does.'

Onion took a small tin from his denim jacket pocket and offered a roll-your-own cigarette. He used a cheap plastic lighter to get them both going. 'Wasn't your nan killed a few years back?' He set a trio of smoke rings on their way towards the high ceiling.

Fishy took a deep drag on his cigarette. 'The number twenty-two bus ran her over outside the Co-op in town.' He turned his head away and chuckled. 'She must have had coffee that morning.'

Onion gave him a playful slap. 'What are you like?'

Fishy relaxed. But only for a moment. 'What was that?' he asked, his head flitting left and right.

'It's just the wind.' Onion watched the broken fans rotate in dusty cages suspended beneath the roofline. 'This place is falling apart.'

'Someone's in here with us.' Fishy let his cigarette fall to the floor. 'What's that horrible stink?' He went deeper into the gloom and shoved at something dangling only an arm's length from his face. When it swung back, he squealed and ducked out of its way. '*Urgh* – there's shit-n-stuff all over me!'

Onion quickly sidestepped and let whatever it was swing into the darkness behind them. 'Get off my jacket,' he said, slapping Fishy's soiled hands. There came the sudden sound of footfall descending the stairs from the metal balcony above. Fishy shifted position and fell against a section of shelving that went to ground with a deafening noise. Onion pulled him to his feet and shoved in the general direction of the exit. 'That way. Shift!' They grabbed at the worn edge of an empty workbench to avoid overshooting the tight turn, Onion slamming the factory door behind them. It squeaked open again as they sprinted across the concrete pad with the ragged gap in the fence looming only metres ahead.

'They're after us!' Fishy screamed.

'The gun!' Onion caught hold of the parka's hood, almost lifting Fishy clean off his feet. 'Shoot him. Shoot the fucker!'

Fishy reached into his side pocket and tried another when he couldn't find it. 'It's gone.'

Onion shoved him hard and followed through the sagging fence, heading for the pavement and the quickest route off the industrial estate.

Fishy sprinted onto the road, oblivious of the vehicle bearing down on him. His trailing ankle caught the nearside wing of the passing patrol car, somersaulting him up and over its bonnet, dropping him onto the wet tarmac in an untidy heap. Onion came to a halt on the white centre lines when the Ford Focus mounted the high kerb opposite, its back end twitching as it swerved to avoid a tree. 'My leg's busted,' Fishy said, writhing with the pain of his injuries. He stretched a limp arm in a plea for help. 'I said my leg's all busted up.'

'They're after us,' Onion warned, and didn't go any closer. 'Come on, stop messing about.'

'I can't.' Fishy pointed at his throbbing foot. 'It's facing the wrong way.'

Onion retreated when the first of two police officers got out of the car and shook himself down. 'Not a word about the gun.' He pressed a finger to his lips and made off in the opposite direction.

Fishy lifted his head off the road. 'Don't leave me.' There was blood on his hands and clothing. Lots of blood. 'I'm dying.' Two faces he didn't recognise appeared out of nowhere, and for the briefest of moments, he thought they belonged to angels. Unlikely, he quickly decided, given that the one to his left was sporting a hefty beard.

'Are you okay?' the officer asked. 'Stay with us, son.'

'Is he okay?' The other officer dabbed at a bleeding nose. 'The daft bastard almost got us all killed.'

'We didn't kill anyone.' Fishy shook his aching head in protest. 'That woman was all cut up before we found her.'

Chapter 2

Detective Chief Inspector Brân Reece descended the winding stairwell from the third floor with an increasing level of menace.

"*You're on gardening leave*," was how the new Chief Superintendent had put it. Or something similar to that. Reece wasn't entirely sure. He'd been far too pissed off to stick around and listen to her rant.

He pushed between two women talking on the narrow landing, knocking a stack of case files from the hands of one of them, sending sheets of A4 paper see-sawing in all directions. The younger of the pair squatted to clear the mess from the floor, while the other officer stood with her hands on hips, struggling to find the right words to complain. Reece offered no apology for his rude behaviour, and neither woman would have expected one now that they'd identified him as the culprit.

He tugged the knot of his black necktie, freeing the stiff shirt collar as a fire door flew open under the command of his boot. When a uniformed constable attempted to engage him in conversation, he raised a finger in warning and uttered one word only: 'Don't.' The young officer's ginger complexion turned a paler shade of white, the poor man turning to flee before the Wrath of Reece descended upon him with little or no mercy.

A few of the murder squad detectives looked up from behind their busy desks, none of them foolish enough to raise their heads too high above the safety of the trenches. They'd let their boss disappear into his office and get the latest cause of angst off his chest. Then someone—Detective Constable Ffion Morgan usually—would take him a milky coffee with two sugars while all awaited calm. The slatted blinds would open five minutes later. The glass door, another five after that. Next, Reece would exit and *walk the deck*; asking questions, issuing orders, and leading from the helm as the heady fog cleared.

That's how things usually went.

But not today.

'The *bastard!*' was all everyone heard before the door to the office slammed shut with enough force to bring the Divisional Shield to ground with a couple of loud bumps.

'I wonder what that was about?' Detective Constable Ken Ward got to his feet and rescued the tarnished silverware before some innocent passer-by did themselves an injury by falling over it. 'The boss looks well pissed off,' he said, finding a temporary home for the shield on top of the nearest filing cabinet.

Detective Sergeant Elan Jenkins tipped back on the rear legs of her chair and patted a new short-back-and-sides. 'That, boys and girls, is all Chief Superintendent Cable's doing.' She rubbed at an annoying smudge of something on the chest of her green bomber jacket. Then spat on a finger and tried again. 'He had orders to go straight upstairs this afternoon,' she said, giving up on the stubborn stain, 'and I'll bet you a pound to a penny he's just had his arse smacked good and proper.'

Morgan held open the lid of the photocopying machine and fed the empty drawer more paper. 'He'll be in deep shit if he doesn't start minding that temper of his.' She checked over her shoulder and said: 'I've heard the new chief super is ruthless when she needs to be.'

Ward agreed and went back to his seat, clapping dust from his pudgy hands. 'The jungle drums say you don't want to cross her. Not if you value your pension, that is.' He groaned as he lowered himself into position. 'Sped through the ranks in the Met, she did.'

Jenkins grinned. 'Yeah, but she'll never have come across anyone like Brân Reece.'

'True.' Morgan puffed her cheeks and let the breath out with a loud pop. 'The poor woman has no clue what she's let herself in for.'

'Right,' Ward said with a clap. He stared across the wide expanse of detectives' desks, to the other side of the room, and promptly announced: 'Do your thing, Ffion-Girl.'

Morgan frowned. 'What thing is that?'

'Coffee and a smile.'

Jenkins watched Ward struggle to pull the hem of an old woollen jumper over what was more than a middle-aged paunch. 'You're cutting back on the crap in the New Year,' she told him. 'Do you hear me?'

'It was like this when I got it.' He gave her his best puppy dog look and opened a drawer in his desk. He lobbed an Everton mint in her general direction. Another arced its way towards Morgan.

'Dream on,' Jenkins said.

Morgan peered over the rims of her newest pair of designer spectacles. 'Like she said, it's soup and salad once Christmas is out of the way.'

Ward rolled his eyes and pointed towards the office door. 'Coffee to the boss. Now.'

'You be my guest.' Morgan gave her head a firm shake, clearly unwilling to back down. 'I've taken one for this team often enough.'

'So that's what lightens Reece's mood. And there's me thinking it was the coffee.' Ward turned to Jenkins and clucked his tongue. 'And her boyfriend is okay with that sort of thing?'

'Apparently so.' Jenkins feigned disappointment.

'Don't.' Morgan went back to her photocopying in floods of blushes. 'You're a bloody pervert, Ken Ward. And *you* shouldn't be encouraging him.'

Ward chuckled to himself. 'It must be your turn then,' he told Jenkins. 'The boss won't shout at you.'

'I'm pulling rank,' she said without the slightest hesitation.

'Ken's right though.' Morgan raised the spectacles onto the top of her head. 'The boss likes you.'

'He likes us all,' Jenkins replied. 'We're a team, and a bloody good one at that.'

'Not me anymore,' Ward said, suddenly serious. 'I'm beginning to think I've fallen out of favour with him.'

Jenkins brought the front legs of her chair down and onto the stained carpet tiles. 'Do you want me to speak with—'

The door to the DCI's office opened with the loud clatter of blinds slapping against glass. The noise cut Jenkins short. Reece loomed in the doorway with his necktie wound to his fists like a boxer's wraps. 'You,' he said, pointing at her with both hands. 'Get in here.'

Jenkins covered the ground between them in a matter of seconds. 'Send in the cavalry if I'm not out by Tuesday,' she told her open-mouthed colleagues.

'Gardening leave.' Reece stood with his back to her, and was dressed head-to-toe in black clothing. Folklore at the station had it he and Al Pacino were one and the same man. 'I got the goatee first,' Reece had joked during lighter times. 'Pacino copied me. Not the other way round.' But Reece wasn't joking now. 'Getting me out of the way while she promotes that fast-tracked tosser is what she's doing.'

Jenkins said nothing initially, but looked as though she thought she should. A faint buzzing from the overhead strip lighting did little to fill what had become an increasingly uncomfortable silence. She gave in. 'I'm sure the chief super wouldn't have—'

Reece turned abruptly, his eyes fixing his detective sergeant to the spot. 'You're sure of what?' He stooped and pressed the knuckles of both clenched fists against the flat of his desk, the necktie stretched between them as though he were preparing to garrotte someone.

Jenkins shifted rearwards toward the door. Might this be the awful moment when Reece finally lost all control of his senses? She took another step, chanced her luck, and said: 'DI Adams won't be here for very much longer. He's just passing through.'

That seemed to work. Reece slumped heavily into a swivel chair, its ageing mechanism squeaking as he rocked back and forth. 'A university degree and a fast-track programme through police college doesn't qualify you as a murder detective.' He loosened his grip on the necktie. 'The man used to be a bank manager, for Christ's sake.'

Jenkins shuffled from one foot to another. 'I graduated from university,' she said with a smile that was gone in an instant.

'You went to Swansea.' Reece was on his feet again, a suit jacket draped over his shoulder. 'I meant a proper university.'

Chapter 3

Reece leaned against the dented door of his twenty-year-old Peugeot 205 and slid the keys across its heavily scratched roof. 'You're giving me a lift home,' he said, getting in.

Jenkins dropped into the torn driver's seat and shifted side-on to face him. 'How do I get back to the nick once I'm done?' She turned the key in the ignition and looked genuinely surprised when the car contradicted its heap-of-junk appearance and started on the first attempt.

Reece fastened his seatbelt and rummaged at the back of the glovebox. 'You went to university,' he said, waving a short screwdriver at her. 'You'll think of something, I'm sure.'

Jenkins kept quiet until they were well established on the A4232 West. 'Is this about Billy Creed?' She stretched to use the back of her hand on the foggy glass, ducking to peer through a porthole of improved visibility. 'Is that what's got the chief super's back up?'

Reece stopped fiddling with the radio. 'It's always about Creed,' he said, shoving the sharp end of the Stubby into a hole that had once played host to the channel select knob. 'Creed or some other scum just like him.'

'But why him in particular?' Jenkins alternated her attention between the DCI and what little she could see of the road ahead. 'You've been after him ever since I've known you.'

Reece left the Stubby sticking part way out of the hole. 'It's been a damn sight longer than that. Creed runs this city,' he said. 'Get rid of him and we go a long way to making it a safer place.'

'You can't be serious about him running things?'

Reece took a deep breath and sighed. 'How do you think he manages to stay one step ahead of the game – shrugging off charges on one technicality or another?'

'Allies in important places?' she ventured.

'Exactly. Welcome to the party.'

Jenkins nodded towards the radio. 'Do you think you should do that? There's a twelve-volt battery powering that thing.'

Reece took no notice. 'Just drive, Sergeant.'

The windshield got another wipe over. The air vents a good tap with a finger. 'When are you getting rid of this thing?' Jenkins asked when the crackle and hiss of radio static gave rise to new levels of irritation for her boss.

Reece shut the screwdriver away in the glovebox and watched the Cardiff City football stadium go by on the other side of the road. 'What's wrong with it?' he asked with a deep frown.

'It's just about ready to fall apart.'

'It suits my needs well enough,' he said. 'Besides, I don't like change.'

Jenkins flicked the indicator stalk and turned at the T-junction, braking hard to avoid a cat with a death wish. 'You should learn to embrace it,' she said cheerily. 'Change will happen with or without you.'

'*Embrace* it?' He gawped at her. 'Don't you bloody start.'

Chapter 4

Belle Gilligham stood at the kitchen sink, scrubbing her hands with a ritualistic compulsion that turned the fingertips pink and sore. She'd worn gloves throughout the kill. Had been careful not to stain herself with Roxie-bitch's spilled blood. Yet still she scrubbed. And when finished, she began over again.

Belle couldn't recall when it was she'd first used the name Roxie-bitch. She liked it. It fit its miserable owner perfectly. The woman was a bitch. A liar too. And one who deserved everything she got.

Roxie wasn't the first of them to be punished. Neither would she be the last. Belle had a list of intended victims. People who were well overdue their comeuppance.

She closed her eyes, savouring the early evening's memories, reliving each individual moment in its entirety. The look of sudden recognition on Roxie-bitch's face had been priceless. Even after the passage of time, the hag had recognised her in an instant. The whimpers of pain were exquisite. The near-silent sound of surgical steel slicing its way through human flesh, divine. Belle shuddered, her mood souring only when her thoughts shifted to how the evening's events might so easily have taken a different turn.

The patrol car had slowed next to her on the industrial estate, its bearded driver warning her to take care as she walked home alone after dark. He had eyed her stockinged legs and made small-talk while scoring her out of a perfect ten. That's what men did when you let them get away with it. It was one of many reasons she despised them all.

Challenging him might well have jeopardised everything she had worked so long and hard to achieve. And so she'd let him stare. Encouraged him even. Waving a shopping bag in his direction while joking that there was enough weaponry inside to kill a small army should the need arise. Had the police officer known the awful truth, he'd have had her face down on the pavement, his knee pressed between her toned thighs, patting her down in the name of the law.

But he hadn't suspected a thing, and had laughed at her lame joke, promising to do a few more circuits of the estate before calling an end to the shift. She'd thanked him for his concern, and at the same time, cursed him with every ounce of her being. She needn't have worried. Roxie-bitch was fashionably late. Presumably missing the patrol car altogether.

The Taser device had been the perfect choice of weapon, incapacitating Roxie long enough to apply bindings and raise her off the ground using a hand-operated winch. The look of terror in her lidless eyes. Pissing herself while mumbling lame excuses. And the blood. So much blood.

The unexpected arrival of the two intruders had made her rush to get things finished. People often made mistakes when acting in haste. She hadn't. Had she? No one would find the shopping bag. She'd hidden it well enough - even with few available options. But she'd been given no time to clean up after herself. Still, the police wouldn't bother with the upper landing. They'd be more interested in the corpse on the ground floor. The nagging doubt had her hurl the soap into the sink. The nailbrush was lost to the kitchen floor as a new wave of anger consumed her.

Chapter 5

REECE CHECKED HIS WRISTWATCH while Jenkins braked and accelerated with monotonous repetition. The Christmas traffic moved along at a snail's pace through the historic city of Llandaff.

'The Romans settled here,' Jenkins said, not taking her eyes off the brake lights of the car in front. 'To link Cardiff Castle with the village of Llantrisant.'

Reece didn't pass comment, preoccupied as he was watching two men drilling holes in the road behind a lopsided barrier of red-and-white plastic.

Jenkins pointed at the overhead decorations without taking either hand off the steering wheel. 'Amy does ours.'

'Waste of time and money, if you ask me.' Reece shifted position in the sunken car seat, getting no more comfortable after several irritable attempts. He gave up trying and went back to watching the men in the hole. 'You two getting on any better than you were?'

'I suppose,' Jenkins said, their eyes meeting momentarily. 'How does that old saying go? *When she's good, she's very, very good. But when she's bad, she's a fucking maniac.*'

'Can't say I'm completely familiar with that one.' They were past the hole in the road, a woman with an orange bucket now Reece's new focus of attention. She wore the colourful tabard of the Noah's Ark Children's Charity.

'Amy is bipolar,' Jenkins said. 'It's not her fault when she gets wound up over things. That's how I look at it.'

When the woman with the bucket came alongside their car, Reece lowered the window and handed her a twenty-pound note. 'Merry Christmas,' he said with as much cheer as he could muster. 'Keep up the good work.'

Jenkins looked suitably impressed. 'Someone's got money to burn.'

'Not really. Half of that donation was yours.'

The grin was quickly swapped for a wide-eyed stare. 'But I'm skint, boss. Ken scrounged another tenner off me first thing this morning.'

'Forget his wallet again, did he?' Reece went back to trying to get comfortable. 'And didn't Ffion have to bail him out with a few quid last week?'

Jenkins nodded. 'The cashpoint near his place was out of action.'

'Yeah, right.' The car rattled over another deep pothole, every nut and bolt holding it together, threatening to break free. Reece was about to mention his mounting misgivings regarding Ken Ward, when Jenkins's ringtone rudely interrupted them. 'Answer it,' he said when she'd made no further attempt after several loud bars of music. 'I'm driving.'

'Hardly. Nothing's moving.'

'It's still illegal.' Jenkins wedged the Blackberry between her shoulder and chin, steering with her knee when the traffic pulled away again. 'I don't suppose you've got this thing set up for hands-free?' she asked.

'And you'd be right.'

'What's up?' Jenkins asked the caller.

Reece could hear precious little of the conversation and sat with his eyes closed. Another night of broken sleep was taking its toll.

'I'll be there just as soon as I've taken the boss home.' She ended the call and fumbled with the handset, dropping it somewhere into the dark footwell of the car. 'Shit.' She reached between her knees but couldn't get a hand on it. Then resorted to using her heel to drag it from under the clutch pedal.

Reece opened his eyes and pinched the bridge of his nose. 'What did the catwalk queen want?'

Jenkins handed him the Blackberry for safekeeping. 'I wish you wouldn't keep calling Ffion that. It's unprofessional, among other things.'

'She's half-plastic,' Reece said with a snort that came from somewhere deep down in his chest. 'That's why you never catch her standing next to the radiators at work.'

Jenkins broke into a fit of loud belly-laughter. 'You're well beyond all available help.'

Reece clucked. 'The chief super said something similar earlier.'

'Are you sure she put you on gardening leave?'

Reece wasn't. 'Does it matter? However they choose to dress it up, it all means the same in the end: they're getting rid of me, and that's that. What did Ffion want?' he asked, changing the subject while a herd of shoppers tried to decide if it was safe to cross the road in front of them.

Jenkins waved them on. 'Uniform found a woman's body off Walker Road in Splott.'

Reece drummed his fingers on the cracked dashboard. 'What are you waiting for? Turn around and get us over there.'

Jenkins must have known she was on a hiding to nothing. 'I'm taking you home. You're on leave, remember?'

'Have it your own way,' Reece said, releasing his seat belt. 'If that's the way you want to play it, then you can head over to the crime scene on foot.'

Chapter 6

A BARRAGE OF FLASHING blue lights greeted the old Peugeot as it slid to a halt on the cracked concrete pad at the side of the factory building. There were vans belonging to crime scene investigators, a fleet of patrol cars, and a pair of ambulances already waiting. Most of them with their engines running. The rain had only just stopped, but a chill wind swirled and blustered, sending sheets of yesterday's news to catch on the chain-link fence like insects trapped on a spider's web. Reece got out of the car and flashed his warrant card at the first person to approach. Jenkins came behind, calling for him to stay the hell away from the crime scene.

'The chief super didn't confiscate your ID?' she asked once she'd caught up. 'That's odd.'

Reece put it away in his wallet. 'Must have passed her by during the excitement of treating me like a school kid.'

A crowd of onlookers were gathered on the other side of the road, rubbernecking, hoping to snatch a glimpse of something they shouldn't. Middle-aged men cracked morbid jokes, while the younger generations used their phones to upload hashtagged images to social media accounts for worldwide discussion.

A journalist walked among them, asking questions and scribbling notes for the evening edition. 'What can you give me, Detective Chief Inspector?'

'It's Maggie Kavanagh.' Jenkins nodded in the reporter's direction, jogging almost, just to keep up with the boss. 'She's here before us again. How does that keep happening?'

Reece ignored them both and marched past a uniform busily stringing crime scene tape between two lamp posts. The officer looked away when he saw who it was.

'Where is she?' Reece asked the nearest CSI. 'Was there a knife involved in the attack?'

The CSI told them to go round the back of the building. 'Suit up before you go in,' she said. 'And make sure you put your names and ranks in the crime scene log.'

Reece glared at her. 'This isn't my first time, you know. I *have* done this before.'

Jenkins shook her head in warning when the woman looked like she might reply. To Reece, she said: 'You can't go in there.'

The factory unit was swarming with activity. A CSI in hooded coveralls took photographs of the body and the immediate environment. Another used video equipment to record the gruesome crime scene. Other specialists came and went with evidence bags and forensic equipment. More still were bent at the knee, numbering things with small yellow cones.

They kept to the metal stepping plates that meandered along the factory floor, leading them to where they needed to be.

'What have we got, Twm?' Reece shielded his eyes from a battery of fluorescent lamps that lit the place up like the inside of a circus tent.

The venerable pathologist removed a thermometer from Roxie May's rectum and did a half-twist at the waist. 'Brân, what are you doing here?'

Reece leaned out of reach. 'Trying to avoid that thing.'

Dr Twm Pryce put the thermometer away and waited for a photographer to finish what she was doing and leave. 'Sorry about that. I thought you were taking some time off?'

Circling the body, Reece was careful not to contaminate anything. 'Good news sure travels fast.' Jenkins shook her head in complete denial when he glanced in her direction.

'I bumped into the new chief super on the way over here,' Pryce explained. 'She was saying . . .'

Reece wasn't listening. He turned to face the steps leading to the overhead balcony. Then went and stood in front of Roxie May's dangling corpse. 'Cause of death?' he asked without a hint of preamble.

Pryce paused, as though collecting his thoughts. He closed a well-worn bag with a double-click of its brass clasps. 'Loss of eyelids aside, I'd say haemorrhage caused by injuries inflicted with a very sharp implement.'

'What's that?' There was an object resembling a rubbery pear sat in a dollop of congealing blood. It was on the surface of the nearest workbench and leaned slightly to the left as Reece viewed it.

'A uterus with a couple of centimetres of fallopian tube on each side.' Pryce stopped to point at the victim. 'It came out of that gaping hole in her lower abdomen.'

The detective's eyes widened. 'Jesus Christ.'

The pathologist looked towards the heavens. 'There's little sign of him coming to the help of this poor soul.' With their gruesome conversation over, Pryce set off, all the while negotiating the stepping plates with due care and attention.

Reece followed and pushed past. He gulped for air and loosened the top button of his shirt. When Jenkins found him some ten minutes later, he was standing against the wall outside, alone, and no less grey in complexion. 'Sorry about that,' he said.

She blew on her hands and turned her back to the worst of the weather. 'I was looking for you.'

'And you've found me.'

'Another flashback?' she asked, coming alongside.

'I'm fine.' He was anything but. The chest tightness and nausea were taking longer than usual to subside. He ran a finger between his shirt collar and neck and took a few deep breaths. 'I needed some fresh air. What happened to that woman reminded me of ...' He didn't finish. Couldn't finish.

Jenkins reached for his arm and missed when he moved away. Their shoulders brushed as he walked around her and set off across the concrete pad. She followed, her pace quickening when he made a sudden beeline for one of the waiting ambulances. 'Stop,' she called. 'You're not allowed anywhere near the witness.'

Maggie Kavanagh was waving an arm from her position on the other side of the crime scene tape. 'Is it true the suspect is already in custody?'

Jenkins caught up as Reece approached a paramedic dressed in dark green trousers and yellow high-viz jacket. 'Boss, please,' she begged.

The paramedic let go of a folding step and wiped her wet forehead on the back of her hand. 'Who are you?'

'Tell him to turn it off,' Reece said when the clackety diesel engine spewed lungfuls of noxious fumes at them.

'And you are?' the woman asked for a second time.

'Police.' Reece used a handrail to pull himself up and into the back of the vehicle. 'Murder Squad.'

'Let me see your ID.'

Reece tugged a blanket off a stretcher, exposing the cowering casualty huddled beneath. 'Would you look who it is.' He tossed the blanket to one side and wrung his hands.

Jenkins climbed in, her attention alternating between the goings-on inside the vehicle, and a black Jag that had just turned in a wide arc on the concrete pad. 'Get out, boss. Come on. Let's go.'

The paramedic got between them and pulled Reece by his jacket. 'Are you deaf? Do as you're told.'

He freed himself and got a handful of Fishy's parka before the paramedic was onto him again. 'What happened in there, you little toerag?'

Fishy sucked on the mouthpiece of a gas and air machine.

'I asked you a question,' Reece said, knocking it out of Fishy's hand.

Jenkins pulled at him with no attempt to be gentle. 'You'll screw up this entire investigation if you're not careful.'

Fishy had the mouthpiece again and turned it away from him to imitate the shape of a pistol. His face lit up. 'I've found it!'

'Give me that.' Reece snatched it away, this time wedging it under his thigh when he sat down. 'Shut up and listen.' Fishy did, his eyes wide and frightened. 'Did you touch her?'

Jenkins's head bobbed in and out of the ambulance. 'Boss, we need to go, and sharpish.'

Reece stood, but wasn't giving up. 'Who was in there with you?'

The paramedic shoved both police officers towards the open rear doors. 'Get out, the pair of you.'

'I saw the footprints,' Reece said. 'It wasn't only you inside that factory.'

'Boss, that's it. No more.'

'You'll be done for murder.'

They were out at last, Jenkins forcing him around the side of the vehicle.

'I didn't see his face.' Fishy sounded close to tears.

Reece thrust his head into the back of the ambulance. 'Did he speak, or leave a waft of aftershave?'

'Boss, make yourself scarce.'

'Well, did he?'

'Detective Chief Inspector!' The call came from somewhere near the parked Jag.

Reece spun; his fists clenched tight to the sides of his head. 'Why can't you leave me in peace to do my job?'

Chief Superintendent Cable strode towards them, her gloved hands holding on to her service hat. 'Go home,' she said above the noise of the busy scene. 'You're not needed here.'

Chapter 7

BILLY CREED SPRAWLED ACROSS a huge leather sofa in his nightclub office, a pair of spray-tanned blondes clinging like limpets to his muscular arms, whispering sweet nothings in the gangster's ears.

'Where's the retard?' Creed asked. His black silk shirt was left unbuttoned to the navel, exposing a thick rug of greying chest hair and a gold rope chain that looked capable of hanging a man should the whim ever take him. Creed's neck, face, and bald head were a canvas of multi-coloured tattoos. A small bluebird inked between his finger and thumb was a memento of his days with the infamous Cardiff City Soul Crew. Football hooligans.

The air in the room was thick with the smell of cigar smoke and—Creed's pungent calling card—patchouli oil.

Onion swallowed on a dry mouth and fought the nagging urge to shit himself. 'A car walloped him, Mr Creed. He's dead.' It wasn't a lie as such. Fishy had been in pretty bad shape when he'd left him sprawling on the cold, wet tarmac. Onion slammed a fist into an open palm, doing his best to simulate the force of the impact with the patrol car. 'There was blood and stuff everywhere.' Opening his balled-up jacket for the gangster to cop an eyeful, he said: 'I did what I could for him, but it was too late.'

Creed took his hands from the swell of the girls' buttocks. 'Tell me you didn't fuck it up.' The light shone off his bald head with such intensity that Onion was convinced someone had spent most of the afternoon polishing it with a cloth.

Denny 'The Shovel' Cartwright was in the far corner of the room, puffing on a thick cigar. The man was enormous. His knee-length leather jacket crunched like boots in virgin snow when he rose from the low chair. Clicking his bruised knuckles, he loosened each mound of a shoulder in turn. 'Answer the question, dumb-fuck.'

Onion clenched his bottom end. 'No one will ever find that gun, Mr Creed. I promise you.'

'Not in front of the ladies.' Creed slapped both backsides. 'Fuck off,' he said, shoving the women away. He got up and watched them exit the door guarded by Cartwright: two near-perfect figures strutting their stuff in tight Lycra bodysuits. 'Where did you ditch it?' he asked once they were alone.

Movement drew Onion's attention to the television screen above Creed's head, a sinking feeling gnawing at the pit of his stomach as the scene played out in neon-blue silence. 'In the sea,' he said, forcing himself to avert his gaze. 'We went on a fishing trip.'

'*Fishing* — are you taking the piss?'

Onion raised his hands in self-defence when the gangster came towards him. 'I wasn't. Promise. It was more of a boat trip, really.'

Creed glanced over his shoulder at the television, and then slowly back again. He tapped ash from the end of his cigar and said: 'Is there a problem?'

The news had thankfully moved on to the next story. Onion desperately needed to open his bowels. 'Not at all, Mr Creed. God's honest truth.'

DS Elan Jenkins stood with her head pressed against the glass front of the hot drinks machine, the gentle hum and rattle of its motor somehow soothing as it sent vibrations coursing through her upper body. It was during times like these she wished she smoked, or at the very least, drank alcohol like most normal people.

Chief Superintendent Cable had only just finished reading her the riot act, making it perfectly clear how close she was to pottering in a garden of her own.

She had tried to stop Reece from entering the crime scene. Had begged him not to interfere with the witness until she could think of nothing more to say in response to his behaviour. But would the man listen? Would he hell. Reece was a law unto himself. His tantrums and mood swings now almost as frequent as those of her partner, Amy. Jenkins shut her eyes and imagined herself lying on a beach where they, and others like them, didn't exist.

'He'll bring you down with him.' DI Adams stalked the corridor, churning pocket change with a repetitive chinking sound. He wore an expensive light-grey suit with oxblood brogues. 'Dinosaurs are extinct for very good reasons.'

Jenkins disliked the man instantly and pressed coffee-two-sugars just because she could. 'DCI Reece is a good copper, sir. The best,' she corrected. 'This last year has been tough on him.' She pushed past, spilling some of the coffee on the linoleum floor. 'His wife was murdered, you know – so you might want to cut him some slack.'

Adams avoided the patches of wet flooring. 'We all have our crosses to bear,' he said with a thin-lipped smile. 'Give my words some thought, Sergeant. Your future on this team may very well depend on it.'

Chapter 8

IT WAS LATE INTO the evening when DI Adams stood at the front of the crowded briefing room. There were several crime scene photographs and a long list of unanswered questions pinned to the evidence board behind him. 'We're here to catch a killer,' he said, pausing for effect, 'and Chief Superintendent Cable has appointed me senior investigating officer for this case.'

An audible rumble of disquiet passed through the room – station rumour and idle gossip, calling for reason and explanation.

'Where's DCI Reece?' someone asked from the back row of seats.

'Suspended on full pay is what I heard,' another responded.

Chief Superintendent Cable appeared from nowhere, her presence a clear sign that top brass had more than a passing interest in

Roxie May's murder. Saying nothing for the time being, she stood with her arms folded. A shoulder resting against the wall.

Adams outlined what they knew so far: which wasn't a bad haul, considering they'd arrived back at the station only thirty minutes earlier. They had a location, a named victim with a preliminary cause of death, two suspects, and a pair of shaken-up patrol officers. Adams searched the room until he found the crime scene manager. 'Any more from Forensics?'

Sioned Williams got to her feet. As the supervisor of a team of ten CSIs, she was the conduit between scientific detail and investigative police work. 'The footprints outside the rear door were a mess,' she said. 'We've made casts, but I don't hold out much hope of them providing anything useful.'

'What else?' Adams asked.

Williams read from her notepad. 'There was a crowbar found in the bushes.' She looked up momentarily and then back down at her notes. 'Lack of rusting suggests it hadn't been there long. But the damage we saw on the door and its frame isn't consistent with it being used to gain entry.'

Adams frowned. 'Fingerprints? Check it anyway.'

'We will,' Williams said. 'All in good time.'

Adams shifted a stack of files to one side of the desk and made himself comfortable on its leading edge. 'I want everything you have as soon as you get it.'

Ffion Morgan raised a hand. 'It says here that the killer left a coin next to the uterus. Is that his calling card, do you think?'

Sioned Williams admitted to not knowing at such an early stage of the investigation. 'You might want to consult a profiler about that.'

'There'll be no profiler.' Chief Superintendent Cable stepped away from the wall. 'We'll be tightening our belts in the lead up to the new financial year.'

Morgan returned her attention to the front of the room. 'It might be significant, don't you think, sir? Worth looking into, I mean.'

Adams slid to his feet, churning pocket change with renewed vigour. 'We'll know just as soon as we've interviewed our suspects. Any sightings of this Onion character?'

Ken Ward came to life and wiped the smudged remnants of a chocolate éclair from his top lip. 'Uniform are out looking, sir. In all the usual haunts, including the ex-girlfriend's place.'

Morgan puffed her cheeks. 'Best of luck with that one. Tasha's as pissed as a fart most days, and as high as a kite the rest of the time.'

'Check anyway,' Adams said. 'I want him under lock and key by the end of tomorrow.'

'We'll need backup. Onion almost got his head caved in the last time he went round there. If it hadn't been for Ken—'

'Do whatever,' Adams interrupted. 'But I want you at the post-mortem first thing in the morning.'

Morgan lowered her head and swore. 'It can't be my turn again.'

Ward nudged her with an elbow. 'Get a good fry-up down your neck before going over there. Works for me, every time without fail.'

She pointed to an untidy mound of paperwork piled atop a desk on the other side of the glass. 'You do the PM and I'll make a start on that lot.'

'Only wish I could,' Ward said between fits of giggles. 'But the DI asked you, and I wouldn't want to make a bad impression this early on.'

Adams had his eye on DS Jenkins. 'Nothing to contribute to the conversation?' he asked.

She took to the floor with an ominous silence descending upon her. 'It's not them. Fishy. Onion.' She waited for Adams to react and continued when he didn't. 'Whoever murdered Roxie May was a cold and calculated killer. This pair are nothing more than opportunistic thieves, there looking for something they could sell on for beer and fag money.'

'It might have something to do with Billy Creed,' Morgan offered. 'Roxie May was his sister, after all.'

Adams silenced them both with a raised hand. 'I wondered how long it would take for someone to mention that name.' His frown was so deeply formed that it made him look like a Pug dog. 'I'd hoped this ludicrous obsession would end in the DCI's absence. Obviously not.'

'They didn't do it.' Jenkins looked at the chief super for support that wasn't forthcoming. 'Trust me on this one.'

'Consider the facts,' Adams said, losing his hands in his pockets. 'If they're as innocent as you'd have us all believe, then how is it that Darren Evans—or Fishy as he's known on the streets—got himself covered in the victim's blood? And then there's the not-so-minor issue of his altercation with a moving patrol car while fleeing the scene of the crime.'

'They had means and opportunity, granted,' Jenkins said, slumping onto her chair. 'But what's the motive?'

Adams cleared his notes from the table. 'As I've already said, we'll know that once we've interviewed them.'

'The surgeon says Fishy will be discharged into our care first thing tomorrow morning.' Ward lifted his foot a few inches off the floor, as though verbal explanation alone was insufficient. 'Nothing broken. Just a dislocation that needed popping back in under sedation.'

'Looks like we'll have this all wrapped up by Christmas Day,' Adams said, chuckling at his own joke.

'And the third person at the factory?' Jenkins again. 'Will we be making any effort to find them?'

Adams sifted through his paperwork until he came across what he was looking for. He skim-read from two incident reports before waving them in the air for all in the room to see. 'The patrol car officers don't mention seeing anyone else. No one at all, in fact.'

Jenkins wasn't giving up that easily. 'Fishy was adamant that a person who, so far, hasn't been accounted for, chased them out of that factory building.'

'You're referring to comments made under physical and psychological duress.'

'It was no such thing,' Jenkins insisted. 'DCI Reece only—'

'The paramedic disagrees with your interpretation of events.' Adams flapped another document like he was waving a flag at a Jubilee celebration. 'I'll read what she had to say, shall I?'

'But that was—'

'But nothing. You know as well as I do that no self-respecting lawyer is going to accept a word of what Fishy says.'

'You don't know that for sure, sir.'

'And you don't know when to accept you're wrong. The suspect was high on gas and air, and pinned to the stretcher under the weight of DCI Reece's fist.' The statement got another wave above his head. 'It's all here, Sergeant, if only you'd get down from your high horse and read it.'

'When do we tell Billy Creed about his sister?' Ward asked. 'He's going to go apeshit when he finds out.'

'Not yet,' Adams replied. 'I want to interview the prime suspects first.'

Jenkins closed her eyes, irritated by the sound of pocket change doing its dance. When she opened them again, Chief Superintendent Cable was nowhere to be seen.

Chapter 9

Onion scarpered like a rabbit freed from a trapper's snare. He glanced over his shoulder—it was little more than that—and saw them watching from a window running the entire width of the Midnight Club's upper level. Creed said something that had Denny Cartwright retreat to the rear of the room. To where the burly doorman kept his shovel in the far corner.

It was all too much for Onion. He went scampering across the empty dance floor, frightening the poor old cleaning lady as he rushed towards her. She raised a wet mop and swung it like a medieval cudgel, driving him away mumbling incoherent apologies.

The soft orange glow of street lighting was visible beyond an open fire door. The sound of a new rain shower audible as it soaked everything outside. Onion ran for the exit, bursting into the empty alleyway to throw up on the wet cobblestones. He coughed, spat, and lit a cigarette to calm his nerves – a foot resting against the damp wall while he contemplated the full implications of what he was into. He'd been there barely a minute when someone came round the corner singing *Delilah* for all he was worth.

The teenager stopped singing to concentrate on what he was doing. 'All right?' he asked with an accent that suggested he was a visitor from the nearby valleys.

Onion edged out of range as just about everything in sight got a good hosing down with warm urine. 'Yeah.'

With a final shake and his jeans re-zipped, the teenager offered him a two-pound coin. 'For a cuppa,' he explained. And with that, he was gone. Off into the night with a crowd of rowdy friends.

Onion hadn't attempted to put the kid right. Two quid was two quid, after all. Besides, the lad hadn't been far wrong in thinking he was living on the streets. Sofa hopping and kipping down at Tasha's place whenever she was out of town was about as good as it got most days. He took a deep drag on the cigarette and once again found himself alone with his thoughts.

If Creed ever paid up on the fifty notes he'd promised, then getting on a bus and riding out of Cardiff might be an option worth considering. But then what? Live on the streets in a place he didn't know and get himself done in by some crazed tosser high on drugs?

He could always wander back inside the club, admit to the monumental cock-up, and plead for mercy. He chose not to do that.

Mostly on account of having no appetite to end his days face down in a muddy field with Denny Cartwright's size twelves pressing hard on the back of his neck.

He'd have to find the gun before the police did. After that, he'd trawl every hospital in the city in search of Fishy. And in the unlikely event he found the useless bastard alive, he'd put all six bullets in him, regardless of who else was watching.

When the first of the patrol cars pulled up outside Tasha Volks's flat, all blues and twos, Onion went out of the back window, leaving his ex-girlfriend jacked up on a green velour sofa. He'd hidden six brass bullets in a pot under the kitchen sink. His job there was done. Dropping to the ground and just managing to stay upright, he made off down a narrow street, toppling bins behind him while zig-zagging from one side of the road to the other.

One of the patrol cars shot ahead. A second blocked his rear, leaving him no easy way out. He climbed onto an overturned bin and ran a hand along the top of the stone wall, thankful the owners hadn't seen fit to crown it with the customary layer of broken glass.

There were police officers everywhere. Most calling for him to stop and hand himself in. He'd do no such thing and heaved himself over the wall, smashing onto a plastic patio set on the other side. The table caved in along its length, four chairs knocked over onto the bow of their backs.

He righted himself on the wet grass and sprinted across the garden, illuminated in a column of white light. He hadn't heard the helicopter arrive, but now he knew it was there, the noise from its engines and rotor blades were deafening.

Dodging the outstretched hands of the nearest uniform, he shoulder-barged what looked to be a flimsy fence separating two gardens. The panel split when he hit it hard, rebounding him towards an army of yellow jackets.

Chapter 10

BILLY CREED STOOD AT the mezzanine window watching the Midnight Club fill with crowds of festive revellers. There were males, females, and others who hadn't yet made up their minds. He'd sell a ton of pills in the lead up to Christmas. Denny Cartwright's army of thick-necked doormen would make sure of that. Creed relit a half-smoked cigar and swirled the remnants of ice round the bottom of an otherwise empty glass. 'Put the news on,' he said, pouring them both another generous measure of Boulard VSOP. 'That little shit had a worried look in his eyes just then.'

Cartwright reached for the battered handset and found the channel with a few clicks of its worn buttons.

There had been a gas explosion at a flat in Caerphilly. The property was damaged beyond all reasonable repair. Its occupants escaping certain death thanks only to them getting up early for the morning school run. Dinner ladies were going on strike in Aberdare that coming Friday - better working conditions the cause of their latest complaint. There was a tractor thief loose in West Wales. More than three hundred and fifty thousand pounds' worth of farming equipment had been stolen from the area in the previous two weeks alone.

Creed sipped his brandy and pressed a finger to his lips when the broadcast came around on its latest loop. 'Turn it up.'

A middle-aged reporter was fighting with a red golfing umbrella, shouting all the while to make himself heard above the chaos at the boundary line of a murder scene. 'Police are keeping tight-lipped about the identity of the victim,' he said, as a gust of wind threatened to turn his umbrella inside out. 'Reliable sources say a man of interest is being held in one of those ambulances over there.' The camera did a full sweep along the length of the building, zooming in on the waiting vehicles for the benefit of the viewing public.

'It can't be.' Creed squinted at the television screen, silvery ash from his smouldering cigar catching in his chest hair. He clenched the brandy glass so tightly that it threatened to shatter in his white-knuckled fist.

'That estate's on our turf.' Cartwright spoke with a deep menace to his voice. 'Someone's been taking liberties.'

Creed kept his back to the angry doorman and gave the reporter his undivided attention. He saw DCI Reece jostling with a woman dressed in green and yellow clothing. She was shouting. Waving her arms in warning. 'They wouldn't have,' Creed said, picking a flake of tobacco from the tip of his tongue. He rolled and flicked it to one side. The ambulance's interior wasn't clear. Darkness, blue flashing lights, and distance, all conspiring against the cameraman. 'Go get that shovel, Denny-boy,' Creed said through a mouthful of clenched teeth. 'You've got yourself a hole to dig.'

It wasn't far off midnight. Christmas Day in less than a week. Reece was behind the wheel of his parked Peugeot, a flat white takeout in hand. His thoughts wandered to the events of earlier that evening. Giving the chief super the middle finger as he'd wheel-spun away from the factory yard hadn't been one of his finest moments. Neither was the continuous blast of the horn until he was well out of sight. But when the dark cloud descended upon him, there was next to nothing he could do to escape its evil clutches.

He and Anwen had sat in this same spot, on numerous occasions, sharing laughter and love. Making plans for a future that was to be snatched away from them in a moment of sheer madness. The old cottage in Brecon lay in a state of disrepair still.

Anwen had been so excited when she first came across it, insisting they stop the car and take a good look around. She didn't care that the slate roof leaked. That the generator was temperamental at best. She'd bullied Reece into buying the place the very same day it came onto the market. He'd promised to do it up. A project they could complete together. But police work was incompatible with renovating a second home. Progress, therefore, had been woefully slow. The failure brought with it a deep sense of self-loathing and shame. His terrible loss made him cry most days. He regularly forgot things and lost his temper with anyone who dared to correct him. And the nightmares. Such awful nightmares. Worst of all were the flashbacks: cruel reruns of Anwen's death playing out on the neon screen that was his mind's eye. They came when he least expected them. At Roxie May's crime scene, for example. He'd better apologise to Jenkins when he next saw her. No wonder top brass were embarrassed and wanted him pensioned off.

He'd earlier driven through the streets of Cardiff, listening to music that he and Anwen had chosen together. Music he now had no choice but to play alone. Unable to face going home to an empty house, he found himself parked next to the Norwegian Church in the bay area of the city.

It had once been a thriving dock, exporting Welsh coal all over the globe, making its owner, The Marquess of Bute, the world's richest man. But Tiger Bay, as it used to be known, was almost unrecognisable now. A multi-million-pound regeneration programme in the nineteen nineties had turned it into *the* place to hang out in Cardiff.

Reece got out of the car and sat on its wet bonnet with his memories and coffee. He stared across the man-made lake towards the fuzzy lights of the tidal barrage system way off in the distance. When laughter passed behind him, he turned to see a group of five young women walking arm-in-arm. He raised his paper cup to them and nodded. 'Ladies.'

'He's lush,' one of them said, wobbling on a pair of impossibly tall heels. She stopped to stare. 'I've seen him on the telly. Sure of it, I am.'

Reece smiled to himself. Read 'em and weep, Pacino.

'Hey mister, you want to come into town with us?' She couldn't have been a day over sixteen and was barely dressed.

'You all take care tonight,' Reece said, watching them stagger into the road to hail a passing taxi. He raised the collar of his jacket against the worst of the wind and slid off the bonnet. He got back in the car, the brief reprieve clearing his head enough for him to make two decisions. Christmas Eve, he'd head out to the cottage in Brecon for the first time since Anwen's death. No more excuses. The renovation would be completed in her memory. Tomorrow morning, he'd drive over to the hospital and beat the truth out of Fishy if that's what it took to find out what really happened to Roxie May.

Chapter 11

Reece took the stairs to the hospital's sixth floor and found the ward he needed with directions given by a passing porter. The man even offered to take him there if need be. Reece declined with grateful thanks. A wall-mounted wipeboard next to the main desk told him where Fishy was located. On guard duty outside the cubicle was a bored-looking constable. The same ginger officer Reece had frightened the day before.

The uniform stood on sight of him, his chair scraping across the stained linoleum floor with a high-pitched squeal. 'I haven't moved, sir. Been here the whole time. The nurse will tell you.'

'Relax. And not a word to anyone, do you hear me?'

'Look who it is.' The woman's voice came from the sluice-room opposite and belonged to the middle-aged staff nurse standing in its open doorway. 'Give me a minute now.' She snapped her fingers repeatedly. 'Your name will come to me.'

Reece smiled, the response warm and genuine. 'Helen, what are you doing here?'

'I needed a change from the other place,' she said, drying her hands. 'It's been four months, almost.'

'I didn't know.'

Helen dropped a paper hand towel into a black bin and shut the sluice door on her way out. 'If you'd only answer your phone once in a while ...' When she attempted to straighten the raised lapel of Reece's jacket, he stepped out of reach. 'Your friends are worried about you. That's all I'm saying,' she said, lowering her hand.

Reece gazed at the floor. 'I'll get round to something in the New Year, I promise.'

Helen looked as though she'd heard it all before. 'You here for that scroat in there?' She nodded at the cubicle door. 'We all know what he did. He's lucky no one's put plain saline in his drip instead of painkillers.'

'I need to see him.'

'I bet you do.'

'And it's probably best you don't document this anywhere.'

The staff nurse pursed her lips. 'You're not here on official police business, are you?'

Reece winked. 'Two minutes is all I need. Then I'm gone.'

Her manner softened. 'You always did fly close to the sun.'

Didn't he know it. 'And got burned every time.'

'That there is the ward round.' Helen pointed to a gathering of people at the main desk. There was a small army of them; several of whom looking far too young to be shaving yet. 'It begins in a little under ten minutes, and there's nothing I can do to stop it once it gets going.'

'Message understood,' Reece said, disappearing inside. He was quick to clamp a hand to Fishy's face and used his knee to pin him flat against the mattress. He whispered in his captive's ear. 'The next copper through those doors is going to do you for murder.'

Fishy tried to free himself, his arms and legs flailing wildly as he mumbled obscenities beneath the weight of Reece's grasp.

'One wrong word and I'll throw you out of that window,' Reece promised, and released his grip bit by bit.

Fishy pressed himself tight against the wall, his hospital gown coming loose and rucking up beneath him. 'We're on the sixth floor.' He used his fingers to count: 'That's one, two, three—'

'Shut up and listen to me.'

'I said we're on the sixth floor.'

'So it shouldn't hurt for long once you've reached the bottom.' Reece snatched a pillow from the bed and forced it over Fishy's face. 'We're going to play ourselves a little game,' he said, checking over his shoulder. 'It's a variation on water-boarding.'

'This is Reece's car. I'm sure of it.' DI Adams walked around the Peugeot, kicking each worn tyre in turn. Its driver-side window was flying half mast and well out of alignment. He picked at the flaking paintwork. 'Check it's got a current MOT.' There was no sign of its owner anywhere. 'Where are you?' Adams said, gazing in all directions. 'I know you're here somewhere.' He refocused his attention on the car's lights and windscreen wipers. 'This piece of junk should be impounded.'

Jenkins stayed where she was. 'It drives a lot better than it looks.'

Adams wasn't listening, and headed for the open doors at the rear entrance to the building. Taking two or three steps at a time, he neglected to excuse himself to anyone who rushed to get out of his way. 'If I find Reece anywhere near our suspect, I'll do him for obstructing a police investigation.'

It took an age for the lift to arrive. A fair while longer for the doors to stop opening and closing without taking them anywhere. Jenkins kept her finger on the illuminated button.

Adams was at the rear of the lift, straightening his necktie in a half-mirrored wall. 'He'll lose his career, pension – the whole damn lot if I'm right about this.'

Jenkins inched her phone from her jacket pocket, angling her body so that Adams couldn't see what she was up to. *No Service*, it said in small white text at the top right corner of the screen.

The automated voice of the lift spoke its every move once it got going—first in English, then repeated in Welsh—the brief journey to the sixth floor, leaving her feeling verbally abused.

Turning in all directions when they got out, Adams said: 'Where now?'

Jenkins pointed to a bilingual wall sign. 'That way I think.'

'Keep up.' Adams hurried along the empty corridor like a missile locked on to its target. 'I want you to be a witness to the downfall of your boss.'

Chapter 12

Reece lifted the pillow and put it to one side. 'Tell me what you saw in that factory.'

Fishy gasped for air. 'It was too dark.'

'You saw something. I know you did.'

Fishy pulled his knees in close to his chest. 'She was like a pig on a hook. Bleeding and dripping smelly stuff everywhere.'

'That was no pig,' Reece said. 'That was Billy Creed's sister.'

'*Roxy?*' Fishy needed no one to explain the consequences of being involved with that one. He looked towards the window as though ending it all might be his favoured option. He wiped dry spit from the corner of his mouth. 'I want protection.'

'This isn't the movies.' Reece got off the bed and readied himself to leave. 'You're looking at fifteen to twenty for what they're accusing you of.'

'Not prison.' Fishy was hyperventilating. 'Please, not that.'

'Where is he?' Adams came to a halt outside the cubicle door, his head bobbing like a nodding dog's.

Ginge rose from his seat. 'Who do you mean, sir?'

'Is he in there?' Adams reached for the door's metal push plate. 'Reece!'

Ginge moved in front of him. 'I haven't seen the DCI since we were back at the station yesterday.'

'His car is parked outside.'

'He could be visiting a friend or relative, sir.'

Jenkins tried not to laugh and looked away. 'Idris Roberts has been in and out of hospital lately. Maybe the boss went over to the chest ward to see him.'

'And what do you think you're doing?' Helen came out of the cubicle next door. When Adams produced his warrant card and attempted to get past her, she mirrored his movements, blocking him. 'The surgeons are about to expose the wound.'

Adams turned to Jenkins. 'I thought Ken Ward said the ankle was dislocated only?'

Helen led them down the corridor before he could question her further. 'You can go in once they've finished.'

Ginge went back to his post. 'There's a coffee machine in the staff room, sir. I'll come and get you as soon as they're done here.'

'That was him,' Reece said, when all outside fell quiet again. 'The man who's looking to fit you up for the murder of Roxie May.'

Fishy leaned one-legged against a bedside cabinet, bemoaning the pain in his ankle now the morphine tablets were wearing off.

Reece went over and pulled on the cubicle door when he failed to respond. 'Your choice – but I doubt you'll make it anywhere near a trial before her brother catches up with you.'

Fishy grasped his head in his hands and dropped onto the end of the bed. 'I'm scared.'

Reece let the door close. 'So quit with the bullshit and let me help you.'

Fishy balled his fists and took deep breaths. 'You promise they won't hurt me?'

'You leave Billy Creed to me.'

Chapter 13

Ffion Morgan stood behind a full-length screen of Perspex waiting for Dr Twm Pryce to arrive. She felt sick to her stomach even before things got started. On the cutting side were white wall and floor tiles; stainless-steel cabinets; fluorescent strip lighting; and air conditioning vents that whispered overhead.

She hated the mortuary. Nothing else came anywhere close on her list of places to avoid when able.

A technician had already collected Roxie May's body from a numbered drawer in the refrigerator and was now whistling Christmas carols as he laid it out on a shiny extraction table. He opened the black bag by dragging its plastic zip from the head to foot end. Then called for help from a short woman. Together, they unwrapped Roxie.

The doors to the cutting room flew open with a theatrical whoosh, Twm Pryce marching in with an inappropriate level of cheeriness. He wore black scrubs, a green plastic apron, and a pair of shin-high white Wellington boots. Morgan's stomach churned. She'd skipped breakfast and had no reason to regret it.

Pryce waved in the direction of the gallery. 'Morning, Ffion.' The man was tall and distinguished. Like an olden-day movie star that her grandmother might once have had a secret crush on.

'Hello, Dr Pryce.' Morgan couldn't be sure that her voice had carried far enough, but the pathologist seemed to have heard her.

'You're still struggling with these things, I see.' Pryce hung his head over the hole in the cadaver and took a few deep breaths. 'The trick is to take a good lungful before you get going. Much better already,' he announced with a wide grin.

Morgan closed her eyes and retched.

The technician went about combing Roxie's hair. Then scraped under her fingernails, collecting and labelling samples while contributing little to the conversation. Next came the photographs, which were accompanied by a battery of clicks.

With Roxie May rolled onto one side, Pryce spoke into a microphone that hung from the ceiling by its coiled flex. 'Do you see the pattern of livor mortis just here?' He pointed at the purple discolouration of the skin. 'When the heart stops beating, the heavy red cells sink to the lowest level of the body, causing a staining effect. On the back and buttocks in this woman's case.'

Morgan took notes. It meant she didn't have to look up very often. 'But we found the victim hanging in an upright position. Shouldn't the blood have settled in the lower legs?'

Pryce ran a gloved hand along each cold shin. 'There is a little,' he said, turning the feet side to side. 'Most of what you see in the flanks would have occurred while she was in overnight storage. Okay, let's get this show on the road,' he said, making a Y-shaped incision from both collarbones to the gaping hole in Roxie May's abdomen.

Morgan wasn't exactly sure what happened next, but found herself sat on a plastic chair in a drafty corridor, sipping cold water from a polystyrene cup. She used her foot to push a vomit bowl further under the seat and peeled a wet compress from her forehead. 'I'll be okay now,' she said, rising to wobble on unsteady legs.

'No bother. Happens all the time.' The technician ran an appraising eye over a soup of brown bile and stomach lining. 'No breakfast this morning?' He tutted his disapproval.

'How do you do it?' Morgan swallowed and made a grab for the bowl. 'I was fine until you opened the skull and spooned out the brain.'

The technician laughed and returned inside to weigh the remainder of Roxie May's internal organs.

The clip-clop of footsteps approaching along an otherwise empty corridor interrupted the brief silence. 'What are you doing out here?' DI Adams checked his watch. 'Even the Great Pryce couldn't have finished this early.'

'I fainted, sir. And hit my head.'

Adams made no response and went through the same door used by the technician. He rapped on the Perspex panel with the back of a hand. 'Anything new for us to be getting on with?'

Pryce turned with surprise. 'Inspector.' He looked beyond the DI, and to an ashen-faced Morgan. 'Are you feeling any better, Ffion?'

'She's fine,' Adams said without bothering to check with his junior.

'That's good to know.' Pryce went back to Roxie, where the technician was busy sewing her closed with a stout needle and heavy nylon sutures. 'There are multiple abrasions to the wrists and ankles, which would be consistent with the bindings found in situ. You know about the uterus and eyelids already.'

'Are you saying the killer is someone with surgical training?' Adams asked.

'Not necessarily. They have knowledge of anatomy—yes—but the execution of the procedure itself was somewhat crude.'

Adams relaxed. 'Right. Good.'

Morgan had since recovered enough to join in. 'And was the victim alive when the worst of the injuries were inflicted?'

Pryce removed his apron and discarded it in a shiny pedal-bin. 'I'd say so, given the amount of arterial splatter at the scene.'

Morgan took a moment to respond. 'The killer forced her to watch her own hysterectomy?'

'If the pain and bleeding hadn't already rendered her unconscious, then yes.'

'Was there a blow to the head, or any other signs of incapacitation?' Adams asked.

'None at all,' Pryce said, washing his hands. 'I've taken muscle biopsies. It might be nothing, but we'll know more once we get the samples fixed under a microscope.'

'When might that be?'

Pryce came closer to the screen, his position in the cutting room a good ten feet lower than theirs in the viewing gallery. 'It is Christmas, after all. I'm not sure the chief super will authorise—'

Adams turned his back on the pathologist and made his way up the steps. 'You won't know for sure until you've tried her.'

Chapter 14

Elan Jenkins looked up from behind her desk and double-took. 'Jesus, Ffion. What happened to you?'

Morgan tossed her bag onto the floor and dropped onto her chair without removing her coat. 'The sick bastard only cut her eyelids off and made her watch the whole thing until she gave up and died.'

Jenkins stood. 'There's a lump on your head.'

Ken Ward rubbed his hands together like he was warming them over a basket of hot coals. 'A little bird told me she did it again.'

Morgan slumped lower. 'That mortuary technician, I bet?'

Ward nodded. 'Apparently, you made a sterling job of pebble-dashing the lower half of the viewing gallery.'

Adams slowed as he passed through the incident room. 'Is that what the awful smell of cheese was?'

Morgan blushed. 'Why did he have to tell you? Why do that?'

Ward tapped his nose. 'Your secret is safe with us.'

'Sod off, Ken.'

Jenkins spoke directly to Adams. 'I heard what Twm Pryce said about the killer having knowledge of anatomy. That's got to put your two suspects out of the running?'

'And did you not also hear that the technique used was crude?' Adams addressed all in the room. 'Who's chasing the lab for those prints?'

'There's nothing back as yet,' Ward said, finger-combing his unruly beard. 'You do know Onion's banged up in a cell downstairs, sir?'

'I'm making him sweat. That way, he's more likely to break down and tell all.'

Jenkins had heard enough bullshit for one day and collected her jacket from the back of her chair. 'I'm off.'

'Where?' Adams asked before she'd made it as far as the door.

'To speak with the crew of the patrol car.'

'Oh no you don't.' He banged the desk with the flat of his hand. 'I've got their statements right here, as well you know.'

'I'd rather hear it for myself,' she said, not waiting for his permission to leave.

She found the pair taking a break in the staff canteen. Both men were complaining—to anyone willing to listen—about the idiot who'd almost got them killed the evening before. Plonking two steaming coffees on their table, she took a seat without asking.

'We've been through this already,' the bearded driver said in response to her opening question. 'Two people ran out in front of us, not three.' Beard's colleague dunked a shortbread biscuit in his coffee and chased after it with a spoon when it broke in two and sunk to the bottom of the mug. 'If there was anyone else there, one of us would have seen him for sure.'

'Not if he made off behind the factory when he saw you arrive.'

Beard shook his head. 'Take it from us, love, there was no one else at that factory.'

'Besides,' said the other officer, 'that area backs onto a thick line of trees and bramble bushes. There's nowhere to go.'

Jenkins took a moment to think it over. 'Okay then, could the killer have made off when you were dealing with Fishy's injuries?'

'It's possible, I suppose.' Beard finished his coffee and made himself ready to leave. 'But you're barking up the wrong tree, love, if you ask me.'

Jenkins fanned the fingers of both hands on the table top. She didn't look up, and spoke loud enough for only the three of them to hear. 'I'm not your *love*, do you understand?' Beard rolled his eyes and nodded. Jenkins made fists and knocked them against the surface of the table. 'I didn't catch that.'

The man buttoned a heavy waterproof coat. 'Sorry, Sarge. Nothing meant by it.'

Jenkins got to her feet and moved uncomfortably close to him. 'That's good to know. Because you've no idea how close you just came to shitting teeth for the next few days.'

Jenkins strutted through the incident room, stopping to make an entry on the evidence board in thick red ink. 'There you go,' she said, lobbing the marker pen into a small cardboard box.

'*Mystery Woman.*' Morgan read it aloud and folded her arms across her chest. 'Are you onto something?'

'There was another person near that factory, and only minutes before Roxie May was murdered – only that pair of morons didn't think to mention it in their report.' Jenkins hung her jacket on the back of the nearest chair. 'There was a woman carrying a shopping bag plenty big enough to conceal a full change of clothes, as well as the murder weapon.'

'Why would they leave that out?'

'Because Adams told them to focus only on persons seen leaving the building. Not events from earlier in their shift.'

The DI appeared in the office doorway, clutching a folded copy of the South Wales Herald. 'Any of you lot seen this?' He read its front-page headline from memory. 'Santa Claws Spotted on Cardiff Industrial Estate. That's Claws spelled with a W.'

'Maggie Kavanagh's at it again,' Morgan said. 'You won't have had the pleasure, sir. She's the local crime reporter and regular pain in the arse.'

Ward unwrapped an Everton mint and popped it in his mouth. 'Maggie rattles sabres with the Police and Crime Commissioner at least once a week. And that means top brass read every word the woman writes.'

'Is that so?' Adams scoffed. 'Then it's just as well we're almost done with this case.'

Jenkins's face crumpled. 'Didn't you hear me? This missing woman has to be a person of interest.'

Adams tossed the newspaper into the nearest bin. 'Sergeant, are you always this belligerent?'

'I don't think I know what that means.' Jenkins looked at her colleagues for help that wasn't forthcoming.

'Hostile. Aggressive. I could go on if need be?'

She told him not to. 'You'd have to agree this changes things?'

'Not one iota.'

'You're kidding me?'

'It would have taken the strength of a man to hang another adult in such a way. Perhaps two men.' Adams spoke with complete confidence in the logic of his argument. 'And to have inflicted such terrible injuries – one with a deep hatred of women.'

Jenkins stared at the ceiling directly overhead. 'Have you seen the size of Fishy? He's nine stone soaking wet. Onion isn't much bigger. And as for them hating their mothers and every other woman they've ever come across . . .' she shrugged, took a breath, and left it there.

Adams shoved a couple of files across the desk towards her. 'I've been catching up with our suspects' backgrounds. Take a look for yourself.'

Jenkins left the files where they were. 'I'm well acquainted with the pair.'

'I insist. Consider it an order. And out loud for the benefit of your colleagues.'

Jenkins thumbed through the first few pages of one. She skim-read only. 'Okay—Darren Evans—or Fishy, as we know him. Has mild autism and other learning difficulties thought to have resulted from his mother's alcoholism. Mum died of liver failure and a stomach bleed before he was six years old. He then lived with his grandmother until she was killed in a road traffic accident when he was sixteen.' Jenkins closed the file with a slap and dropped it back onto the desk. 'I know this already, sir. He's totally reliant on Gary Pask.'

'And I'm thinking he'd be willing to do anything for Pask?' Adams tapped the other folder. 'And this one. Read.'

Jenkins could have sworn the man was playing Jingle Bells with his loose change. She fought the overwhelming urge to kick it way up into his chest, along with his balls. Instead, she pacified herself by imagining his face, not Roxie May's, staring out of the photograph on the evidence board. 'Okay. Both were let down by society. But that doesn't mean they went on to kill because of it.'

'Are you familiar with the term Occam's razor?' Adams asked.

Jenkins wished he'd speak in simple, everyday English. 'No, sir, I think it's another that's passed me by.'

'It's a problem-solving principle stating that the simplest solution will most often be the correct one.' He raised his voice for all in the room to benefit from his great wisdom. 'When presented with competing evidence, the investigator must choose the answer with the fewest assumptions.'

Jenkins hid a pair of clenched fists behind her back and wondered how long it would take the others to drag her off him once she got going. 'Two long-in-the-tooth coppers speaking face-to-face with a potential suspect isn't an assumption, sir. It's a fact!'

'I want no more time wasted on your silly mystery woman.' Adams turned to Morgan and Ward. 'You two go and put Onion through his paces. He should be good and ready to squeal by now.' To Jenkins he said: 'You and I are going to hear what Paddy May has to say for himself.'

Chapter 15

JENKINS PULLED AWAY FROM a metal gate that spanned the entire width of the muddy lane. 'Get a leash on that dog,' she told the owner.

'Says who?' The man looked like a weasel—all pointed chin and beady eyes—and spat in the nearest puddle. A long-haired German Shepherd stood its ground alongside him, barking at the visitors while salivating through bared teeth. Weasel aimed a kick at the animal's hindquarters, and missed, screaming for it to: 'Shut the fuck up.'

'Cut that out.' Jenkins rattled the gate with a hand gripping its horizontal rail. 'Now!' she demanded when Weasel raised his boot for a second time.

'It's my dog.' Weasel chased the animal until he'd trapped it in a corner formed by the wire fencing. 'My yard.' He turned and spat again. 'And *my* fucking rules.'

'You do and you're nicked,' Jenkins said, exposing a pair of restraints attached to her belt. 'And you'll quit with the attitude if you know what's good for you.'

'We're looking for Paddy May.' Adams leaned against the nearside wing of his Volvo, a shiny brogue resting in what might well have been liquid dog shit.

'And we've found him, sir.' Jenkins glanced over her shoulder to see he hadn't yet followed her. 'First impressions?'

Paddy rubbed his rheumy eyes. 'If you're here about the boys, then you're wasting your time.'

Adams ventured closer and wiped the sole of his shoe on a patch of green grass at the foot of the gatepost. 'This isn't about your sons.'

'I don't know why you keep letting 'em out.' The scrap dealer used a short length of frayed rope to secure the dog to the fence and gave it another stern warning before leaving it be. 'You're not nosing round the yard. Not unless you've got a bit of paper that says you can.'

Jenkins closed the gate behind them and picked her way through a minefield of watery dog excrement. 'We're not here about stolen property. Not this time. This is about your wife, Roxie.'

'Ex-wife.' Paddy stopped to wag a filthy finger in her face. 'And a lying bastard to go with it.' With a growl, he was off again. Stomping through muddy puddles and swearing like a sailor.

'You threatened to kill Roxie.' Jenkins turned to speak with Adams. 'I had the pleasure of nicking him last year, sir. For threatening behaviour. That's one nasty piece of work you see there.'

'The woman took money that was rightfully mine.' Paddy kicked open the door to a battered Portakabin. 'The office,' he said, going inside.

Onion had thieved, lied, and cheated most of his twenty-seven years, but had never previously spent the night in a police cell on charges of kidnap and murder. What should have been little more than a five-minute job had somehow turned into a nightmare. He and Fishy had screwed up big time, and he was as sure as he could ever be that Billy Creed knew. The way the gangster had watched from his office window. The deliberate turn of the head as he spoke to Denny Cartwright. Creed knew all right.

But thoughts of his absent friend had given Onion the kernel of an idea. It was unlikely that Fishy had died from his injuries. It was only a smashed foot, after all. He was probably sitting in a hospital bed right now, eating cheese and pickle sandwiches and chatting up the nurses.

There was a way out of this predicament, Onion decided. But it meant only one of them could walk free. He worked and reworked the ifs and buts until they were clear in his mind. Life had never offered him a break. He'd have to make his own good fortune instead.

A drunk shouted abuse from the adjacent cell, disturbing Onion's train of thought. It didn't matter; he already had things straight in his head. Someone called for the man to be quiet, goading him into another outburst of vicious threats and childish name-calling.

Doors slammed and keys jangled. And so it continued until they came for him.

Morgan pressed the record button on a wall-mounted digital interview recording device (DIR). She waited for the loud beep to end before running through introductions and preliminaries.

Onion—Gary Pask for the formalities—winked at her.

'Do you understand why you're here?' Morgan asked.

'Because you wanted to be alone with me?' Onion leaned across the table and blew her a sloppy kiss. 'I'm game. Chubbs here can watch.'

Ward stifled a yawn. *Fatty. Lard arse. Chubster.* He'd heard them all and more, and no longer cared.

Morgan went for it from the outset. 'What do you think Billy Creed's going to do when he finds out you killed his sister?' She sat back and waited.

Onion's head snapped up; all signs of humour gone. He pointed a finger and struggled to get the words out. 'That's not what happened. No way.'

'Of all the women you daft dipshits could have chosen.' She closed her eyes and laughed at him.

'We didn't. I didn't.'

'You came onto Roxie like you did me.'

'No way.'

'She turned you down like every other woman you've tried it on with.'

Onion pulled at the cuff of a grey sweatshirt he'd been made to wear when they'd bagged his clothes. 'You're talking bullshit.'

'Roxie is being examined for evidence of sexual assault. How long do you think you'll last in prison as a rapist and woman killer?'

'Fuck you!'

'You're doing it again. Talking dirty. You obviously have no respect for women.'

Ken Ward banged the table. 'Sit down!'

Onion slunk onto his seat.

'You cut Roxie open,' Ward said. 'Left her hanging there when she threatened to tell her brother about you.'

'I'm no murderer. It wasn't me.'

'Then tell us who did this.'

Onion put his hands to his face and peered through the gaps between his fingers. 'Fishy's not like the rest of us. He's not right in the head.'

Chapter 16

Paddy May took a generous swig of cheap whisky from a half-bottle and drew the back of a hand across his cracked lips. 'Shut the door,' he said when they came through behind him. 'Were you born in a barn?'

Jenkins pushed it closed. Again, when the wind blew it open. She leaned against the handle and let the DI start with the questions.

'Roxie's dead,' Adams began. 'Where were you last evening between the hours of four and six?'

Jenkins clucked her tongue. 'I've seen that done with a lot more compassion.'

Adams paid her little attention. 'Mr May doesn't look to be the grieving type.'

'And you ain't wrong there.' Paddy screwed the top of the whisky bottle on tight and then loosened it again.

Adams had left his jacket on the back seat of the car and shivered with the cold. He moved closer to the two-bar electric heater and warmed his hands over it. 'Yesterday. Between four and six?'

'I was here.' Paddy took another gulp of whisky. 'Filing my tax returns,' he said, bursting into a fit of phlegmy laughter.

'Can anyone vouch for that?' Jenkins asked.

'Aye, the dog.' Paddy exposed a crooked row of rotting teeth. 'Go ask him, why don't you. He loves a good chat.'

Jenkins leaned on the desk. 'Stop pissing about. This is serious.'

Paddy slammed the bottle down next to her open fingers, missing them by a narrow margin. 'You saw what Billy did to me last year.' He caught Adams's eye. 'Creed had Denny Cartwright break both my arms.'

'Because you assaulted his sister,' Jenkins said. 'The same woman who's now lying dead in a hospital mortuary.'

'It was only a slap.' Paddy looked as though he genuinely believed that justified the act. 'Couldn't wipe my arse for the best part of a month.'

Jenkins didn't dare try to imagine how he'd overcome the inconvenience. 'You refused to give a statement.'

'Because Billy would have buried me out there somewhere.' Paddy hooked a thumb towards the woods and slumped onto an old car seat that was propped on top of a couple of milk crates. 'Imagine what he'll do if he thinks I'm involved in any of this shit.'

'And are you?' Adams asked.

'Do I look nuts?'

'We haven't informed your brother-in-law as yet,' Jenkins said. 'Next of kin only at this stage.'

Paddy got up and limped over to the window. 'Make sure you give me plenty of warning before you do. I wanna be well away from this place when that bomb goes off.'

'You won't be leaving Cardiff,' Adams said. 'I'll make sure Creed does you no harm.'

Paddy laughed at him. 'When Billy wants you dead, it kinda happens that way.'

'Then things are about to change round here.'

The scrap merchant went and looked out of the windows on all sides of the Portakabin, as though watching for something. Or someone. 'How was she killed?'

'You didn't see today's newspapers?' Adams asked.

'I don't read much.'

'I'm afraid we can't go into any more detail,' Jenkins said.

Adams pushed on the door. 'Remember what I said about you not leaving Cardiff.'

Paddy swallowed more of the fiery liquid and grimaced. 'And you remember what I said about giving me good warning.'

Onion leaned on an elbow and picked at a split in the desk's wooden veneer. 'Fishy's mum always said the midwife dropped him on his head and broke something.'

'What was she like?' Morgan asked. 'Were the two of them close?'

'Nah. She beat seven shades of shit out of him most days. We were all too scared to go anywhere near her as kids.'

'And his nan? Did he have a better relationship with her?'

'He loved that woman to bits. Broke his heart when he lost her. That's when I started looking out for him.'

Ward lay a colour photograph on the table and slid it across. 'Did Fishy's mother turn him into someone capable of this?'

Onion pushed the photograph onto the floor. 'You can cut that out. It had nothing to do with me.'

'You don't dispute being at the scene of the crime?' Morgan asked.

'That's impossible for him to deny,' Ward said. 'Two serving police officers positively identified him as being there.'

'Are you listening to anything I'm saying?' Onion leaned and stretched his neck towards them. 'Fishy's been doing some stuff for that pikey up at the breaker's yard.'

'Paddy May?'

'That's right.'

'What's that got to do with Roxie?' Morgan asked.

'You must know what happened last year? Paddy's lucky it was only his arms that got busted up.'

'What are you saying?'

'That he's not stupid enough to get rid of her himself.'

'Are you saying Paddy May had Fishy kill his ex-wife?'

'If you're looking for someone who *is* stupid enough.' Onion threw his arms in the air and let them fall at his sides. 'He's your man.'

'I don't buy it.'

'A pack of fags and a few cans of cider is all it would have taken to convince him.'

Ward shook his head. 'He doesn't have it in him.'

'Remember what I said.' Onion tapped his knuckles against his temple. 'He doesn't know what's what unless I'm there to help him.'

'But you were there,' Morgan replied. 'Why didn't you stop him when you found out what he was up to?'

'Because I got there later than he did.'

'How come?'

'He's been acting all weird lately. Disappearing for hours. Thieving for Paddy May. I heard he'd gone over to the factory for a look around.'

'And?'

'I went over there to see what he was up to.'

Ward tossed a clear plastic evidence bag onto the table. Inside was Onion's bloodstained jacket. 'You were there all right.'

'It was too late by then.' Onion pointed at the photograph on the floor. 'There was nothing I could do to help her.'

'And Fishy?'

'He turned on me. You should have seen his eyes. It was like he was on something.'

'Let's be clear about this,' Ward said. 'Fishy tried to kill you?'

'I got her blood on my clothes when he came at me with the same knife. If I hadn't done a runner, I'd be in that morgue with her right now.'

Ward scribbled something on a yellow notepad. 'And that's the only reason you were both sprinting from the building. Not because you were being chased by a third party?'

Onion nodded. 'I was running for my life. There was no one else there but us.'

Chapter 17

FISHY WAS SITTING ON a plastic chair in another of the station's interview rooms. He shifted position, unable to find its sweet spot. The walls were painted a drab green, much like the military vehicles he'd seen on the telly. Opposite was a long rectangular window that gave no clue as to who might be watching from the other side.

'They keep you waiting on purpose,' he told his brief. 'To wear you down before twisting everything you say.' He winced and swore when he caught his foot on the leg of the table. 'Like in the movies,' he said, nudging the woman with an elbow. The latest round of painkillers were wearing off and his ankle throbbed like a bad case of toothache.

The brief smiled politely and tried to move her chair a few inches further away from him.

'You can't,' he said when it didn't budge. 'They screw them to the floor to stop you whacking them with one.' He grabbed the underside of the table and heaved. 'See. You'd have to be King fucking Kong to swing that.' He rubbed his ankle. 'Do you like King Kong?'

A middle-aged police constable waited near the door, yawning with annoying repetition while the minute-hand of the wall-clock crawled its way nearer home time.

'I need a smoke.' Fishy checked the desk and then along the shelf next to the DIR machine. 'I said I need a smoke.'

The brief had nowhere to go, the legs of her chair refusing to shift no matter how hard she tried. 'They don't allow it in here,' she said, nodding at a red and white sign on the far wall.

Fishy was about to ask why that was when the door to the interview room opened without warning. He recognised the newcomer as one of the detectives from the back of the ambulance. He watched her take a seat and set her things out on the table. She wasn't the type to mess with, he could tell.

'I'm DS Jenkins. DI Adams was called home at short notice,' Jenkins told the brief. 'One of the other officers will join us soon.'

'Is that thing working?' Fishy pointed towards a camera mounted on the wall high above them, his paper coverall rustling like a crisp packet whenever he moved.

'Smile,' Jenkins said. 'You never know who might be watching.'

He didn't. 'Can they hear us through that window?'

Jenkins reached for a small rocker switch. 'If I press this, they can.'

'Don't.' Fishy swivelled his back to the camera and cupped a hand over his mouth. 'Al Pacino said I could trust you.'

Jenkins stared at him. 'Who?'

'He came to see me this morning.' Fishy grinned wide enough to almost swallow his own ears. 'He's a right baddass.'

Jenkins rested her phone on the table top and let her breath out slowly. 'And what did this Pacino fella have to say for himself?'

Fishy turned to his brief. 'You can piss off now. I've got some talking to do.'

Chapter 18

As funerals go, Jack Stokes's was nothing to write home about. There couldn't have been more than a dozen mourners in total. Family mostly, a few friends, and the odd copper not put off by rumour and reputation. There were more crows perched in the nearest tree than there were people in attendance.

Reece arrived, slipping and sliding on patches of mud and wet grass. 'Sorry I'm late.'

Idris Roberts glared at him. 'Where the hell have you been? We've already started.'

Reece fastened his top button and folded down his shirt collar. 'Hospital.' He nodded an apology to the deceased man's wife and daughter. Another to the dour-faced vicar.

'Which one?' Roberts asked.

'What does it matter?'

'It matters to me.'

'Why?'

Being graveside on a Welsh mountain in the middle of December was doing nothing to lift Roberts's mood, and Reece winding him up for the fun of it, was helping even less. The vicar stared; an unspoken point of order made before lowering his head to read from a damp bible.

'I'll tell you later,' Reece promised, averting his eyes when the vicar looked up for a second time. The clergyman went on with his reading, no doubt as eager as the rest of them to escape the sheets of horizontal rain making its way down the valley. No one else there knew, but it had taken every ounce of resolve Reece possessed just to turn up. Sitting on his bed half-dressed, he'd broken down and cried. At the front door, he'd been rooted to the spot, unable to open it. And when at last he'd finally got going, he'd stopped at the side of the road to throw up. But arrive, he had. Digging deep inside his coat pocket, he once more found himself in the vicar's sights. The hip-flask of Penderyn Sherrywood whisky not yet meant to see the light of day.

The coffin lay on a square of green carpet next to a hole containing an ankle-deep puddle of rainwater. 'They'll have to throw a snorkel and flippers in with him if they don't get this over with soon,' Roberts said.

Reece came forward on the vicar's prompt, took up the slack on a strap running between carpet and coffin, and lowered Stokes to his final resting place. When it was done, he took his turn in line, waiting to cast grit on the lid. He shivered, not only because he was cold.

'I'm next,' Roberts said as they made their way along a winding path to the car park. He coughed and used a handkerchief to wipe blood-specked spit from his mouth. 'I'm waiting for the ground to warm up a bit before I get in. And a dry day,' he said, looking overhead with a palm turned to the sky.

'You'll outlive us all.' Reece supported the retired DCI's elbow until they'd passed the worst of the potholes. 'You're like a creaking door.'

'Stripped and dipped.' Roberts lifted his shirtsleeves to expose a pale arm. 'Skin and bone is all that's left of me.'

Reece couldn't think of anything that hadn't already been said between them. Roberts moved the conversation along. 'How's work?'

'It is what it is.'

'Maggie hasn't lost her touch if this morning's newspaper headlines are anything to go by.'

'I wouldn't know.' Reece checked they weren't being watched before producing the hip flask. 'That vicar was a miserable sod.' He offered Roberts the first nip, then took some himself.

'You're telling me.'

'What's wrong with his sort?' Reece asked. 'Apart from being stuffed full of self-importance, that is.'

'I'm buggered if I know.' Roberts blew his nose in his handkerchief. 'I'm going for something upbeat at my own funeral.'

'Upbeat?'

'Yeah. Like an Elvis impersonator.'

'Why him?'

'Why not?'

Reece couldn't think of a good enough reason. 'I'll bring my guitar, shall I?' The rain came down hard just then, sending them both to shelter beneath the bare limbs of a towering oak.

'That's decided then.' Roberts looked to the heavens and used the same stained handkerchief to wipe down his wet neck. 'Cremation it's gotta be,' he said with a loud clap. 'Out the back of the hearse and off to the fires of hell.'

'To what song?'

'Burning Love, of course.'

Reece was about to reply when someone called to him from a row of cars parked opposite. He marched over to the black BMW and faced up to its oversized driver. 'What are you pair of arseholes doing here?'

Billy Creed shifted in the passenger seat, leaning forward to see past Denny Cartwright's bulging chest. He called over Reece's shoulder and waved. 'My man's brought his shovel, Idris. Pick your spot and we'll bury two pigs in one day.'

Roberts checked the vicar wasn't in sight and gave Creed the middle finger.

Reece wasn't anywhere near as careful. 'Fuck you,' he said, rattling the handle of the car door.

Cartwright got out and loomed over him.

Reece stepped in closer, itching to go toe-to-toe with the big man.

Creed laughed. 'Denny, play nice now.'

Cartwright wound his neck in and squeezed himself back behind the steering wheel.

'All this talk of dead coppers gets him overexcited.'

Reece double-tapped his palm against the roof of the BMW and turned to leave. 'You might need us way more than you think in the coming days, Billy.'

Creed had to ask why that was. Couldn't help himself.

Cartwright gripped the steering wheel and sped across the junction without slowing to check for traffic coming from his right. 'What we gonna do, Billy?' He didn't wait for an answer. 'Someone round here needs proper fucking up.'

Creed hammered a clenched fist against the dashboard of the car. 'You still got that bolt cutter in the boot?'

Cartwright nodded. 'Course I have.'

The dashboard got another thump as they sped through a set of red traffic lights. Horn blaring as they joined the main carriageway with a squeal from the wide tyres. 'Get us over to Paddy May's place.'

'What about my shovel?'

'You won't be needing it,' Creed said through gritted teeth. 'There'll be fuck all left to bury once I'm finished with him.'

'Yee-haw,' Cartwright called over another loud blast on the horn.

Creed lit two cigarettes and handed one over. 'I wanna know why we're only just hearing about this, Denny-boy.'

'I'll get Ken Ward on the blower.' Cartwright let go of the steering wheel to search his pockets. 'We pay the fat bastard way too much for him to be keeping things from us.'

Creed grabbed for the steering wheel when the BMW strayed across the centre-lines of the road. 'Use the hands-free, you fucking moron!'

Chapter 19

THE LOCAL RUGBY CLUB played host to the wake. Stokes had been captain and a pretty decent openside-flanker in his younger days. Reece got back from the toilet to find Roberts perched on a stool by the bar. When still a rookie detective, he'd been bollocked by the older man for doing the very same thing. 'What happened to your mantra of *"Never sit with your back to anyone"*?'

'They'd be doing me a favour if they came and did me in,' Roberts answered.

'Speak for yourself. We're moving.' Reece took both drinks and made his way towards a table in the far corner of the room.

'You shouldn't have told Creed about his sister. Not without checking with the team first.' Roberts lowered himself onto a wooden chair, burping on the first sip of his pint. 'They might have been planning on keeping that one quiet for the time being.'

'I'll give Jenkins a ring later and warn her.' Reece checked the room. 'Poor show from headquarters.'

'What did you expect?'

'More than this.'

'Stokes was unconventional.' Roberts raised a bushy eyebrow. 'Rubbed shoulders with the wrong sort, some might say.'

Reece rested his glass on the table. 'Do you think the rumours were true?'

'Corruption?'

'Yeah.'

It took Roberts a while to respond. 'You'll find something lurking beneath every rock if you look hard enough.' He knocked Reece's arm with an elbow. 'Those were different days back then, and methods change with time.'

'Not always for the better.'

Roberts watched him agonise over the detail. 'What's this about, Brân. The moods. Not picking up the phone when I call?'

Reece gulped the rest of his whisky and held his breath for as long as the fire burned deep in his belly. 'It's like I'm on a runaway train that won't stop to let me off.'

'Anwen's gone, man. Move on.' The words were characteristically matter of fact. 'She wouldn't have wanted you moping around the place, always playing the victim.'

Reece brought the empty whisky glass down onto the table with enough force to turn the nearest heads. 'If you were any other man, I'd—'

'Drag me outside and thump me?' Roberts rested a hand on his. 'I'm saying it for your own good. You've got to pull yourself together. It's what she'd have wanted.'

Reece moved his hand away. 'I'll get us both a plate of food.'

'Another pint of Dark is all I need.'

'You have to eat. You said it yourself — all skin and bone.'

'That's right,' Roberts called after him. 'You're willing to give out advice. It's the taking it you have problems with.'

Reece made his way along a table covered with a white cloth. He stopped to spoon a few silverskin pickled onions onto two paper plates. A couple of ham rolls followed. A pork pie and a chicken drumstick after that. He added cheese and pineapple cubes on sticks. And finished with a fistful of salted peanuts.

'Someone's hungry?' The voice sounded as though its owner had recently gargled with razor blades; the air suddenly contaminated with the odour of smoked cigarettes.

'Half of this is for Idris.'

Maggie Kavanagh was short, despite her beehive hairstyle. 'That'll last him all bloody week.'

Reece glanced across the room to where Roberts was sitting. 'He needs feeding up.'

'Look at you playing family doctor.'

'I'm being serious, Maggie. The man's on his last legs.'

Kavanagh forked a bowl of rice and turned her nose up at it. 'Funerals do that to some people. Makes them all maudlin.'

Reece moved with the shifting queue, stopping at a platter of custard slices and chocolate eclairs. He took one of each. 'How did you find out about Roxie May so quickly?'

Kavanagh tapped her nose with the end of the plastic fork. 'You know I'm never going to tell you that.'

He went back to his seat with the journalist close on his tail and put a plate of food in front of Idris Roberts. 'Try that.'

'I can't.' Roberts pushed the plate away.

Reece pushed it back. 'Pick at the bits you like. Leave the rest.'

'Brân said I could join you both.' Kavanagh lay her plate on the table and leaned to peck Roberts on the cheek. 'You know how warm and welcoming he is.'

'Maggie. Nice to see you after all this time.'

'I did no such thing.' Reece repositioned his chair, making it next to impossible for Kavanagh to sit beside him. 'Bugger off and leave us be.'

'Leave her alone.' Roberts patted the seat of the empty bench. 'Come around my side, Maggie. He's in one of his moping moods again.'

Reece lowered the chicken drumstick and wiped his mouth on a paper napkin. 'I'm not.'

'Too much time on his hands now they've suspended him.' Kavanagh poked out her tongue.

Reece's eyes widened. 'Will you shut up.'

Roberts looked concerned. 'Brân? You mentioned nothing about being suspended.'

'Well, it's not the sort of thing you brag about, is it?'

'What did you do this time?' Kavanagh asked. 'String some paedophile up by the gonads and torture a confession out of him?'

Reece balled his napkin and dropped it onto his plate. 'Leave it, Maggie.'

She turned to Roberts and said, 'I bet it's got something to do with Billy Creed. It's always about Billy Creed with him.'

Roberts nodded. 'Like a dog with a bone, he is.'

Reece rose from the table. 'That's enough, both of you.'

'If you're not on the case, then there's no reason we can't all chat about it.' Kavanagh gave up on chasing a pickled onion round her plate and used the cocktail stick to poke between her teeth.

'Where are you going now?' Roberts asked.

Reece spoke over his shoulder as he walked away. 'The bar. I need another drink.'

Kavanagh wasted no time at all in rearranging the seating. 'Gin and tonic for me,' she called. 'A large one. We'll have ourselves a right proper catch-up when you get back.'

Chapter 20

KEN WARD SAW THE BMW within seconds of him entering the supermarket car park. He found a space not far away from it and pulled to a full stop. He stretched his legs on the wet tarmac, straightened his shoulders, and made himself look like any other divorcee calling in for a week's supply of microwave dinners.

Denny Cartwright was behind the wheel of the Bimmer—a cork in a bottleneck—the vehicle listing to one side under his weight. The bald head of Billy Creed was just visible through the dark tint of the glass.

The side window came down with a hum of its motor, venting copious amounts of cigar smoke into the cold and damp air. 'Get in, Copper,' Creed said. It wasn't an invitation. He twisted in his seat while Cartwright repositioned the rear-view mirror to get a better view of the new arrival.

Ward was well beyond nervous and had every reason to be. Inside was the pungent smell of patchouli oil mixed with cigar and the body odour of three big men. 'Best make it quick, Billy, I need to—' He managed no more than that before the hot end of Creed's cigar burnt a hole in the knee of his trousers. 'Jesus!'

Creed pointed in warning, a gold bracelet the thickness of a bike chain weighing heavily on his left wrist. 'Don't you ever try rushing me, Copper.'

Ward stuck a finger through the hole in the material, stopping short of his blistered skin. 'They're ruined.'

'That's the least of your worries.' Creed blew smoke at him. 'You've been keeping secrets.'

Ward's attention flitted between both men in the front seats. 'What's he saying, Denny? Tell him. You and me talk all the time, don't we?'

Creed growled his sister's name, the veins in his neck straining like thick cords beneath his taut skin. 'Are you playing both sides, Copper?'

Ward cleared his throat. 'Course not, Billy.'

Creed swung the back of his hand and missed the detective's face by only a short margin. 'You've got ten seconds to explain before I throw you to Denny.'

Cartwright winked at the mirror and cracked each of his knuckles in turn.

'I was waiting for the right time,' Ward said. 'It would have done our arrangement no good if you two had gone blazing in there with both barrels cocked.'

'I'll tell you about our arrangement, shall I?' Creed forced his head between the seats to face the rear – a pair of bloodshot eyes set against a patchwork of blue ink. 'You're in debt to the tune of eighteen grand, and I bought that debt. So until you've paid it off in full, I own you, Copper.'

'Fat chance of that ever happening.' Ward scratched his beard. 'Six thousand it was before you got your hands on it.' He looked out of the side window, wondering how his life could have spiralled so low. He'd recently gone through a messy divorce after accruing gambling debts owed to the meanest man in Cardiff. Life was a bitch who had more claims on him than his ex-wife did.

'It's gone up by another two,' Creed said with a nod. 'Penalties for being a twat.'

'Twenty-grand. Are you nuts?' The gangster was known to double debts whenever the whim took him, and Ward knew he'd be an idiot to argue the toss. 'Who told you about Roxie's death?'

'Reece.' It was a single word, but then, so much more.

'You're kidding me?'

'Do I look like I'm in the mood for a fucking joke?'

Ward pressed himself tight against the upright of the leather seat, adding another inch of distance between them as the bracelet whizzed by his chin. 'He's off the case now. The new chief super suspended him for bad behaviour.'

'Did you know that?' Creed turned to Cartwright, who shook his head. 'Copper's at it again. Keeping secrets from us.'

'He needs a good slap, Billy.'

Ward went grey. 'For fuck's sake, guys, it only just happened.'

Cartwright pulled on the handle of his door, the vehicle rocking violently as he moved to get out. 'We warned you.'

'Not so fast, Denny-boy.' Creed squeezed the big man's knee. 'Reece suspended. I like the sound of that.'

'You're not the only one.' Ward kept both eyes fixed on the back of the burly driver. 'Reece has been watching me ever since we raided your club. He's got my card marked. I'm sure of it.'

Creed tapped the side of his head. 'He knows nothing and you'll keep it that way.'

'Do you think I'm not trying? If he'd entered that room any sooner, he'd have caught me stuffing a murder weapon down the front of my trousers.' He pinched the bridge of his nose between finger and thumb. 'I could have lost everything. That has to be worth what I owe you.'

'You've got a lot more than that left to lose, and don't you forget it.'

Ward knew it was true. They could destroy him any time they wanted. Pull the last few pieces of his life and career apart. He needed an insurance policy, or better still, a rock solid way out of the mess he was in. For a while no one spoke, all three wrestling with their individual thoughts before Ward broke the silence. 'Did you get rid of the gun like you promised?'

'It's sorted,' Creed said. 'That's all you need to know.'

Ward felt a sinking feeling deep in the pit of his stomach and thought he might vomit. 'Please tell me you didn't. Not that pair of idiots?' He lowered his window when neither man answered. 'We've got ourselves a big fucking problem,' he said, and set about explaining.

Creed bounced up and down in his seat. 'I want them out!'

'How do I manage that?' Ward asked. 'DI Adams is about to charge them for Roxie's murder.'

Chapter 21

For the briefest of moments, the young constable must have thought an enormous dark cloud had parked itself on the other side of the front desk. 'Can I help you?' he asked, looking up from what he was doing.

Denny Cartwright hovered over him like some giant harbinger of doom, stooping to force his head through the open hatch. 'I fucking doubt it.'

The constable retreated a good arm's length away, looking decidedly unsure how best to play this one.

Cartwright offered no introduction or apology. 'Fetch me DI Adams,' he said with the best scowl he possessed from a repertoire of many.

'Could I ask what it's about?' The counter creaked under the weight of the visitor's elbow. 'Tell him Billy Creed's come to rip him a new arsehole.'

Adams had no intention of letting the pair anywhere near the briefing room and exhibits pinned to its evidence board. In fact, he'd be giving Creed little more information than the minimum required at this point in the investigation. The chosen room was an empty office on the ground floor. 'You asked to see me,' he said, straightening a red and white striped tie. He took a seat and offered two more.

Cartwright stood with his back pressed against the office door while Billy Creed prowled like a cat in a cage.

The gangster came to a stop and pointed at Adams. 'Word is you're in charge now.'

'I'm heading up the murder squad, if that's what you mean?'

Creed's eyes narrowed. 'Then it's you who should've told me about Roxie.'

'Next of kin only at this stage, I'm afraid. Standard procedure and all that.'

'I am next of kin.'

Adams shook his head. 'Your sister and Mr May never divorced.'

'You told that piece of shit before telling me?' Creed poked holes in the air. 'I'm her brother!'

'Makes no difference in law.'

Cartwright took a menacing step away from the door. 'He's pissing me off already, Billy.'

'And they have children,' Adams continued. 'The boys would be next in line to know if there wasn't a Mr May.'

Creed bit on a clenched fist. 'Feral cats is what they are.'

Adams waved a hand dismissively. 'Even so.'

Every tattoo on Creed's face merged into one. 'Are you trying to wind me up, Copper?'

Adams wondered if staying upstairs for the meeting might have been a better option. He was trapped, and the atmosphere was becoming increasingly tense. 'How did you find out about Roxie's death?'

Creed told him about the funeral and the altercation in the car park.

Adams made a mental note to deal with Reece later. 'Where were you both between the hours of four and six pm yesterday?'

The question caught Creed off-kilter. 'I'm on a short fuse here.'

'Routine. To eliminate you from our enquiries.'

'We were with that security guy,' Cartwright said.

Creed nodded. 'CCTV's been playing up at the club. Rats nibbling at the old cables.'

Cartwright balled his fists. 'And it's still fucked, even though he said he'd fixed it.'

Adams took a scrap of paper and hovered the nib of a pen above its surface. 'I'll need to speak to him.'

'You and me both,' Creed said.

'Company name?' Adams insisted.

'Denny'll sort you out with it once we're back at the club.'

'Could Roxie's death have been meant as a warning to you?' Adams rested the pen on the desk and rolled it under a finger. 'A rival looking to muscle in on your business interests?'

Creed gave the question little consideration. 'No one would fucking dare.'

'Find me Reece,' Adams said, stomping through the briefing room.

Jenkins looked up from her laptop screen. 'I know he went to a funeral this morning.' She checked her watch. 'He should be home again by now.'

'Get your coat. We're going out.'

Jenkins followed. 'Paddy May's?'

'He can wait.'

'But I thought—'

'I said Paddy May could wait for now.' Adams stopped so suddenly that Jenkins had to sidestep to avoid colliding with him. 'I've got a bigger fish to fry.'

Chapter 22

Paddy May was out in the yard, shifting a pile of old tyres, when the sound of the car first caught his attention. It was powerful—he could tell—a high performance engine growling as it negotiated a good mile or more of snaking bends and potholed dirt track. Nothing unusual there. People came and went all the time. But in clapped-out vans and junk cars, mostly.

Police, was his first thought. Was always his first thought. Territory that came with the life he lived. Making a quick mental check of what he knew he had hanging around the place, he relaxed for little more than a moment. Something wasn't at all right. The dog sensed it too, barking and leaping in circles as it strained to break free of its rope leash.

But the police normally arrived with a fanfare of noise and flashing blue lights. Besides, they'd already been and gone that day.

Not the police then.

Paddy caught flashes of something dark in colour through the patchy gaps in the semi-naked hedgerow. And then it was out of sight again, lost behind a sweeping rise of wet landscape. He watched the thing play an annoying game of peek-a-boo. Polished chrome reflecting weak daylight wherever it penetrated the cover of the overhanging trees. There was no need for him to be legging it just yet. Those coppers had promised to give him good warning before telling Billy Creed that Roxie was dead. They'd given their word and sounded convincing.

And then the SUV broke free of the last bend, charging at him like an angry bull in a field. Big, black, and coming his way.

Paddy's office was less than twenty yards off. He ran and slammed the Portakabin door shut behind him, regretting his choice of hiding hole when he slipped on the wet flooring. He was trapped with nowhere to go. A mistake he knew would likely cost him his life. He went to the dirty window and watched Denny Cartwright take a bolt cutter to the looped chain on the front gate while the dog tried to get a bite of him.

'I didn't tell him much,' Reece said with little emotion.

Adams gripped the armrest of a green Chesterfield sofa in Reece's front room. Jenkins was sitting next to him, taking notes and keeping her mouth shut. 'I should arrest you for interfering with an ongoing police investigation?'

Reece had his back to them, staring out of the window. 'I gave Creed nothing he couldn't have found for himself in the newspapers.'

'Not true.' Adams rested his coffee mug on a short-legged occasional table and wiped both palms on the knees of his trousers. 'You gave him the victim's identity. *You,* not Maggie Kavanagh.'

Reece shrugged, suddenly preoccupied with something more interesting outside. He followed the track of a dark cloud as it lumbered across the purple sky and pressed his face against the cold glass until it was out of sight. He wasn't sure why, but he'd started dreaming of the things recently. 'Do you know how many people in this city are in Billy Creed's pocket?' He turned away from the window and faced them. 'Lawyers. Councillors. Coppers, even.'

'That's not what we're discussing here and you know it.'

'Isn't it?'

Adams pointed an accusing finger. 'And don't think I'm blind to what you were up to at the hospital. You're treading on thin ice, Reece.'

'That's DCI Reece to you. Boss or sir will do just the same.'

Jenkins did well not to spill her coffee when Adams forced himself upright without warning. 'If I find you're withholding information relevant to this case, then I will arrest you. For obstruction, at the very least.'

Reece laughed. 'What case? You don't have a fucking clue what to do next.'

Chapter 23

Paddy May came to and peered through a pair of swollen eyes. It hurt to blink. Even more so to breathe. For a moment, he couldn't remember where he might be. Billy Creed slapped his face, screaming for him to wake up. Paddy was able to make out a few things if he squinted. They had him tied to a chair. Both ankles bound to an oily engine block. His arms bothered him the most. They were stretched out at his sides with his hands caught in the tight grip of two large bench vices.

Cartwright opened the sharp pincers of the bolt cutter, ready to get going.

Creed struck Paddy with a backhand full of sovereign rings, splitting his bottom lip and freeing a decaying incisor in one swift move.

He had no memory of them entering the Portakabin. Nor of being dragged around its dirty floor by handfuls of hair. But now he was wide awake and witness to every vicious punch and kick.

'Is this how my sister looked when you did her in?' Creed loomed, teeth bared, eyes staring maniacally.

'I didn't,' Paddy croaked. 'I never went near her.'

The gangster took the bolt cutter from Cartwright's hand. 'Open his fingers so that I can get at them.' Cartwright caught Paddy by the balls and squeezed down hard. Screaming, Paddy straightened all four limbs like a cat going through its wake-up routine. Creed took his opportunity and snapped the jaws of the cutter closed, leaving a stump spurting bright red blood onto the vice and desk. It burned, and hurt, and stung, all at the same time.

Cartwright went over to the window, checking for unwanted visitors drawn to the yard by the awful screaming.

'Nine left.' Creed grabbed a fistful of Paddy's hair and jerked his head up and back. 'You'd better start talking before you run the fuck out of them and I start on your toes.'

Paddy struggled under the gangster's tight grip. 'What do you want to know?'

'The retard.'

'Fishy – what about him?'

'You paid him to kill Roxie.'

Unable to move his head, it was only Paddy's eyes that rocked side to side. 'I never did.'

Creed called to Cartwright and readied the bolt cutter. 'Eight!' he shouted over the screaming. 'Get me one of them Jerrycans.'

Cartwright went to the far side of the Portakabin and helped himself. 'This one's full.'

'Give it here.' Creed opened the can and poured its contents over his victim.

Paddy had been unconscious, but the cold fluid and pungent smell soon had him awake again. He heaved, and gasped for breath like he was having a heart attack.

Cartwright dragged the two-bar floor heater into place alongside Paddy's chair. 'You're about to have yourself an accident,' he said with a wheezy chuckle.

Paddy wanted to die. But not like this. He closed his eyes and prayed the end would come soon.

With both electric elements going full pelt, Creed lifted a foot and rested it in the middle of the scrap merchant's chest. 'I warned you last year. No second chances.' He pushed and stepped out of the way. There was the instant smell of clothes igniting. Then something far worse. As the scorching flames enveloped Paddy, his high-pitched screams became bouts of deep howling. Then he fell silent and still. Creed stopped at the door to toss the Jerrycan into the raging fire. 'That's what happens when you fuck with me and mine.'

Adams put the phone to his ear and went out into the kitchen. When he came back, he shook his head at Reece. 'We're on our way,' he said, ending the call.

Jenkins stood. 'What is it, sir?'

'Someone's torched Paddy May's place.' He gave Reece his full attention. 'Get yourself down the nick and find Ken Ward. I want a full statement on my desk by the time I get back. Everything you told Billy Creed about this case.'

Chapter 24

There was intense activity on the site of Paddy May's breaking yard. Blue flashing lights illuminated the lane and nearby fields. In attendance was an ambulance, two patrol cars, a couple of silver vans, and a full-sized fire appliance. It looked as though the news people had forecast the end of the world. Adams steered his Volvo tight to the steep bank, groaning as gnarled fingers of hedgerow clawed at the vehicle's paintwork. 'Next time we bring a damn pool car.'

Jenkins grabbed for the hand strap above her left shoulder, hitting her head against the side glass when the car's tyres caught in the deep ruts made by the emergency vehicles. 'I doubt there'll be a next time. This looks as serious as it gets.' The air smelled acrid. Thick folds of black smoke hanging lazily beneath the low-level cloud. On foot, they picked their way between dirty puddles and vehicles waiting with their engines running. 'There's pretty much nothing left of it,' she said, shaking a wet foot.

Earlier in the day, the building had stood with a lopsided tilt. But it had stood there, nonetheless.

Adams showed his warrant card to a uniform, who pointed in the direction of the watch manager. The man was busy directing his crew and wore a white helmet, and two silver pips on each shoulder of his coat.

Adams interrupted him mid-conversation. 'If we're dealing with a murder here, that'll put me in charge.' He wrestled his arm loose of the firefighter's grip and followed when the man walked off. 'Are you listening to me?'

When the watch manager was finally able to talk, he showed both detectives to a place of safety. 'You were saying?'

'I'm expecting no more than a single victim,' Adams said above the rumble of the diesel engines.

The watch manager studied the smouldering remains of the Portakabin. 'What makes you think it might be murder? All that fuel stored next to an electric fire — an accident waiting to happen.'

'An accident, you say?'

'I'm saying nothing until we've had a proper look around.'

'And when will that be?'

'Just as soon as you're out of my face.'

Jenkins had plenty of experience in diffusing awkward situations. Working with Reece had made her an expert in the field of *smoothing things out*. 'We should bring Billy Creed in. See what he's got to say for himself.'

Adams was on his way back to the car. 'You saw Paddy downing that whisky.'

'I did. But sir.'

'He got pissed, fell, and knocked the petrol onto the heater. That's good enough for me.'

'Sir.'

'Leave it, Sergeant. This one's done.'

Reece was sitting on the wrong side of an interview desk. 'Get on with it, then.'

Ken Ward looked decidedly sheepish sitting opposite him. 'Apologies, boss, but DI Adams insisted I take a statement from you.'

'You look worried.'

Ward swallowed. 'Just a bit overwhelmed. It being you and all.'

Reece lay his hands on the desk in front of him. 'Relax and get on with it.'

Ward opened his pocketbook and doodled on a blank page. 'I think the DI is only interested in your conversation with Billy Creed.'

'*My* conversation with him, or conversations involving other officers working at this station?'

'Boss?'

Reece leaned forward and whispered: 'This place is leaking faster than a sieve.'

Ward dropped his pen on the floor and puffed under the effort of bending to pick it up. 'I've been meaning to talk to you about that, but didn't know how to broach the subject.' He folded his arms across a soft belly and locked his fingers together. 'Maybe now's not the right time or place.'

'Try me,' Reece said. 'I've nothing better to do.'

'What's your take on Ffion Morgan? The flash cars and holidays in Dubai. That jewellery doesn't come cheap. And all on a constable's salary.' He shook his head. 'I know I can't afford any of that. I hope I'm wrong,' he said with a tut and a deep sigh. 'But there's been some strange shit going on recently.'

'And none more so than during our raid on the Midnight Club. I know that handgun was there when we went in,' Reece said. 'We had good intelligence.'

'Exactly. But we never came across it?'

Reece leaned on his elbows and stared at the other man. 'I've a theory about that.'

Chapter 25

Billy Creed held his playing cards close to his chest and poured himself another two fingers of brandy. He passed the bottle to the man on his right, watching the other players through a thick veil of cigar smoke. All had been present by the time he'd got back from the scrap yard. There to provide him with an alibi whenever the police arrived. He knew they would, of course. His would be the first door they'd come knocking on.

Jimmy Chin took a good measure of spirits and sent the bottle on its way. 'Where's Denny?' he asked.

'Giving the car a once-over.' Creed fanned his cards and squinted. 'You can't be too careful these days.'

Chin nodded. He'd grown up in Tiger Bay, like the rest of them, and wasn't of oriental descent. His nickname was down to a bottom jaw that would have given Desperate Dan a run for his money.

Wiggley-Jones was the local undertaker; known to those sitting around the table as Worms. 'Anyone we know?' He swore at his duff hand and tossed it onto the table, face up.

'He's already cremated,' Creed said with a wide grin.

'Not looking to start your own business, are you?' Worms asked, pretending to be worried.

Jimmy Chin took another card and promptly folded. 'Denny gave you that doctor to bury the other week. How much more work do you expect us to put your way?'

Worms chuckled. 'You mean the one who couldn't cure his mother's cancer?'

'That'll be him.'

The undertaker pulled a face. 'The poor bastard looked like a bag of spanners when I had him collected from the mortuary.'

'Top floor of the hospital car park,' Chin said, slapping his hand against the table top. 'Like strawberry jam when he landed.'

'And all the clever people claimed to have seen it coming.' Creed scooped the winning pot towards him. 'The newspapers said he'd been suffering with depression for years.'

'There you go.' Chin retied his greying hair with a thin length of leather lace. 'Our Denny put him out of his misery.'

The door to the office opened without warning, a tall ginger police constable entering the room alone.

Creed tapped his cigar over an empty foil tray. 'If you're here for the curry, Copper, then you're a good twenty minutes too late.'

All eyes were on Ginge. He'd stepped into the lion's den and pissed off the alpha male. 'There's a car waiting outside, Mr Creed. If you'd like to make your way downstairs.'

The gangster stood. 'Can you believe they'd send this lanky string of piss to fetch me?' There was laughter in the room, but not of the happy kind.

'I'll ask you again, Mr Creed. This way.'

The door swung open, knocking Ginge off balance. The entrant was young and wore her blonde hair in a short ponytail.

'The stripper's arrived, boys,' Worms said to a rapturous round of applause. 'Who's for the first lap dance?'

Chin threw himself out of his seat and caught hold of the front of his jeans. 'Get the Games Room open. I need some exercise of the sexual kind.'

The officer kept her hand on a shoulder-mounted radio, her finger poised, ready to call for backup at a moment's notice.

'It's okay,' Ginge told her. 'Mr Creed was about to get his coat.'

'You're either very brave, or you've no idea what you've got yourselves into,' Creed said, pushing his way into the police officer's personal space. There was footfall on the metal treads outside. The office floor vibrating beneath its occupants' feet. 'The big man's coming to grind your bones.'

Ginge held his ground. 'We're expected to make a progress call in . . .' He turned to his colleague for confirmation.

'Less than two minutes from now,' she said, looking behind her.

'Billy!' The door almost came off its hinges as Denny Cartwright burst into the room with his habitual wheeze. 'There's filth outside.' He straightened on sight of the police officers, and scowled. 'What the fuck are you two doing up here?'

'Security ain't what it used to be,' Creed said over the sound of a short radio burst.

The female officer acknowledged the order from base. 'We're to stand down.'

'Why?' Ginge asked.

'That's all the control room said.' She took a step nearer Creed. 'But DS Jenkins wants the CCTV man's contact details before we leave.'

Chapter 26

The Volvo had been blocked in by the arrival of the pathologist's car. Adams had tried to get someone to move it. Finally admitting defeat, he'd agreed to Jenkins's suggestion of joining Dr Twm Pryce during his examination of the body.

When they found Pryce, he was already at work and not speaking much. Jenkins knew the object under scrutiny was a person's face, mostly because that's where the body part should have been in relation to the rest of Paddy May. A hefty mound of black remains represented the shoulders and upper torso. The abdomen and its soft contents had been almost obliterated by the intense heat. The upper limbs were contracted in a tight, pugilistic pose.

Turning his attention to the pelvis, Pryce said: 'It's V-shaped and therefore male. I can tell you that much, at least.'

Adams hunted for somewhere dry to plant his feet. What had once been a four-walled Portakabin was now a flatpack of disintegrated panels and dirty mush. 'Young or old? You can tell from the teeth, can't you?'

'I'm afraid that's not so straightforward once an individual is beyond their mid-twenties.' Pryce gave him a questioning look. 'Is there any reason to believe this isn't who we think it is?'

Adams shook his head. 'No reason at all.'

Reece waited in front of the evidence board upstairs, his finger drawing an imaginary line from Roxie May's photograph to an entry marked *Mystery Woman.* 'Interesting.'

'Get away from that.' Adams searched the room, then his office – Reece's office. 'Where's Ward?'

'Who is she?' Reece asked. 'A new suspect?'

'I said leave that alone.'

Jenkins entered with a Starbucks coffee in her hand and must have caught the tail end of what Reece had said. 'A patrol crew saw her outside the factory. Right time, right place.'

'Just someone on their way home from work.' Adams gave up looking for the absent detective constable and forced himself between Reece and the evidence board. 'Is that statement done yet?'

'Go ask Ward.'

'Very funny. Did he say where he was going?'

'Nope, but I could probably hazard a guess.'

Adams turned to Jenkins. 'Call and tell him to get his fat arse up here, and pronto.'

Reece kept his back to them as he crossed the room. 'Find your mystery woman,' he said. 'If only to eliminate her from enquiries.'

'You stay out of this.' The comment earned Adams a raised middle finger, and a loudly blown raspberry. 'I'm warning you.'

Reece stopped in the doorway. 'You might want to change out of that posh suit of yours. You're starting to smell like a kipper.'

Chapter 27

'SHOULDN'T YOU BE ON your way over to the hospital by now?' Jenkins asked.

Morgan was sprawled across her desk. Her head resting on folded arms. 'The man's got it in for me.' She stood and slipped the strap of her bag over a shoulder. 'Second sodding post-mortem this week,' she said, gagging on a finger. 'Christmas bloody eve as well.'

Ken Ward looked up from what he was doing. 'If you think Roxie May was a mess, then wait until you've set eyes on her other half.'

Jenkins joined in the banter and took a waste bin from under her desk and made a play of retching into it.

Morgan stood rooted to the spot. 'Not that bad, surely?'

'Worse than I could ever describe,' Jenkins said.

'Thanks for that, both. Thanks a bunch.'

Ward chuckled. 'And the smell. God, the smell.'

'Stop it.' Morgan put her hands to her ears and ran for the door.

Once she'd quit laughing, Jenkins powered up her laptop and sat watching the cursor blink in the username box. The reflection of Ken Ward behind her was clear to see. 'You seem preoccupied this morning. Anything wrong?'

Ward checked the empty doorway. 'What do you make of that one?' His voice was hushed, the tone conspiratorial.

'Ffion? Head in the clouds most days, but her heart is in the right place. She'll make a decent detective given time and coaching. Why do you ask?'

Ward took a bag of mints from a drawer and offered one. 'Something the DCI said yesterday.'

Jenkins declined. 'What did he say?'

'He thinks she might be on the take from Billy Creed.'

'Shut up! There's no way he'd say that.'

Ward looked for somewhere to put the sweet wrapper and settled on his empty mug. 'Not those exact words, but I got his drift.'

Jenkins was having none of it. 'You must have got the wrong end of the stick.'

Ward sucked on his mint. 'Maybe we should be a bit more careful with what we tell her from now on?'

They were interrupted by a ringing telephone. Jenkins answered it. She ended the call and stretched in her chair. 'Well, Creed's alibi checks out. The CCTV guy says that he and Cartwright didn't leave him alone the whole time he was there.'

'Shame.'

She drew a line through their names and got up and went over to the evidence board to stare at her *Mystery Woman* entry. 'I know I'm right about this.' She took a red marker pen from a pot of other colours and began listing her thoughts: Random Killing; Jealous Wife; Unpaid Debts; Other Grudge. That last one got her thinking. A Pro-Life campaigner, maybe? She added Anti-Abortion Activist to her list. With a swipe of her finger, she erased the first entry. Roxie May's murder was anything but random. And a jealous wife? Unlikely. Walking in wide circuits of the room, she tapped the pen against her teeth. 'Come on, think. The coin. The uterus. What's the connection?'

Reece wandered outside the old factory unit, blue and white crime scene tape ticker-tackering next to him. Overhead was a sheet of corrugated roofing that rose and fell on the wind. He moved out of range, concerned it might break free at any moment and do him a serious injury. Just about every window in the building had been broken. Each wall was a cracked canvas for a gung-ho spray can enthusiast. But Banksy hadn't visited Splott. Not unless he'd taken to painting rudimentary images of male genitalia complete with homophobic slogans.

'You shouldn't be over there.' There was a middle-aged man dressed in grey overalls, with an oily rag held in one hand and a heavy wrench gripped in the other. 'Police didn't come back this morning.' He put the tool to one side and wiped his hands on the rag as he spoke. 'The whole world has gone to pot, if you ask me.'

Reece wandered over and introduced himself. 'How long has the place been out of action?'

'Couldn't say exactly. Couple of years maybe.'

'Any idea why no one else moved in?'

'It's supposed to be haunted.' The mechanic swapped the rag for a smaller socket-wrench and went back to a car supported on orange axle stands. 'And this will do nothing to help its cause.'

Reece waited at the garage door. 'Were you at work when the murder took place?'

'I was here until six-ish. Then outside with the rest of them until we got bored staring at blue lights and bugger all else.' He flicked the switch on an electric kettle and offered a fresh brew and some digestive biscuits.

Reece accepted, his eyes wandering across an expanse of wall covered with posters of muscle cars and exploded diagrams of engine parts. They stopped and lingered on a pair of gigantic breasts sported by a calendar girl waving a cricket bat. He tilted his head to one side and frowned.

The mechanic handed him his tea. 'I know. It's a wonder she gets upright packing those.'

'Do you fix radios?' Reece asked, dragging his attention away from the breasts.

'Fit rather than fix. What have you got?'

Reece pointed towards the old Peugeot. 'That's it over there.'

'Ah.'

'I'll take that as a no?'

'A new one's gonna cost you more than the car's worth.' After rummaging through the drawers of a metal cabinet, the mechanic returned with something that was dusty and sprouting lots of coloured wires. 'You can have this for thirty quid fitted.'

'Does it have buttons?'

'Wouldn't be much good without them.'

Reece thanked him. 'I'll let you know.'

Chapter 28

KEN WARD HAD LONG since made his excuses and left Jenkins to bang her head against the evidence board. His rusted Vauxhall was parked opposite the bookmaker's shop off City Road. While he did his best to alternate between a good half-dozen different bookies, their turn came around quickly enough. He'd previously made the mistake of using independent agents, stupidly thinking his addiction could be hidden by blacked-out windows and handwritten record keeping. How wrong he was. His mounting debts had passed to Billy Creed when the shop's proprietor had tripped on the stairs and broken his neck in an *accident.*

The usual clientele loitered beneath wall-mounted television screens, turning betting slips into confetti before skulking home to their wives. He wondered what they made of him. If they knew or even cared that he was a police officer. He doubted they did, and what difference would it have made in any case? He went to the counter to lay his bet. 'Chantelle, looking as gorgeous as ever.'

The blonde blew a huge pink bubble that popped over half her face. She went back to chewing just as soon as she'd peeled the gum away and shoved it in her mouth again. 'All right, Kenny-boy?'

'Living the dream, and you?'

'Don't get me started. You know how it is.'

Ward came away from the counter, slip in hand, loitering with the rest of them. Someone tried to make idle conversation, but he wasn't listening. The result of this particular horse race would be the difference between him having an MOT and not. The gas bill could wait another couple of weeks. With the race over, he dropped confetti in the bin and made for the door.

'Better luck next time,' Chantelle screeched.

'Oi.' Ward went after the traffic warden when he crossed the busy road without stopping. 'Are you deaf?'

The warden pointed overhead. 'The sign says thirty minutes and no return within two hours.'

'Come on. I'm only five over.'

'Eight, to be exact.'

'Give me a break.' He showed his warrant card. 'Can't we say I was on police business?'

'Say what you like – it's still a seventy quid fine.'

'Are you serious?'

'It's in the system now.'

Ward fought the urge to punch the man. 'Look, I'm having a really bad day. I wouldn't normally ask, but—'

'You and me both,' the warden said, already entering the details of another number plate into his handheld device.

'Is there nothing I can do?'

'Short of asking Santa to fetch you a better watch – no.'

Reece had moved on from the garage and was now standing in the open yard of a garden fencing specialist. 'Ed, the mechanic said you both saw a woman walking near the factory the other night.'

The owner scratched his arse. 'Aye, but I'll be buggered if I can tell you what she looked like.' There was a small camera above the door to the premises, and a domed version just below the guttering on the side wall.

'Do those work?' Reece asked.

'Too bloody right they do. It's like Beirut round here once the sun's gone down.'

'Are they on a recording loop?' Reece hoped not.

'Downloads to a laptop in the office, then gets uploaded to an online server somewhere in India,' the man said, rolling his eyes. 'Just about everything does these days.'

'But you can access and watch it whenever you want?' Reece asked.

They moved inside and sat at a desk, watching a fourteen-inch screen come to life with a flicker of white lines on a black background. 'The twenty-second of the month, wasn't it?'

'Around five o'clock.' Reece waited as the files were searched and loaded.

'This is the one. Let me fast forward to the right bit.'

'No. Go back,' Reece told him. 'Further. There she is.'

'How can you tell?' The image was grainy and little more than a grey silhouette set against greyer surroundings. The woman moved with purpose, checking over her shoulder and lowering her head from sight of passing traffic. She carried a shopping bag in her left hand. 'That's her,' Reece said. 'Could you send a copy of that file over to DS Jenkins at the Cardiff Bay station?'

Ken Ward was over his altercation with the jobsworth traffic warden on City Road. Loitering in the alleyway next to a children's playground, he didn't have long to wait before Tasha Volks arrived — a can of cider held to her mouth, a regulation shell-suit in off-white polyester hanging low on her hips. One of the oddest things about the woman, and there was plenty odd with her, was the way she walked with an up-down, quick-slow, lolloping gait that had her look like she was stepping barefoot on hot coals. Volks slung the empty can over a shoulder and disappeared inside her flat.

Ward crossed the road and knocked on the front door. It opened without warning, a baseball bat travelling ahead of the figure wielding it. Wrestling it from Volks's grip, he pushed her aside and went in. She came at him again, this time armed with broken fingernails and a few black teeth. 'I'm not after your shit,' he said, parrying a succession of flailing blows. 'This is about Onion.'

'He ain't here.'

'I know that. When did you see him last?'

Volks staggered into the squalid living room, oblivious to the amount of red thong she had on show. 'I needs a spliff before my fucking head explodes.'

'Has Onion been round here lately?' Volks took a paper bag from her pocket and emptied a dozen or more used cigarette butts onto the arm of the chair. Several of the filters were stained with lipstick and brown rings of tar and saliva. All would have been collected from the gutters and parklands of the city. 'You get a present if you help me find what I'm looking for.'

The addict let out a phlegmy laugh. 'I ain't heard it called that before.'

Chapter 29

THE RECORDING CAME TO an abrupt end; the file offering a Play Again option in bold white letters across the middle of the laptop screen. Jenkins sat back and folded her arms. 'And there she is, folks, our mystery woman. Good ole Reece.'

'It's a bit grainy don't you think?' Ken Ward hovered over her shoulder. 'A woman in a hat and coat, and that's about it.'

Jenkins couldn't disagree. But on the positive side, it was more than they had a few minutes earlier. 'Maybe one of the geeks downstairs can have a go at enhancing the facial features.'

Morgan finished licking the foil lid of a yogurt pot and looked for somewhere to put it. 'I can go ask them if you want me to?'

Ward caught Jenkins's attention, his eyebrows rising and falling. 'I'll do it.'

Jenkins took a sip of coffee and spat the cold liquid back into its mug. She closed her laptop and turned to face him. 'Where were you earlier?'

'When do you mean?'

'Earlier. You went out when there was no reason to.'

Ward offered his wrists. 'All right, you caught me in the act. I went to see a man about a dog. There – happy now?'

Less than thirty minutes later, Jenkins was holding the floor in the briefing room.

Adams glared at her from a front-row seat. 'You do know that Reece is going to screw-up this whole investigation.' His comment was directed at Chief Superintendent Cable.

'And why didn't *you* find this?' was her curt reply.

'I would have done, but we got caught up with the Paddy May incident.'

Jenkins fought the urge to laugh. 'It looks like DCI Reece saved you the bother, sir.'

Adams went bright red and, for once, had nothing to say.

Cable checked her watch. 'We're running out of custody time for that pair downstairs.'

'I'm well aware of that, ma'am,' Adams said, dragging his gaze from Jenkins.

'Then you'll also be aware that the additional twelve hours I granted is the maximum permitted without a magistrate's warrant?'

'Yes.'

'And in light of what you've heard today, do you still intend to charge them?'

Jenkins beat him to an answer. 'The CPS are going to laugh us out of the room. It's the mystery woman we should be—'

Adams cut her off mid-sentence. 'I'll need the full ninety-six hours, ma'am.'

Cable shrivelled. 'You know that's next to impossible? And on Christmas Eve of all days.' She went and joined Jenkins in front of the evidence board. 'You really think this woman is somehow involved in Roxie May's murder?'

'I do, ma'am.'

'And DCI Reece agrees with you?'

'I've every reason to believe he does.' Jenkins ignored Adams tutting in the background. 'Roxie May was killed for a motive we haven't yet figured out. Even the presence of a patrol car in the area wasn't enough to deter the killer. This was pre-planned and couldn't be put off for another day.'

'Go on.'

'Then there's the uterus, as well as the coin found at the scene. There'll be a reason for it being left there – one that only the killer is likely to know.'

'She's talking nonsense,' Adams told the ceiling tiles. 'The coin could have been lost or left at the factory by anybody, and at any time in its past.'

'I don't believe that's the case.'

'What then?' Cable asked. 'What's your theory?'

Jenkins's shoulders rounded. She shoved her hands in her pockets and shrugged. 'I don't know as yet, ma'am. Maybe the killer's playing a game with us.'

Adams scoffed. 'The only person playing games here is you.'

Cable turned to Sioned Williams—crime scene manager—and asked for her thoughts on the significance of the coin.

Williams explained that it was an old ten pence piece. The kind replaced by a smaller version in nineteen ninety-two. And subsequently demonetised in nineteen ninety-three.

'It could have been clanking around in the bottom of an old money box?' Ward suggested. 'Or dropped while the factory was still open for business.'

Adams shifted in his chair. 'Isn't that what I just said?' No one responded.

'What date did you say it was minted?' Jenkins again.

'I didn't,' Williams replied. 'But nineteen ninety now that you ask.'

'Ken, go check for similar crimes from that year,' Jenkins said. 'And while you're at it, find out if there was any abortion legislation passed at that time.'

Ward scribbled an entry in his pocketbook. 'Any reason why?'

'Humour me.'

Adams left his seat and jockeyed for a position out front. 'This has hate crime written all over it. Both suspects had abusive childhoods. Both were caught at the scene. And both had clothing stained with the victim's blood. It couldn't be more cut and dried than that.'

'Sergeant?' Cable said.

Jenkins knew she was losing ground. 'I'm asking you to trust me on this, ma'am.'

'It has nothing at all to do with trust. I have to weigh up the evidence and, right now, yours is looking pretty thin.' To Adams, she said: 'If you want that extension, then you'd better get yourself across to the Magistrate's Court before it closes for the Bank Holiday.'

Chapter 30

Reece accelerated hard off the hairpin bend, Bob Seger singing as loudly as a few turns of a Stubby screwdriver would allow. He knew every word and sang at the top of his voice while the harsh winter wind hurled hail at the old Peugeot with the snap-and-rattle of coarse grit. He was on the Brecon Beacons—an area of outstanding natural beauty set in over five-hundred square miles of national parkland—and already it felt like he'd come home.

He wiped the windscreen with a damp rag and watched the low cloud base shroud the twin summits of Pen y Fan and Corn Du. The road ahead spiralled upwards and into it, disappearing from sight altogether, leading him to a place that held many memories and mixed emotions.

He hadn't been able to travel this route since Anwen's death.

Fluffy sheep with green rear-ends stood at the roadside, their heads lowered to the worst of the weather, thick fleeces dripping with an ice-water mix. To the east the sky was the colour of ripe plums, and beyond that, a storm was announcing itself with a deep rumble of thunder. There was good reason the SAS used the Beacons as a survival-training ground.

A few miles further on, he slowed to navigate a potholed dirt track, the car rocking side to side on its squeaking suspension. He turned in a wide arc outside the cottage, the Peugeot's tyres sliding to a full stop on an open patch of loose gravel. A quick glance at his watch confirmed there was no chance of him having the old generator up and running before morning — meaning he'd spend some of Christmas Day getting dirty with spanners and oil drums.

He went round the back of the vehicle, dodging puddles frozen over with thick sheets of ice. It was cold. Much more so than it had been in Cardiff. With an overnight bag in hand, he searched for the spare key beneath a cracked plant pot, and let himself in. There wasn't another property for miles.

The compact boot room smelled of damp and a year's worth of neglect. The kitchen smelled of something far worse. Islands of black mould spores clung to the ceiling and walls. With a groan, he reached behind a short gingham curtain that hung untidily beneath a Belfast sink, and lay his hands on a pair of squat candles. He used a thumbnail to scrape away the wax damp-proofing from the head of a match and struck it against a dryish section of kitchen wall. His route to the living room was negotiated by candlelight alone.

The warped door refused to budge in its swollen frame. A firm shoulder popped it like a cork from a bottle of plonk. He was picking bits of dust and flaking paint chips from his clothing when the phone rang in his back pocket. 'Where the hell are you?' he asked. 'It sounds like there's a riot going on.'

'Outside the Rummer Tavern,' Jenkins said. 'You sound out of breath?'

'An altercation with a door.' Reece gave no further explanation.

'Who won?'

'Split decision,' he said, checking the damage and adding it to an expanding list of jobs to be done.

'You coming out tonight?' Jenkins was shouting to be heard. 'It's last office drinks before Christmas Day.'

'This year I'm spending it in Brecon.'

'You there now?' she asked. 'All on your own?'

'It's not by choice.' Reece paused for thought. 'I'm planning on getting some work done. Haven't been here in a long while.'

'Good for you. Hey, you almost gave Ginge kittens at the hospital yesterday. You should have seen how he dealt with Adams.'

'That boy's gone way up in my estimation. Get him a pint if he's out with you.'

'You paying?'

'Of course. Get the whole team a drink while you're at it.'

Jenkins promised she would. 'Fishy told me about your visit. What are you up to, boss?'

Reece sniffed. 'A fiver says you already know.' He hurried the conversation on before she could have another go at him. 'Any progress with the mystery woman angle?'

'None at all. DI Adams won't let us follow it up on it.'

'What does Cable say?'

'For now, she's supporting her man.'

'She'd lose face if she didn't.'

'There are rumours circulating that the Assistant Chief Constable is chewing her ear over it.'

'Harris is as big a clown as Adams is.'

'It's getting busy, boss. Let me move out of the way of these people. Can you hear me any better now?'

'A bit.'

'I know this mystery woman is involved somehow. I'm just about certain of it.'

'Go find her then.'

'My orders are not to. Adams even talked the magistrate into extending the custody warrant to ninety-six hours.'

'That's practically unheard of.'

'I suppose the evidence against that pair is pretty damning to anyone who doesn't know them like we do.'

'So why doesn't he charge them instead of pissing about with extended warrants?'

'I think deep down even he knows he's wrong, but won't dare admit it.'

Reece perched on the arm of a chair and drew a grubby net curtain across a loose rail. 'Then you'll have to find her before she kills again. We both know she will.'

'Adams won't let me.' The frustration was clear to hear in Jenkins's voice.

'Who says you have to tell him what you're up to?'

'Are you suggesting I disobey an order given by a senior officer?'

'I'm saying that going it alone can sometimes have its advantages.'

Chapter 31

'There you go.' Jenkins came away from the bar and handed Ginge a bottle of frothing Peroni. 'DCI Reece sends his thanks for all you did to help yesterday.'

'That's kind of him.' Ginge licked froth from his fingers. 'You're not drinking?'

Jenkins tapped a glass of tonic water, ice, and a slice. 'Alcohol does all kinds of weird shit to me.'

'That's true of most people,' Ginge said, watching someone crowd-surf their way across the dance floor.

'The smallest amount is like poison to my system.'

'No way.'

'Yep. I hear you and Billy Creed had yourselves a showdown at his place.'

'It was touch and go at one point.' Ginge rested his drink on the edge of the bar and made a pair of pistols with hands. 'Like a scene from one of those mob movies when there's a standoff before everyone starts shooting.'

'That bad, eh?'

'Not really.' He took another swig from the bottle. 'Can I speak off the record, Sarge?'

'Go ahead, everyone else seems to.' Jenkins rapped him on the chest with the back of her hand. 'But do us a favour, will you, cut it with all the Sarge shite.'

Slade wished everyone a Merry Christmas for the third time since they'd arrived, the place erupting in a frenzy of dance and song. Ginge shouted in Jenkins's ear. 'I think there's more to this Roxie May murder than first meets the eye.'

'You've got a theory?'

'I do.'

She leaned closer, not wanting to share details of an open case with the drunken occupants of a heaving pub. 'Come on then, Sherlock, let's have it.'

'It's shambolic, isn't it?' Ginge belched and excused himself. 'I mean symbolic.'

'You were probably right the first time.' Jenkins struggled to open a packet of crisps one-handed and resorted to using her front teeth to good effect. 'Sorry, I interrupted you.'

Ginge steadied himself when someone pushed past. 'I don't think Onion and Fishy are the woman-haters DI Adams made them out to be. After all, Fishy loved his nan, and Onion had a girlfriend. Even when Tasha Volks beat him up, he never went back there to do her any harm.'

'I agree. What else have you got?'

'I think the killer hated Roxie as a person, not as a woman.'

'There are far easier ways to kill someone you don't like. Far quicker too.'

'That's why I'm saying it's symbolic. The coin or its date — has to mean something, otherwise why go to the bother of using an old one?'

'We already searched HOLMES and came up with nothing similar in terms of MO.'

'True,' Ginge said with another suppressed burp. 'But that database is limited to crimes committed within the UK and Northern Ireland. Nothing further afield.'

'We can't go to Interpol with this. Not with Adams breathing down our necks.'

'I suppose not.'

'Don't look so deflated,' Jenkins said. 'For now, let's accept there's a reason the killer removed the uterus. We just don't know what it is yet.'

'Okay.'

'And the coin is . . .' She puffed her cheeks, not knowing what else to say.

'It's the clue to all this,' Ginge said. 'It has to be. The killer is highlighting a specific date for a reason.'

Jenkins nodded slowly. 'If we work out what happened back then, we might have a fighting chance of learning who was involved.'

'That's what I was thinking.'

'Fancy yourself as a detective, do you?'

'I was going to ask DCI Reece yesterday.' Ginge lowered his head and picked at the foil at the neck of his bottle. 'He shut me up before I could open my mouth.'

'He's a bit preoccupied just now.' Jenkins tapped him on the shoulder. 'But you did yourself no harm at all at the hospital.'

Ginge leaned closer and spoke in her ear. 'Can I get you another drink, or maybe—'

'Whoa, slow down, tiger. You're not my type.' She stepped away and handed her empty glass to the barmaid.

'That's not what I was going to say.' He pointed towards a leggy blonde in a tight black dress. 'I'm with my girlfriend over there. I was going to ask if you wanted more crisps.'

Jenkins blushed, hopeful that the festive lighting in the room would have hidden it. They both laughed. 'Sorry,' she said.

'No offence taken.' He leaned again; this time, careful not to make contact with any part of her person. 'So, what is your type?'

Jenkins turned her head towards the blonde thrashing about to the Time Warp. 'Be afraid, Ginge. Be very afraid.'

Reece munched on a bright-red apple and stared into the flames of the log burner. A handful of candles lit the small living room, the old Aga oven heating only enough water to afford him a quick swill in the bathroom sink. The armchair wobbled under his shifting weight, an old book not quite the perfect fit for its broken front leg. He put the apple on a low table and took the lid off a worn shoebox wedged between his knees. He rummaged through several layers of pink tissue paper until he found what he was looking for.

The ornament was the purest white, save for a gold halo hovering above its head on a short piece of stiff wire. He took the angel and held it in the open palm of his hand, turned it over and caressed its delicate form. With a heavy heart, he placed it on the oak mantelpiece, his thoughts returning to the earlier conversation with Jenkins. The mystery woman was an interesting angle. The killer didn't have to be a man. Women could be every bit as violent. Even more so when the motive was strong enough. But try as he did, he couldn't help but think that Billy Creed was somehow involved.

Reece's phone pinged and caught him off guard. He opened the text, setting free a myriad of cavorting emojies. *Merry Christmas, boss*, it read before fizzling to nothing. He put the phone away without replying and turned his attention to an array of shapes forming in the depths of the hot flames. There were faces in there that came and went. One of them belonged to Helen, the staff nurse at the hospital. Next was Anwen. Even Ken Ward's ugly mug made a brief appearance.

Then a new image. One as cruel as it was vivid. Anwen, lying in a pool of her own blood, the moped rider wearing a Billy Creed face mask while brandishing a knife. Blinking made no more difference than shaking his head. Creed refused to pass and let him be. Reece looked away from the flames, then back again. Anwen was dying in his arms. Her lifeless eyes staring up at him. He flew out of his chair and hurled an empty whisky glass into the fire. 'You're going down, Creed — dead or alive.'

Chapter 32

THE BEDROOM LIGHT WAS on, and that alone should have served as ample warning. Jenkins's phone showed 1.35am — way past her partner, Amy's usual bedtime. But Amy wasn't due home until much later that afternoon. Things had obviously changed without prior warning. Jenkins paid the taxi driver his fare and stepped out onto the pavement. She shivered with cold, the hairs on her arms standing erect. She kept an eye on the upstairs curtains and jumped when the outside downlighter announced her arrival by bathing everything in its reach in a soft yellow glow.

Letting herself inside, she closed the door behind her with a level of stealth a seasoned burglar would have been proud of. She held her breath and listened to the silence. There was an unnerving stillness in the house. Something wasn't right. She was still trying to fathom what it was when Amy pounced without warning from the dark shadows beneath the stairs.

'Where the fuck have you been?' She hammered the plasterboard wall with a clenched fist, its booming echo reverberating through the narrow hallway. 'It's Christmas morning, as if you didn't already know.'

What Jenkins did know, and with the utmost certainty, was the fact she wouldn't get back through the front door in time to escape physical injury. Talking her volatile partner down was her only option. 'I told you I was out with work colleagues tonight. Even asked you to come along and join us. Don't you remember?'

'I've been working,' Amy said. Gone was her usual soft Irish lilt, replaced with something far harsher. 'How the fuck could I come out with you if I wasn't here?'

'I mentioned it before you got your rota. People were asking about you.'

'Who?'

'Ffion for one. She still hasn't met you. Not properly.'

'Tell her to fuck off.' Amy ran a trembling hand across her bald head, moving skittishly as she pulled at handfuls of imaginary hair. In the gloom, her white nightdress gave her the appearance of someone returned from the grave. Her attitude was just as cold. 'Who were you screwing tonight?'

Jenkins recognised the signs. All the signs. Amy was dangerously close to blowing her fuse. Not good in anyone's world. 'I told you, I was out with colleagues. Coppers, mostly, and a few of the support staff from the labs and offices at the station.'

Amy closed the distance between them. 'Liar.'

'Not this again.' Jenkins pressed her back against the front door, its handle digging into the flesh above her right hip. She tried to sound confident and in control. She failed miserably. 'You did take your medication away with you?'

'You're doing it again, Elan. Making out this is all me.'

'Nonsense, I was trying to explain that—'

'*Silence!*' Amy clenched her fists above her head and came closer still. 'You know I have to punish liars.'

Reece woke with a sudden start and couldn't remember the last time he hadn't. His body went through its usual wake-up routine while his brain lagged and got its bearings. He massaged the back of his neck, rising from the threadbare armchair in stages – like an Evolution of Man character printed on the front of a cheap T-shirt. He yawned, and rubbed his shoulders, crossing to the kitchen where the heart of the stove was as lifeless as the log burner in the other room. That generator needed fixing, and sharpish if he was to remain at the cottage with any degree of home comfort. Brecon wasn't at all forgiving in winter.

He squatted over his travel bag, rummaging inside until his hand closed around breakfast. He took a bite of the bruised apple and gave thought to his latest nightmare. They were getting worse. Playing out in vivid colour. No matter how often they repeated, he could never alter the outcome and save his dying wife.

Outside, the early morning sunlight was making its pilgrimage across the land with the dogged determination of an army marching into battle. There was a light dusting of snow. The higher ground had copped for a lot more, making the summit of Pen y Fan off limits for the time being. The new light caught the edge of something next to his chair in the living room, drawing him towards it with the pull of a powerful magnet. When he saw what the object was, he went down on his knees and took the two pieces of broken angel into the palm of his hand. Closing his fingers over them, he sobbed for all he was worth.

Jenkins sat at the kitchen table while Amy fried bacon and hummed along to the radio version of Lady Gaga's 'Born This Way'. Jenkins put a finger to her bottom lip and ran the tip of her tongue along the split. It could have been worse. The lip wasn't that swollen. She'd tell them at work that the cold weather had chapped it. Just as a slip on the icy patio had caused a bruised rib only a month before. She had lists of excuses available to her and was ticking them off faster than she could ever have imagined. Amy scared her whenever she got like she was now. Her issues were both deep and complex, and she'd never been willing to open up and speak about them. Jenkins knew their time together was almost done.

'What was that, darling?' Amy turned side-on, a wooden spatula dripping pig fat onto the enamel surface of the cooker.

Jenkins let her lip be and forced a smile. 'I didn't say anything.'

'You've hurt yourself.' Amy leaned over and kissed her. 'Any better?'

'Yes.' Jenkins went to the refrigerator and returned with two juice cartons: one apple, the other, orange. She rearranged bottles of ketchup and brown sauce, making room for the juice at the centre of the table. 'Anything else I can do to help?'

'The rolls are ready to come out of the oven.' Amy moved to one side. 'Careful not to burn yourself.' It was how things always went the morning after a fight. There was never a word said in acknowledgement of the violence. No remorse or apology given.

You've such a shock coming. Jenkins slid the bread off the hot tray and took the basket to the table. 'These look good.'

'You're troubled today,' Amy said. 'I can tell.' She straightened her newest wig—a shoulder-length redhead parted down its centre—and took Jenkins's hand in hers. 'You wouldn't be keeping something important to yourself, would you?'

Jenkins suppressed a rising wave of panic and handed Amy a bacon roll before taking a seat. 'Not at all.'

Amy licked grease and ketchup from her fingers. 'Did you miss me while I was away?'

'Of course I did.' Jenkins poured orange juice for herself, then apple into a second glass. 'Three weeks is a fair amount of time for you to be living out of a suitcase.'

'I've got used to it. It comes with the territory.'

Jenkins trod carefully. 'You were home earlier than we both expected.'

Amy finished the apple juice in one go and helped herself to another glass. 'I changed my flight.'

'I thought everything coming out of Germany was full until this afternoon?'

'I wanted to surprise you.' Amy smiled. It looked contrived. 'You know how I like surprises.'

We'll be testing that claim soon enough. 'You're home now, and that's the main thing.'

Amy reached a finger. 'You should put Vaseline on that lip of yours. It's started bleeding again.'

Jenkins flinched under her partner's touch and pulled away. 'Don't. That hurts.'

'You're not blaming me, are you?' Amy's tone was harsh, her mannerisms stiff and edgy.

'I was asking you to be more careful, that's all.'

'Good. For a moment then, I thought you were trying to spoil Christmas.' Amy got up and put her dirty plate in the sink. 'We'll do nice things today. A long walk in the park, perhaps?'

Jenkins poured the tea and added milk and sugar to both cups. She hated walking. And running. The gym especially. She was naturally small and most days didn't eat many more than twelve hundred calories. Exercise, she'd decided long ago, was for people with time on their hands and fat round their middles. She had little of either. 'What about Roath Park Lake?' she suggested.

Amy clapped the air like an excited child and spun on the spot. 'That would be perfect. I'm so lucky to have you, Elan.'

Chapter 33

REECE DIDN'T KNOW WHAT was happening back in Cardiff and, for the most part, couldn't give a shit. He leapt the narrow stream, crunching through the icy mud on the other side. He grabbed at the long grass, using it to get purchase and climb the steep bank side-on. After taking a moment to get his bearings and absorb the raw beauty of the snowy landscape, he was off again, headed towards a small outcrop of trees in the distance.

He'd spent the best part of the morning working on the generator, though the term work had proven to be something of a misnomer. He'd mostly stood in front of it, scratching his head and swearing at the top of his voice. The thing looked like a battered chest freezer: waist high and only a little wider than he could stretch his open arms. Once a clean white, the unit was now a shade of dirty cream, with flaking patches of rust on all sides. He'd eventually prised open the lid with a flathead screwdriver, only to find that beneath the foil covered heat-blanket, was a tangle of chewed fuel and power lines. Whacking the metalwork with a large socket-wrench, he'd given up, deciding instead to exorcise his demons with a brisk run along the Beacons.

Reece had contemplated suicide in the aftermath of Anwen's murder. He'd waited on a platform at Cardiff Central Station, intent on throwing himself under the next incoming train. But that would have been unfair to the driver. And so he'd taken up running; the activity most likely saving his life, if not yet his sanity. He cleared another ditch—this one full of solid ice—pushed and pulled by a wind that carried an alternating load of hail, sleet, and snow. There was no protection to be had for several miles, save for a few outcrops of jagged rock and a forest treeline still so far away. He lifted his knees and pumped his arms, fighting against the weather in an exhausting battle between man and environment. His face stung and his chest burned, but he hadn't felt this alive in far too long.

Anwen's voice carried on the buffeting wind, calling his name, drawing his attention. Stopping, he doubled over to catch his breath, turning in small circles as he hunted for the source of the sound. Overhead, a buzzard rode the gale like a surfer on the crest of a giant wave. It called as it went, and Reece knew the message was for his ears only. He waved and went chasing after her as though his life depended on it, laughing and crying all at once.

Jenkins and Amy walked hand-in-hand around Roath Park Lake, the meandering pathways busy with children on shiny new bicycles, and parents looking just about dead on their feet. Amy stopped to point. 'Look at the gulls, they're everywhere.' The rooftop of the boathouse opposite was littered with them. More still on the Scott Memorial clock tower next to the promenade. 'I don't like them. They scare me.' She ducked and squealed when a pair swooped to feed nearby.

Jenkins shooed the gulls away and took a chance. 'Can we talk?'

Amy tossed a piece of bread into the water and watched a swan barge its way through a flush of mallards. 'Here they come.' She threw another pellet. 'Swans are my favourite.'

Jenkins tried again. 'I wish you'd open up about your past. It might help me understand you better.'

Amy stiffened, a piece of bread poised between finger and thumb. She cocked her head to one side and tapped it with her knuckles. 'Do you know how many people have been inside this already?' She lifted the hairpiece, exposing her bald scalp to the elements. 'And not one of those meddling fuckers gave me any answers to my problems.' There were people watching. Some steering children off in the opposite direction. 'You want to talk – let's start with this murder you're involved with. Tell me about you and your job.'

'You know I can't divulge the details of an ongoing case.'

'Can't, or won't?'

'Both. I could lose my job.'

Chapter 34

MARTIN THORNE WENT FOR dinner at his mother's house every December twenty-fifth, and had done for as long as he could remember. It was the only day of the year he could get his young family anywhere near the woman they collectively referred to as the *Wicked Witch of the East*. Truth was, Thorne dreaded the annual visit more than they did. He took a deep breath and waited on the unwelcoming doorstep.

'Maybe she's done us all a favour and died in her sleep?' his wife said, crossing the fingers on both hands when a third round of knocking brought no reply. 'On second thoughts, let's hope it was something excruciatingly painful.'

'Stop it, you know she's got ears like fag paper.'

'I didn't mean it,' his wife said. 'Not really, anyway.'

Thorne rang the bell even though he knew his mother had previously removed the batteries out of spite for visiting Jehovah's Witnesses. "*Haven't they got better things to do with their time?*" she'd asked in a fit of rage one Sunday morning. "*Parading their brainwashed kids in clothes that are far too old for them. There should be a law against their sort.*"

He went back to knocking. 'I bet she's on the other side of that door, making us wait for the sheer hell of it.'

Lifting the flap of the letterbox, his wife peered through. 'She's cooking sprouts again.' The flap slammed closed. 'I thought you told her none of us wanted sprouts?'

Thorne nodded. 'And I would have done if she'd answered the sodding phone.' He knocked again and called to his mother.

'Can we go home now?' his eldest asked. He turned to his younger sister: 'Gran's gonna make us eat sprouts.'

She shuddered. '*Urgh.*'

'Not this year,' their mother promised. 'Nobody's having sprouts.'

'Ssh.' Thorne took a step away from the house and checked the upstairs windows. The curtains were closed. Downstairs too. He tried to get a peek through the drab netting but saw nothing except for a few flies on the glass and frame.

'I'm taking the kids back to the car,' his wife said. 'It's far too cold to be standing out here twiddling our thumbs.'

Giggling, the little girl tugged at her mother's sleeve. 'Mammy, you said bums.' She gripped her doll's ankle with the other hand, its head swinging precariously close to the lip of the stone step.

'I'm bored.' The teenager had a whine to his voice and walked with rounded shoulders to exaggerate his point.

'I'll try Mrs Pearce next door.' Thorne cocked his leg over the dwarf-wall and climbed a short flight of steps that led to a weather-worn frontage. At the top, he turned to see his wife and daughter wave from the warmth of the car. His son was nowhere to be seen. He couldn't blame the boy.

He rang the bell and knocked at the same time. There were signs of life on the other side of the frosted glass panel, followed by the rattle of a chain as a catch travelled on its runner. Next came the squeaking of hinges as the door opened to reveal an old woman no taller than his thirteen-year-old. 'It's Martin,' he said, trying to sound friendly. 'Libby's son.' He pointed in the direction of his mother's house. The old woman disappeared from sight, closing the door without explanation. Thorne fingered the bell until Mrs Pearce shouted something he didn't quite hear. The door opened again with a pronounced judder.

'I told you I was coming.' Mrs Pearce waved a fistful of arthritic fingers at him. 'You think it's easy managing with these?'

'I'm sorry.' Thorne stepped across the threshold and wiped his feet on the doormat. 'I was wondering if you'd seen or heard anything from Mam today?' Mrs Pearce didn't answer and made off down the hallway without inviting him in. He closed the door, shutting out the draught, and followed the old woman into a warm living room, waiting until she'd got herself seated. 'I can't get an answer next door and she's not picking up the phone.'

Mrs Pearce put her hands in the front pocket of a nylon pinafore. 'I haven't seen your mother since the day your sister called in.'

'I don't have a sister.' Thorne watched her reach for a drawer and rummage through a lifetime of safekeepings. 'I'm an only child.'

'You'll be wanting the spare key.' Mrs Pearce tried the next drawer down, and the one after that when she couldn't find it. 'It's in here somewhere.' She frowned. 'I came across it straight away when your sister called in.'

A car horn tooted outside. 'What about the hook next to the back door? Do you hang it out there with your own keys?'

Mrs Pearce ran a cold hand over his cheek. 'You look just like her.'

'Most people say I'm more like my dad.' Thorne lowered his head, a tinge of melancholy colouring his voice. 'Not that I ever knew him.'

'Not your mother, you silly thing.' She gave him a playful tap on the arm. 'I meant your sister. Oh, what's her name now?'

Thorne went into the kitchen and checked the tags on the keys. None belonged to his mother. 'What about Dai?' he asked. 'He'll know where it is.'

'Dead a whole twelvemonth.' *Cancer*. Mrs Pearce mouthed the word, not daring to speak its name aloud.

Thorne swore under his breath at the sound of a second sharp blast of a horn, and willed himself not to throttle all remaining life out of the old woman. 'I'm sorry about that. I didn't know.'

Mrs Pearce nodded at a Welsh dresser. 'It was in that teapot when your sister came. I remember now.' He took the lid off to speed things along and handed it to her. She shook her head and refused to take it from him. 'There's no point in you giving me that. Your sister never brought the key back.'

They were tucking into turkey and all the trimmings when Jenkins's phone rang. She excused herself from the table and took it in the front room. 'This had better be important.' She pushed the glass door closed and left it as it was when it popped open again.

'They've found another body.' Ken Ward was outside somewhere. Jenkins could tell from the amount of background noise.

'Female?'

He spoke to someone else before answering. 'You guessed it, and she's a real mess this time.' He sounded busy and wasn't paying Jenkins full attention. Crime scenes were often like that. There was always something to be done, asked, or said.

'That puts Fishy and Onion in the clear.' Jenkins settled on the arm of a large sofa and wondered how well smug grins travelled down phone lines. 'Let's see Adams argue his way out of this one.'

'Not so fast.' There was another delay as Ward juggled multiple conversations. 'Sorry, Jenks, but this woman was killed well before that pair were taken into custody.'

'Shit.' She slid off her perch and kicked at the air. 'You sure?'

'Wait and see for yourself.'

She took a purple paper crown off her head, crumpled it, and tossed it to one side. 'Shitface there yet?'

'He's on his way back from the Midlands. Been visiting family, apparently.'

She stared through the front window, watching traffic and pedestrians passing in blissful ignorance. 'You know what this means, don't you?'

'It's got all the makings of there being a serial killer out there.'

'Spree killer, at the very least.' She took her pocketbook and pen from a leather satchel. 'Give me the address.'

'Going somewhere?' Amy stood in the doorway sipping a glass of bucks-fizz.

'There's been another one.' Jenkins went to the far end of the room and pushed her arms into the sleeves of a thin jacket. 'Sounds like it could be the same killer.'

Amy stayed put in the only doorway out of there. 'And you're going, just like that, Christmas Day and all?'

'I've no choice.' Jenkins edged towards her. 'As a murder detective, I work when the killer works.'

Amy ran a wet finger around the top edge of her glass, making it sing. 'I'll let you go this time, but only if you promise to tell me all about it tonight.'

Chapter 35

IF ELAN JENKINS DID the job for a hundred years or more, she'd never get used to the smell of a corpse gone ripe. She was standing on the victim's doorstep, swatting at the flies that got up her nose, in her mouth, and just about everywhere else. Trying not to imagine on which putrid parts of the deceased they'd feasted before refocusing their interest on her. She rested a hand on the shoulder of a CSI, wobbling on one leg while applying an elasticated overshoe to the other foot. 'Don't you keep some sort of air freshener in that bag of yours?'

The CSI handed her a face mask to go with the head-to-toe coverall. 'Even if I did, it wouldn't help much with what's circulating in there.'

Jenkins delved into her jacket pocket and waved a small glass vial at the CSI. 'Forest Glade — doctor's orders.' She sprinkled a few drops of the green liquid inside her mask and reapplied it. 'They sell it for colostomy bags, apparently. Does the job nicely.'

The CSI waved a hand when Jenkins offered her some. 'I'm just about done here. Almost ready to get back to the lab.'

'Lucky you.'

DI Adams barged his way up the steps and made a grab for a coverall. 'Have you been inside yet?'

Jenkins moved out of his way. 'No, sir, but I've logged in and taken a briefing from the officer on the door.' She waited for the DI to get dressed and made no mention of the wonders of Forest Glade.

Adams gave the street a brief once-over. 'Where's Ward?'

'Taking statements and trying to avoid Maggie Kavanagh, sir.'

There were several white vans parked wherever they could outside the terrace of houses, most having satellite dishes and tall aerials attached to their roofs, all belonging to the local news channels. Reporters prowled the pavements like opportunistic thieves, knocking on doors to ask the same pointless questions.

'Tell him to keep his gob shut and to get over here, pronto,' Adams said.

'Yes, sir.'

Ward came puffing up the steps when called. He raised the hood of his coverall and applied new overshoes with help from Jenkins. 'I've been in there once already,' he said with a look of disgust. 'And it ain't pretty, I can tell you.' He followed Adams into a busy living room where the stench went up a few notches. 'Her name is Elizabeth Thorne.' Ward pinched the mask tighter to the bridge of his nose. 'The son broke in through the back door and was first to find her like this. Poor sod.'

'Why did he break in?' Adams asked.

'He couldn't get an answer round the front.'

A CSI moved to let them pass.

'Pryce here yet?' Adams again.

'I'm behind you.' The voice was deep and unmistakably that of the pathologist. 'And a Merry Christmas to you all.' Jenkins and Ward answered likewise.

The DI pointed to the kitchen and said: 'Shouldn't you be in there doing something medical?'

Pryce leaned over and whispered in Jenkins's ear, 'You didn't share our little secret with him, did you?'

She winked. 'You always told me it was best to take a few deep breaths before you get going?'

Pryce chuckled. 'Ffion wouldn't agree with us on that.'

'True. I heard she went spark out again yesterday?'

Adams pushed between them. 'Whenever you're both ready.'

Elizabeth Thorne was lying half-naked on the kitchen table, her arms and legs splayed. Beneath her was what would once have been a significant amount of blood. It had formed puddles, congealed and dried, then cracked open and gone bad. There was dark staining of the table and linoleum floor, together with areas that were orange and yellow. Adams waved at a sortie of buzzing flies and let Pryce enter the kitchen ahead of him.

'Can't we get some fresh air through here?' Adams asked.

'Not yet.' The woman was young but obviously knew her job well enough to insist on things being done properly. 'A few more surfaces to check for prints, and then it's all yours.'

Adams made no reply and moved for another member of the scientific support team to get behind him and take measurements of blood spatter on the nearest wall. The back door was ajar, part of its frame split where Martin Thorne had used force to gain entry.

'Don't touch that!' The young CSI shook her head. 'Patience, Detective Inspector, I've already told you we'll be finished soon.'

Adams apologised in his own clumsy way. 'What's that?' He watched the CSI peel something off the blackened floor. It broke into a few smaller pieces. 'Might have been toast once.' She bagged and labelled it. 'Bit difficult to tell now.'

'You can put that down to rodent activity.' Pryce looked up from what he was doing. 'They've been in here too, by the looks of things.'

Adams edged towards the kitchen table, moving from one metal stepping plate to the next. 'Rodents?'

Pryce poked a metal probe deep inside a wound that gaped just above the pubic hairline. 'Of the long-tail-sharp-teeth kind.'

'Rats?' Adams stopped where he was and turned pale. 'They're not still in there, are they?'

'Not that I can see.'

'And the uterus? Is it intact?'

Pryce came away and removed a pair of surgical gloves. 'You'll have to wait until we get her back to the mortuary before I can say for sure.'

Adams checked the kitchen counters. 'I don't see it anywhere out here.'

'Eaten long ago if ever it was left for us to find,' the pathologist said.

'What's the soonest you can get the post mortem done?'

'Will two or three days do you?'

'What's wrong with today?'

Pryce stared. 'You do know it's Christmas afternoon?'

Adams didn't seem to care. 'And this is a murder investigation.' He turned to Jenkins and Ward. 'Or has no one else here clocked that yet?'

Jenkins kept her mouth shut. She was preoccupied at the other end of the table, inhaling lungfuls of Forest Glade. She angled her head to get a better view of the marbled face on its stiff neck. There were long lengths of darkish hair trailing to the floor, a deep plough-line of grey running along its wide centre-parting. 'What did you see before you died, Elizabeth? Who did this to you?' The woman gave no answer, her mouth forced open by a purple tongue that was far too large to be a proper fit. There was a curled piece of tape hanging from one side of it. Jenkins leaned closer. 'Someone come and take a look at this.'

A CSI called for a photograph to be taken before pushing past the swollen tongue with a pair of long-nosed forceps. 'It's a ten pence piece,' he said, turning it under a bright light.

'Date?' Jenkins asked. 'What date is on it?'

The man inspected it with an exaggerated squint. 'Nineteen-ninety.'

Jenkins crossed the kitchen and interrupted the DI's conversation with Dr Pryce. 'Sir, there's something I need to show you.'

Chapter 36

JENKINS GOT TO HER feet. 'Let me help you with that.'

'No need to fuss.' Mrs Pearce rested a steaming teapot on the table with only a small amount of its contents spilled. 'Can I get you a biscuit, dear?'

Jenkins thought it best to pour for them both. 'Not right now, thank you.' She doubted she'd ever eat again; images of putrid flesh and swollen tongues filling her mind.

'And what about that handsome gentleman in the smart suit?' The old lady clucked. 'Are you two an item?'

'I'd rather have a go with the corpse next door.'

'What was that, dear?'

Jenkins hadn't realised she'd spoken out loud. 'I asked if you wanted milk?'

'Just a spot.' Mrs Pearce prised the lid off a tin of biscuits. 'I've got your favourites. You always did like shortbread — ever since you were a little girl.'

Jenkins handed over a cup that she'd only half filled. 'Who lives here with you?'

'My husband, Dai.' The old lady shook her wristwatch and checked the wall clock opposite. 'He's late home from work today.' She went to the window and looked up and down the street. She wasn't a day under eighty-five, and had either nabbed herself a toy boy, or things were decidedly worse than Jenkins had first thought.

'Where does Dai work?'

'Tower.' Mrs Pearce spoke with an obvious show of pride. 'A collier all his life.'

Tower Colliery had once been the oldest continually worked deep-coal mine in the world. That was before Maggie Thatcher and a Conservative government saw fit to decimate the entire industry in the nineteen eighties.

'And how old is Dai?'

'Thirty-six'. Mrs Pearce glanced at the clock again, clearly troubled by her husband's non-show. She got up and then sat down almost immediately. 'Oh, what am I doing?' she asked in a shaky voice. 'Dai's not coming home for his tea. Not today. Not ever.'

Jenkins reached for the woman's hand and gave it a gentle squeeze. 'Is there no one else to help you?'

'Well of course there is. Dai will be home soon.' Mrs Pearce smiled. 'Your brother was here earlier. He'll be pleased you've brought back the front door key.'

'How the hell can that be?' Jenkins put her hands on top of her head and spun in a circle on the pavement outside the row of terraced houses. 'One woman dead for weeks, another clearly dementing, and no one round here gives a flying fuck.' She glared at the onlookers. 'What's wrong with you people?'

Ward tried to move her on for her own good. 'It's happening everywhere these days.'

Jenkins gawped at him. 'What a stupid thing to say. What does that even mean?'

'It means we're police officers, not social workers.'

'I'll tell you this for nothing: you can shoot me if that shit happens to me. Do you understand?'

'Loud and clear.'

'Good. I wanted that out in the open.'

'And now it is.'

'I've reported it.' Jenkins took a deep breath. 'I feel awful, but it's the right thing to do.'

'Of course it is.'

'It won't be the way poor old Mrs Pearce sees it, though. She's lived here all her adult life. Then one day—wham—she wakes up in a council-run nursing home not knowing where the hell she is.'

'You couldn't have left her there and done nothing.' Ward lay a hand on her shoulder. 'You did the right thing.'

'Did I? She'll go downhill quickly now and that'll be the end for her.'

'You don't know that.'

'It's what happens.'

'You get too attached to people. A sucker for anyone with a problem.'

'No, I'm not.'

'A magnet for the needy.'

'Sod off.'

'What happened to your lip?' Ward asked. 'I noticed it when you took your facemask off earlier.'

'It's this bloody weather,' Jenkins said. 'I blame it on my father — I'm meant for sunnier climes.' She put her fingers to it. 'Is it that noticeable?'

'Not really. I thought you'd overdone the mistletoe.'

'Yeah, right.'

'How *is* Amy, anyway?'

Jenkins puffed, but said nothing.

'Like that, is it?'

'I'm not sure she's taking her medicines. Not consistently. She's all over the place at the moment.'

Ward nodded at her split lip. 'You be careful.'

Jenkins looked away.

'DI Adams. Do you have a moment?'

'You must be Maggie Kavanagh?' Adams extended a hand in greeting. 'I've heard a lot about you.'

Kavanagh squinted and tossed a cigarette butt into the road. 'Not so much about you, I'm afraid.' She took his hand in hers and thought of wet lettuce. 'You're holding the fort for Brân Reece, I'm told.'

The remark got no reaction. 'Quite a crowd for a Christmas afternoon.'

Kavanagh laughed, loosening a fair amount of phlegm. 'This beats the Queen's speech hands down by my reckoning.' She lit another cigarette and inhaled so deeply that for a moment she turned a worrying shade of blue.

'You're not a fan?'

'Oh, I love a good murder, me.' She exhaled slowly, bathing the DI in a veil of thick smoke. 'Nothing quite like it, especially at Christmas.'

'I didn't mean—'

'I know you didn't.' Kavanagh face-palmed. 'It was a joke, for Christ's sake.'

Adams ducked under a drooping line of crime scene tape to join the reporter on the other side. 'I can see why some of my colleagues might find you intimidating.'

'Little old me?' Kavanagh pointed at her Mercedes parked further up the road. 'Let's get in out of this cold,' she said, pressing 'record' on a device she kept hidden in her coat pocket.

Chapter 37

Belle Gillighan watched the news broadcast come to an end, wondering how bad Libby's corpse must have stunk after lying in wait for the best part of three weeks. How blue and bloated it would have been as she liquefied and quite literally fell apart. The reporters said very little on that front. And what they did say was mostly supposition. Belle could only imagine. Rising from the sofa to take her empty glass to the kitchen, she stopped to stare at the table, her mind flooded with images of her first victim laid out on one that wasn't dissimilar.

It had been easy once Belle had identified the correct address.

'You're so like your mother,' the mad old bat said before handing over the key to the front door. Belle hoped not. She hadn't seen Libby in over twenty years, and even then, the woman had been the chewiest of mutton dressed as lamb.

The front door shut with a quiet click. There was a musty smell inside, and threadbare carpets with peeling flock wallpaper. A radio played somewhere: a commercial station repeating the Christmas songs of yesteryear with a cloddish monotony.

The coverall and overshoes took little more than a minute to apply. That was good to know when planning for the next victim.

Libby was in the kitchen burning cheese on toast and smoking cigarettes, and to say she was caught by surprise would be something of an understatement. It isn't every day, after all, that someone wanders through a person's house dressed head-to-toe in a blue paper suit, Taser device gripped tightly in their hand. Not that Libby would have had a clue what the black and yellow thing was until the current hit and made her dance like a demented frog. And even then, Belle might have forgiven her that initial look of ignorance.

Libby let go of the plate and attempted to flee. It hit the floor and broke into four sharp pieces, the bread landing cheese-side down with her writhing next to it on the hard linoleum.

The bindings came next: wide plastic bag-ties fastened to her ankles and wrists. Arm in arm, Belle heaved Libby against the table. It shifted away from them, Libby falling head first against the side of a cabinet door. A slap across the face and a firm shake of the shoulders woke her up. 'Not until I open you up. You owe me that.' Belle pushed the table against the far wall, where it couldn't slide any further. She grabbed handfuls of long, greasy hair and used it to pull Libby to her feet. Then shoved her on top of it. More juice from the Taser meant the required crucifix pose was easily accomplished.

Belle reached and turned the radio up loud, laughing until it hurt her ribs and lower jaw. 'How fucking ironic is that?' she asked when able. 'Last Christmas — by Wham.' She set herself off again.

Tools and victim were ready. Every sinew in Libby's body was stretched to just short of rupture point. Her eyes bulged grotesquely without lids to hold them in place.

Belle took the scalpel and held it to the overhead light. 'I was once like you are now. Tied down and violated against my will. You could have stopped it. Any one of you could have stopped it. But no one even tried.'

Libby lifted her head and mumbled something from behind the duct tape covering her mouth. She let her head drop when her pleas for mercy brought no response.

Belle turned the radio off before George Michael got to finish his song. 'I want to hear every last whimper you make.' There was more head thrashing and muted screams as Libby's skirt and underwear were peeled away. 'I'm ready,' Belle said, plunging the knife into her victim's lower abdomen. 'How about you?'

Chapter 38

The euphoria of the memory quickly wore off. Replaced by one that was far darker. One that haunted Belle every day.

It was the summer of 1981.

There were young children shouting cruel names as they searched the tall grass in pursuit of her. She wasn't a witch. How dare they call her such a thing? And was her mother really a whore? As an eight-year-old girl, Belle wasn't sure what the word meant. She crouched over the wriggling corpse of a cat and kept very still. After an intolerably long time, the shouts became less frequent and more distant. Then they were gone altogether, leaving her with only the dead animal and her secret friend for company.

'Poke it,' said her secret friend.

Belle turned, but as was always the case, she couldn't find the owner of the voice anywhere. The boy was the best hider ever. 'I don't think I should. It's icky.'

'I said poke it!' He sounded impatient.

With a short stick, she stirred a sea of wriggling maggots, unperturbed by the awful smell. Lifting the dark pelt, she tapped the animal's exposed ribs and got closer for a better look.

'The other children are evil.'

'Liars, too,' Belle agreed.

'They deserve to be punished.'

Her secret friend was always right. 'Yes, they do.'

'Would you like to hurt them?'

She thrust the stick through the rotting animal and into the soft earth on the other side. 'Yes, I would.'

'You could make them look like that cat.'

'Oh, yes.' Belle got up and danced in circles, willing the boy to come out of hiding and play properly. He didn't. He never did. 'Who's the first to die?' she asked, excitedly.

'What about Amelia?'

Belle clapped her hands and squealed. 'Oh yes. Let's start with her.'

Across the fields, Belle skipped. And up the garden path to her mother's house. Those wicked children would leave her alone soon enough. Amelia Hosty especially.

From her position in the kitchen, she heard voices overhead. Not voices exactly. But mother crying in tune with a rhythmic squeaking that got louder and faster the further Belle climbed the narrow stairs. Her secret friend warned her to be quiet. She put an eye to the keyhole and took a loud gasp of air. Mother was clawing at the back of a man who had her pinned to the bed. A man who was hurting her.

'Let her be,' Belle demanded, with a stamp of her foot.

The bedroom door flew open only moments later, a bony hand catching her little arm so tightly she screamed. The man dragged her into the room and pushed her onto the boarded floor. He was tall and thin, and naked except for a dog collar and dark-green socks.

Mother pulled a thin white sheet close to her body and shifted hair from her wet face. 'Father Quinn was only—'

The priest silenced the woman with a fearful look and dragged Belle to a wicker chair in the far corner of the room. 'You're the devil's child,' he said, putting her over his knee.

Belle struggled as he exposed her, throwing her arms open wide, screaming for love and protection.

A leather strap passed between mother and priest. 'It's for your own good, my dear. Father Quinn says it's the Lord's will.'

Belle heard them pray together and took herself off to her safe place before the beating began . . .

Belle blinked. It was no longer 1981. She was standing at the kitchen sink, waiting for the water to run hot and steam. She gripped the nailbrush and soap in her hand. And then it began. The ritual cleansing.

Chapter 39

THE BUZZARD WAS LONG gone. No doubt roosting on a roadside post somewhere. Reece stopped to take a drink and rest at the Tommy Jones Memorial along the route to the summit of Pen y Fan. He'd read the inscription a hundred times or more. He read it again.

THIS OBELISK
MARKS THE SPOT
WHERE THE BODY OF
TOMMY JONES
AGED 5, WAS FOUND.
HE LOST HIS WAY

BETWEEN CWM LLWCH
FARM AND THE LOGIN
ON THE NIGHT OF
AUGUST 4TH 1900.
AFTER AN ANXIOUS SEARCH
OF 29 DAYS HIS REMAINS
WERE DISCOVERED SEPTEMBER 1ST.
ERECTED BY VOLUNTARY
SUBSCRIPTIONS
W. POWELL PRICE
MAYOR OF BRECON 1901

'No one deserves such a terrible thing.' The man came from beyond the other side of the stone and spoke in the Welsh language. 'Not least a small child.' He removed his flat cap and leaned on a shepherd's crook.

Reece replied in their mother-tongue. 'Still gets me every time I read it. Poor kid all on his own up here, waiting to die.'

'Such beauty,' the man said with a deep nod. 'But if not respected, it'll bite like the devil himself.'

Reece couldn't argue with that. The summit had been bad tempered that morning. Snow and strong winds forcing him back before he got there. They talked a short while longer. About the weather, and rugby mostly. After bidding the man farewell, he crossed over the rise and made his way downhill towards Llyn Cwm

Llwch — Dust Valley Lake. He stopped at the water's edge to bathe his face and, for the briefest of moments, thought he'd glimpsed the invisible island said to exist at the lake's centre point. A place purported in local folklore to be inhabited by fairies and other magical creatures. *Fairies.* He scoffed at the notion and tightened the straps of his rucksack. *But the devil - he walks among us every day.*

Reece was on his way again. Building to a jog, his eyes on the sky, in search of that buzzard.

Chapter 40

MARTIN THORNE SAT OPPOSITE Adams and Jenkins, his wife and children tucked safely away in one of the station's waiting rooms.

Jenkins thought the man must have been in shock, such was the lack of grief he'd shown since arriving back at the nick. 'When did you last see or hear from your mother?' she asked.

'This time last year. We aren't . . .' Thorne corrected his use of present tense. '*Weren't* particularly close.'

'You had a falling out, or an argument of some kind?'

'No, nothing like that. My mother was a difficult woman to be around.' Thorne turned his head to Adams. 'By the sound of your accent, you're not local?'

'Bewdley, Worcestershire.'

'Ah, right. We took the kids there during the summer. To the safari park.'

Adams looked as though he couldn't care less.

'Anyway,' Thorne continued, 'Cardiff Bay hasn't always looked like it does now. All bars and restaurants. Pleasure boat trips and fancy apartments. In my mother's day, you had to grow up fast. People scrapped and scraped just to survive.'

'I've read the history,' Adams told Jenkins. 'Shirley Bassey was born just round the corner from here.'

Jenkins ignored him as best she could and went on with her own line of questioning. 'Could someone from your mother's past have been harbouring a grudge?'

Thorne wrung his hands. 'You could pick just about anyone in the street. She'd have had a ding-dong with them at some time or another.'

'Was she really that bad?' 'Unfortunately, yes. Even I avoided her like the plague.'

'But not today,' Adams said. 'You even took the whole family there.'

'And every Christmas Day since I left home. Like some Catholic Penance. Only this time we couldn't get an answer, so I went round the back and—'

Jenkins stopped him. 'Sorry, I just want to be clear on something before we move on. When was it your mother was last seen or heard from alive?'

Thorne scratched his head. 'It would have been some time in November, I guess. First week. Had to be, because I was in Tesco buying last-minute fireworks when she rang.'

Jenkins scribbled a note. 'Earlier you said the two of you hadn't spoken for the best part of a year?'

'I'd forgotten about that one. Blanked it out probably.'

'And how did she sound?'

'Like she always did. The usual moaning at me for not ringing her first.'

'Did she mention anything out of the ordinary?' Adams asked. 'Crank calls, a stranger at the door, or another argument with a neighbour?'

'Not really.'

'However insignificant, it could be important.'

'You have to remember that my mother was a compulsive liar.'

'So, there was something?'

Thorne took a deep breath. 'She thought she was being watched whenever she went out. Fanciful, I know.'

'Now we're getting somewhere.' Adams shifted in his chair. 'Did she say where this was happening?'

'All over. Supermarket, chip shop, bus stop. You name it, she claimed to have seen her there.'

Jenkins pounced. 'A woman?'

Thorne scratched his chin. 'You don't think it was the same one who took the key from Mrs Pearce, do you?' He lowered his head and shook it. 'I can't believe another woman did that to her?'

Adams stood and brought the interview to an abrupt end. 'We don't know that yet. We're exploring all possibilities.'

When they got back to the briefing room, Jenkins drew a pair of red arrows connecting the crude outline of the mystery woman to the photographs of both victims. 'There she is again,' she said, making sure Adams heard her.

'Elizabeth Thorne was killed long before the arrests of our suspects,' he protested. 'There's still no reason to believe it wasn't them.'

Jenkins was tired of the DI's refusal to accept what was staring them all in the face. 'And on whose behalf did they kill this woman, sir? The son; daughter-in-law; grandkids, maybe?'

'Mind your tone, Sergeant.'

'We're wasting our time on the wrong people.'

'In your opinion.'

'Two women murdered. Both with links to Billy Creed, and you've got us fannying about with the village idiots.'

'Enough!'

Jenkins looked out of the window, wishing she was someplace else. 'Well then.'

The other occupants of the room kept their heads down and mouths shut, wise not to get involved. Adams churned pocket change. 'What's that supposed to mean?'

Jenkins grabbed her jacket. It was either that or take him by the throat and squeeze hard. 'I don't know exactly, but I won't be sitting here any longer with a thumb stuck up my arse.' She made her way to the ground floor corridor with her phone held to the side of her head. 'Answer for God's sake.' Reece, not doing so, was winding her up that bit tighter. She put the phone away and slammed a hand against the glass of the vending machine. 'Twat!'

'Hope you're not referring to me?' The desk sergeant stood opposite, fiddling with a sweet wrapper.

'No, not you, George.'

'Glad to hear it.' He checked the corridor was clear, and said, 'DI Adams, by any chance?'

Jenkins folded her arms across her chest. 'Reece on this occasion.'

'Why? What's he done?'

She was about to reply when Adams came through the door at the foot of the stairwell. George nodded and headed off in the direction of the custody suite.

'I needed a break,' Jenkins said, coming away from the vending machine. 'This case is starting to get to me.'

Adams thrust his hands in his pockets. 'I've finished reading through all of yesterday's statements . . .'

She watched him and waited. *And you're ready to look for the mystery woman.*

'I want to reinterview Fishy and Onion.'

Jenkins clapped the air and spun on her heels. *Of course you do. You're a fucking A-Grade idiot.* 'Why would you do that?'

'Because I know they're somehow involved.'

She could think of nothing else to say and walked off in silence.

Chapter 41

THEY BEGAN THE INTERVIEWS with Fishy. Jenkins lay two colour photographs flat on the table. Both of them depicted heavily made-up women in their late fifties. 'Do you recognise either of these?' she asked.

'That's Libby.' Fishy studied the image at arms-length. He put it down again and pushed it away. 'I don't like her. She shouts and calls me bad names.'

'What sort of names?' Adams asked.

'A retard.'

'Speak up. I can't hear you.'

Fishy blushed. 'She said I should've been strangled at birth.'

'And was that why you killed her? Because of the things she said about you?'

'I didn't kill no one.'

'What about this woman?' Adams rested the tip of his finger on Roxie May's forehead.

Fishy turned away from the photograph. 'I'd never hurt Roxie.'

'Onion says he caught you at it.'

'He didn't.'

'Yes he did. And when he tried to stop you, you went for him with the same knife.'

'He wouldn't say that. It's not true.'

Adams tossed Onion's statement onto the desk. 'Read it for yourself. It's all there. Every word of what he said about you.'

Jenkins snatched the single sheet of paper. 'Don't do that, sir. You know he can't.'

Adams took the statement from her and pointed to a paragraph at the bottom of the main block of text. 'He says you attacked him with the same knife you used on Roxie.'

'What knife?'

'You're not getting this, are you?' Adams said with a deep sigh. 'The one you used to kill her with.'

'I didn't kill anyone.' Fishy put his head in his hands and rocked in his chair. 'You're trying to trick me. Trying to make me say things I never did.'

'You killed her,' Adams insisted. 'I know you did. And Elizabeth Thorne before her.'

'It's not true. I wouldn't.'

Fishy's new brief spoke after a long period of inactivity. 'You're clutching at straws, Detective Inspector. My client has already admitted to being in the factory, and explained how the victim's blood came to be on his clothing.' The woman looked towards Jenkins. 'He has a mental age of twelve — only just above the threshold for criminal responsibility.' She summarised the victims' injuries using the relevant sections of the pathology reports. She tilted her head towards her mumbling client. 'Do you really think he'd have the wherewithal to execute any of that?'

It was Onion's turn in the hot seat. Jenkins concluded formalities and withdrew her hand from the DIR's record button. 'Why did you lie to us?'

'What?' He managed a thin-lipped smile only. 'Who says I did?'

She leaned on her elbows. 'I've been wondering why you'd invent such a cock-and-bull story.'

All trace of the smile was quickly gone. 'I told you what happened.'

'And I said you're lying.'

'Prove it then.'

'I know somebody chased you out of that factory building.'

'Fishy did.' Onion looked at Adams for help. 'Shut her up. She's talking through her arse.'

'It wasn't your friend who came running after you. That would have been impossible.'

'Ex-friend. And what makes you think that?'

'Common sense alone.'

'Huh?' Another glance at Adams. 'What's she talking about? Have you got any clue, coz I haven't?'

Jenkins locked her fingers together and pressed her elbows firmly against the hard surface of the desk. 'Fishy was well ahead of you. Out into the middle of the road and hit by the patrol car well before you even reached the pavement.' Onion and Adams frowned in sync. 'He wasn't chasing you. The killer was.'

Chapter 42

Reece tossed and turned during another fitful sleep. The dream had him back in Rome. Inside the cramped music shop strumming open chords on an old Blueridge acoustic guitar. The place had been such a lucky find. It was dark and dusty, and crammed from floor to ceiling with more music memorabilia than he'd ever previously seen stacked in one room. He'd returned there several times during their stay, insisting Anwen join him on what became the fateful last day of their honeymoon.

The shop owner—in the dream—was Carlo Collodi's Geppetto. The old man sat behind a counter carving wood, looking up occasionally to applaud the accomplished guitarist. 'Bravo. Bravo.'

'Pinocchio?' Reece asked, muting the strings with the palm of his hand. It always began that way; innocent small-talk shared between two like-minded people.

Geppetto nodded. 'He'll be such a fine boy. You wait and see.'

Reece didn't doubt the old man. The carving had come on tremendously since his previous visit.

He could see Anwen walking along the pavement, taking photographs and practising her limited Italian whenever the opportunity arose. He loved her dearly and was happier now than he could ever have imagined.

He spoke with Geppetto about what it took to carve a child from a large block of wood. It was worth knowing. Anwen hadn't fallen pregnant despite more than two years of them trying. When everything outside went inexplicably dark, he took the guitar to the window, Geppetto joining him when there was insufficient light to continue his carving. The two men raised eyebrows at one another. There was a whale passing overhead. Huge and grey.

Anwen was out of sight. Reece mumbling incoherent warnings to her in his sleep. When he turned to speak with the woodcarver, the kindly old man had disappeared, replaced by the bearded hulk of Stromboli. Reece shoved Stromboli away and headed for the door in an attempt to alter the course of history – knowing that no matter how hard he tried, he wouldn't be able to. He'd been there a thousand times before and had failed on every occasion.

And then he heard it. That noise: the whine of a four-stroke modern scooter engine somewhere off in the distance. There were calls of warning from other pedestrians, but Anwen's attention was fully taken by the passing whale. Reece ran, but the cobblestone pavement had since become a travellator set in reverse gear. He pumped his arms and legs, desperate to close the distance between them. It was like running under water, his limbs propelling him nowhere near the speed he knew they should. Calling to his wife, his tongue swelled to the size of the prime fillet steak he'd eaten the previous night, and as such, was next to useless.

And here it was: the man riding pillion reached for Anwen's camera. Instead of letting go, she yanked at it, pulling the scooter and its riders on top of her. They lashed out, one of them striking her just below the ribs. She didn't scream, but staggered forward, searching for her husband.

Reece called for help, his tongue no longer swollen, his pleas when spoken in English not fully understood. He tried again; this time in pigeon Italian. 'Aiutarla.' He pointed in the direction of the beautiful woman slumped on her knees. 'Aiutarla — help her.'

Reece fought to wake up, unwilling to yet again witness his wife lying in that expanding pool of her own dark blood.

Jenkins eased herself behind her desk, a Starbucks coffee in hand, an angry drummer let loose in her head. She'd driven the entire way to work that morning with the car window down, convinced she had a hangover. It was impossible under normal circumstances, given that she didn't drink alcohol.

Amy had insisted they stay up late the night before, discussing the case as promised, both of them getting to bed somewhere after 2.30am. She knew she shouldn't have—that to do so was a disciplinary offence—but what she didn't need right now was another war between them.

'Morning Campers.' Morgan danced into the room with a greeting stolen from an '80s sitcom. She dropped a Gianni Conti Forli shoulder bag onto her desk and sat down with a satisfied sigh. Seconds later, she was on her feet again, collecting empty mugs. 'Who's for coffee and nibbles?'

Jenkins had a small waste bin wedged between her knees. Her head was angled over it. She raised the Starbucks in answer and passed on the food. 'Did you have a good Christmas?'

Morgan shook a wrist at her on the way to putting the kettle on. 'Josh spoiled me rotten, as always.' She rolled her eyes. 'What's a girl to do?'

Jenkins had no clue what brand watch her junior colleague was wearing, but guessed it must have cost close to a month's wages. 'It's all right for some.'

'It certainly is.' Morgan used her thumb to extract a mince pie from its foil tray. 'George downstairs tells me you found another body. Christmas Day, as well.'

'A right stinker.' Jenkins reached for the bin and took several rapid breaths. 'I shouldn't have said that.'

Morgan left the broken mince pie where it was. 'You're not usually like this after seeing a corpse. Me, on the other hand, well—'

'It's got nothing to do with the corpse.'

'What then? Not pregnant, are you?'

Jenkins peered over the top edge of the bin. 'Highly unlikely, don't you think, given Amy doesn't carry the right equipment?'

'Fair point.'

'I think the turkey must have been a tad undercooked.' Jenkins knew that wasn't true, but it sounded plausible enough as an excuse.

Morgan used the back of her hand to push the mince pie to one side. 'Oh shit, you know what another victim means, don't you?' She slumped forward onto the desk with her head buried deep in the crook of her elbow.

'Relax, I've sent one of the others,' Jenkins said. 'I thought it was only fair.'

'Was it Ken? It'll do him no end of good being off his food for a few days.'

Jenkins shook her head. 'He's not back in until tomorrow.'

'And what are *you* doing in work?' Morgan asked. 'Boxing Day is supposed to be your day off, isn't it?'

'I'd rather be here at the moment.' Jenkins used the corner of the desk to steady herself when she got up. 'Come on, we're going out.'

'Where?'

She put the empty bin to one side. 'I think it's time you and me had a good look round Roxie May's place.'

Chapter 43

KEN WARD WAITED BENEATH a widescreen television in the City Road betting shop, watching his horse limp home like a donkey on Porthcawl beach. He tore the losing slip in two and dropped it in the nearest bin. 'Shat on again.'

'No luck?' Chantelle quit with the rapid-fire selfies and put her phone down. 'You should try the lottery instead. Might be more your thing.'

Lottery. Dogs. Nags. Ward did them all. He'd even bet on a snail race once – his choosing not to move the entire time. 'This next one,' he said with a finger pointed at the screen. 'You wait and see.'

'What would you do if you won a few million?' Chantelle had started, and that usually meant the subject wouldn't change for the best part of ten minutes. 'I'd AstroTurf the back garden,' she said, fully absorbed in a new daydream.

Ward moved out of range but found her still banging on when he returned to the counter a short while later – something about a mobile tanning unit she'd take to supermarket car parks.

'Tan-in-a-Van,' she said proudly. 'What do you think?'

Ward couldn't bring himself to say. 'Told you my luck would change some time soon, didn't I?' After collecting close on three hundred quid, he made his excuses and left Chantelle to it.

Jenkins hadn't counted on Seamus May being at his mother's house when they got there. And wherever Seamus went, then so too did his brothers.

'Oi,' she shouted when the door slammed in her face. She still felt queasy, the pounding headache showing no signs of letting up. 'Open it. Now!'

Something came out of the window above them, exploding when it landed next to Morgan's foot. 'There's pee in that,' she squealed, kicking the shredded condom to one side. 'Filthy sods.'

'I'll give you a count of ten to open this door, Seamus.'

The letterbox flapped up and down. Then stuck in the up position. 'What are you going to do then, dyke?'

'Open the bloody door or I'll nick all three of you.'

'For what?' Seamus stood in the narrowest of gaps, peering into the daylight through beady eyes. He was his father's son, all right. 'Come on. For what?'

'Oh, I don't know,' Jenkins said, barging past. 'How about for being thieving gobshites as starters?'

'You can't come in here,' he said, following her down the hallway. 'Not without a fucking warrant.'

'And that's where you're wrong. Don't you want us to find your mam's killer?' The living room curtains were closed, empty cider cans and pizza boxes piled high next to the sofa. It smelled of cigarette smoke and stale farts. 'Open those windows,' Jenkins told Morgan. 'I'm close to passing out.'

Seamus went to the bottom of the stairs and hollered. 'Aiden, Brady, get your-fucking-selves down here this minute.'

Jenkins knew from experience that Aiden was the most volatile of the three brothers. Seamus was the eldest and liked to shout his mouth off, but Aiden was quick with his fists and good in a fight. 'We're not here for anything you've done,' she said when the boys appeared. 'We just need to find out why someone would want to hurt your mother.'

Aiden was short and stocky, and wore a ginger buzz cut with a stained vest top. 'There'll be plenty of fucking hurt when I get my hands on them.'

Morgan came away from the window. 'There'll be no need for threats.'

'Then you'd better catch the bastard who did this,' Seamus said, drawing a finger across the front of his neck. 'Because if you don't—'

Jenkins took him by the elbow and steered him out of the room and towards the stairs. 'Come on Rambo, show us where your mam kept her stuff.'

Chapter 44

'We came across it in the drawer of Roxie May's dressing table.' Jenkins waited as Chief Superintendent Cable read the short note.

'It's not much to go on.' Cable handed back the evidence bag and its paper contents. 'Take a seat.'

Jenkins did. 'This means Roxie had contact with her killer before the night of her murder.'

'Someone she knew, do you think?'

'It looks like she might have done, ma'am. It would've been hellish risky to turn up to a disused factory unit if she didn't.'

'And you're sure that's Roxie's writing?'

'One of her sons confirmed it was. She's obviously written the date, time, and venue down, in case she forgot.'

Cable reclined and folded her arms, thinking out loud. 'Lured to the factory by someone she knew?'

'Or someone pretending to be.'

'Two bodies in six days. Three, if you include the ex-husband.'

Jenkins took advantage of her opportunity. 'And all the while, DI Adams has us focusing resources on a pair of delinquents who had nothing to do with this.'

'But the evidence against them is—'

'Even Onion's changed his tune—' Jenkins stopped herself. 'Sorry, ma'am, I interrupted you.'

There was a moment's silence shared between them. Then: 'You don't like him?'

Jenkins needed more time to come up with a response that wouldn't get her sacked. The best she managed was, 'Who do you mean?'

'DI Adams.'

'With all due respect, I think he's way out of his depth.'

Cable leaned in a lopsided pose on the arm of her chair. 'You know I appointed him, as well as had him act up as SIO for this case?'

'I thought you wanted my honest opinion, ma'am?'

'I did, Sergeant, but the thing is—'

'Then we need DCI Reece,' Jenkins said, interrupting for a second time. She forced her point before the chief super could stop her. 'Can you really afford to have your best murder detective on gardening leave while Cardiff plays host to a serial killer?'

'Reece isn't on gardening leave.' Cable sat upright, her chair objecting to the sudden movement with a series of annoying squeaks. 'It's for the good of his own health, and some might argue, the wellbeing of colleagues that I've put him on a period of forced rest.'

Jenkins screwed her eyes shut. 'Oh.'

'Oh, indeed.' Cable was staring when Jenkins opened her eyes. 'Why would you think the DCI was suspended from duty?'

Jenkins couldn't wait to get her hands on him. 'A misunderstanding is all.'

Chief Superintendent Cable raised a finger to stop Adams from entering her office and swivelled her chair so that she sat with her back to him. Pushing the telephone handset tight under her chin, she spread the newspaper across both knees. 'The bank holidays have impacted on progress, sir, not to mention the cutbacks on overtime.' She let Assistant Chief Constable Harris continue his rant from the other end of the line. 'Reece is nowhere ready to return to duties,' she said for a second time. 'I will, sir.' She hung up and sat staring at a grey sky. Her chair turned slowly on its axis. 'Adams!' She waved, and when that didn't work, tossed a pen against the glass.

'DS Jenkins said you wanted to see me.' Adams helped himself to a seat without waiting to be asked.

'What the hell did you think you were doing?' Cable threw the folded newspaper at him. 'Definitely not your finest hour.' Adams read in silence. 'Didn't the team warn you about Maggie Kavanagh? I know I certainly did.'

Adams didn't look up. 'I thought I could improve things between the station and local journalists.'

Cable gawped. 'You're a murder detective, not a fucking press relations officer.'

'All I was trying to do was—'

'Wasting time is what you've been doing.' Cable stood and went to the window. 'You're letting them both go.'

'You can't be serious?'

'I'm not arguing with you, Robert. You'll follow DS Jenkins's line of enquiry from now on. Do I make myself clear?'

Adams's brow furrowed. His left eye closed. 'She's been to see you?'

'Because you're too stubborn to listen to anyone but yourself.'

'I thought you were with me on this? You even granted a custody extension.'

'And now I'm telling you to get their arses out of this station.' Cable let the air clear. 'Elan Jenkins is a good detective. She has a keen eye for detail and a willingness to go that extra mile.'

'And I don't. Is that what you're saying?'

Cable came away from the window and held open the office door. 'Grow up.'

Adams took his cue and left in a huff.

'And I want twice-daily progress reports,' she called after him.

Jenkins opened a large white envelope and removed Elizabeth Thorne's post-mortem report. 'Here it is.'

'I owe you one,' Morgan said, looking up from her laptop screen. There was no opportunity for Jenkins to answer.

'You went running behind my back like a little snitch.' Both women turned to see Adams looming towards them. 'You "*just happened to bump into the chief super on the stairs*," is what you said.'

Jenkins got to her feet. 'And what would have happened had I brought the note to you? I'll tell you shall I – we'd still be arguing the toss over it.'

Adams's pocket change got a good shuggle. 'We're supposed to be a team, not a one-man band.'

'You don't give a shit what the rest of us think, just as long as you get a quick result.'

'I'll go put the kettle on.' Morgan was out of there before anyone could stop her.

Adams looked like he might explode with rage. 'Are you accusing me of framing that pair?'

'I'm saying you're wrong; that I've worked these streets for years and know most of the scum who walk them. Fishy and Onion are a royal pain in the arse, true enough – but murderers, they're not.'

'How can you be so sure?'

'Because. Because I just am,' Jenkins said, throwing her hands in the air.

Adams headed towards his office. He stopped before he got there and came back. 'I think your mess of a private life is clouding your judgement.'

For a time, Jenkins stood open-mouthed. 'What did you say?'

'Your girlfriend is obviously a—'

'Whoa. Don't go there.'

'Amy. Isn't that her name?'

'I said stop.' Jenkins's voice was trembling. She promised herself she wouldn't break down and lose it completely. 'How do you know anything about Amy?'

'She sounds a right one from what I've heard.'

Jenkins pointed a finger. 'I'm warning you.'

'I found some biscuits to go with the coffee.' Morgan stood in the doorway, a blue plastic tray and mugs held out in front of her. 'Some of them are in bits, but beggars can't be—'

'You. It was you who told him.'

A couple of the mugs slipped sideways, spilling some of their contents. 'It wasn't like that, Jenks. I promise.'

'You had no right.'

'I was worried.' Morgan found room on her desk for the tray. 'The bruised ribs and split lip were the final straw.'

'No fucking right at all.'

'That's enough.' Adams went to his office again. 'I want a word with the pair of you about tomorrow's press conference.'

Jenkins wasn't concentrating, her mind awash with emotion. 'This doesn't end here.' She glared at her junior colleague as she went past. 'You've let me down, Ffion. Big time!'

'On your feet.' Ward spoke through the small serving hatch in the cell's door. 'Your mate Fishy's been gone a good ten minutes already.'

Onion rubbed his eyes and threw his legs over the side of the narrow bench-bed. 'Why didn't he wait for me?' He sounded put out and massaged both calves simultaneously.

'It must have had something to do with you trying to stitch him up for a murder he didn't commit.'

For a moment, Onion looked like he might argue the point. In the end, he didn't. 'Did he say where he was going?'

'Nope.' Ward moved out of the way for the custody sergeant to open the door. 'Funny that, don't you think?'

'Have you lot spoken to Paddy May yet?'

'No can do.' Ward waited until the uniform was out of sight. 'Billy caught up with him.'

'Dead?'

'And cremated.'

Onion bit down on his bottom lip. 'Fuck.'

'I've a feeling your troubles are only just beginning.'

'*I* know who you are. I've been wracking my brain ever since the interview. You're on Billy Creed's payroll with the rest of us.'

Ward shoved him back into the cell—out of sight of the surveillance camera—and grabbed him by the throat. 'Where's that gun?'

'I don't know what you're talking about.'

'You've got three seconds to stop being a prick.' Ward let go and took his phone from his pocket. He hovered a thumb over Creed's number. 'One. Two.'

'The killer's got it.' Onion caught his breath. 'He must have, if your lot don't.'

Chapter 45

JENKINS SLAMMED HER FIST against the steering wheel of her car. It caught the horn and earned her a two-fingered salute from a startled pedestrian. How dare that prat Adams tell her to wear something more feminine for the following day's press conference. How fucking dare he! And Ffion Morgan . . . Jenkins couldn't go there as yet.

The Principality Stadium went by on the right-hand side of the road, the castle to her left, its battlements lit up with brightly coloured lights set against an impenetrably dark night sky. Wire-mesh reindeer-and-sleigh combinations were fixed to its outer walls—beyond the reach of drunken hands—a bloated inflatable Santa swaying atop the castellated tower. She checked the dashboard clock: 9.10pm already. She'd earlier told Amy she'd be in by 9pm at the latest. There were speed cameras dotted at regular intervals for another mile or so yet, and no easy way of avoiding them on the route home.

Amy wouldn't be interested in excuses, regardless of how justified they were. Jenkins's heart skipped a beat. Not tonight. Not before tomorrow's press debacle.

She gave thought to not going home at all. To turning the car in the opposite direction and driving off, never to return. Anywhere would do. She could find a hotel, bed-and-breakfast, or sleep on the back seat of the car if need be. There was a blanket and an overnight bag in the boot. Kept there for that very reason. She drew a deep breath and pressed on the accelerator pedal. Fingers crossed the roadside traffic cameras had snapped their day's quota of speeding motorists.

When she got home, Amy's car was nowhere to be seen. Amy had mentioned nothing during their earlier telephone call. Jenkins parked clear of the driveway, leaving enough space for her partner to swing on whenever she got back. Letting herself in via the front door, she waited in the hallway with bated breath, half expecting Amy to fly at her, fists first. She flicked the light switch and saw a note pinned to the newel post at the bottom of the stairs. She tore it free and went through to the kitchen, putting the back of a hand against the kettle. It was warm still. She tossed her jacket onto the upright of a chair, a sugar-free 7UP liberated from the American-style fridge. Passing on ice, she read the note.

Elan,

Running errands.

Not sure what time I'll get back.

Don't wait up.

Love and hugs,

Amy

Errands at such a late hour. What was Amy up to? Jenkins turned the note over, took a gulp of lemonade, and burped loudly. Her parents watched from a framed photograph on the opposite wall: an attractive couple walking hand-in-hand beneath a Caribbean sunset. 'Don't judge me, you guys.' She burped again, but this time more quietly, and with a hand held to her mouth.

There were no photographs of Amy's family to be found anywhere in the house, and only one of the woman herself. Jenkins studied it. 'What brought you to my door? Turning up the way you did?' She rested the bottle on the note and went upstairs to take a shower.

Onion knew they'd come for him, and couldn't be sure the fat copper wasn't pulling his chain and trying to get him killed.

"Get yourself round to Tasha's flat and stay there," Fatty had told him. "*Creed doesn't know diddly-squat about her. You'll be safe if you keep your head down.*"

Onion's eyes had popped almost as wide as Fishy's. "*Are you nuts?*" he'd replied. "*She'll fuck me up worse than Denny Cartwright will.*"

But Fatty had insisted, and it seemed like he hated Billy Creed almost as much as he did.

Onion ducked for cover and descended the front steps from the police station. He kept low as he went, careful not to draw attention to himself. If he could only get to the pavement unseen, then there was a dwarf wall and some bushes to hide behind.

The BMW was parked further along the street, listing to one side with its lights and engine switched off. Denny Cartwright was on board, watching and waiting for his moment to pounce. The car being there came as no real surprise. Fatty's phone call to them could be delayed for only so long without raising Creed's suspicion.

Onion peeked over the top of the wall. So far, so good. He crept behind the sixty-foot lighthouse sculpture—purchased with seventy-five thousand pounds of taxpayers' money—and used it to block Cartwright's line of sight while legging it down the nearest side street. He'd done it. Got away without being seen or followed.

Or so he thought.

Ward parked round the corner and walked the short distance to Tasha Volks's flat. Two kids wearing expensive trainers rode circles in the middle of the road, watching the stranger's movements, ready to race off at a moment's notice to warn those further up the food chain. Paying them little attention, he blew on his hands and passed through a narrow alleyway running adjacent to the property he was interested in. He had to take the risk. This might be his one and only opportunity to get that gun back before any of his colleagues got their hands on it. Reece especially. The nets were reeling in fast, and Ken Ward had no intention of ending up as *catch of the day*.

He knocked on the door for a second time, calling for Tasha to open it. He thumbed the letterbox and saw movement inside. 'Come on, Tasha, I've got you that present.' He was getting angry, but trying hard not to show it.

The safety chain slid in its catch, then two bolts, the door opening to reveal a woman who looked more than twenty years beyond her true age. 'What you got me?' She clawed at him. 'You brought me my goodies?'

Ward pushed her inside. 'First, we talk.' She followed him into the living room – if ever such an awful hovel could be described as one. It stank worse than he remembered, the air thick with cigarette smoke and the vinegary odour of heroin. 'Onion's on his way round.'

Tasha went behind the sofa and returned, tapping a baseball bat against an open palm. 'Bring it on.'

Ward took the bat from her and rested it against the wall. 'He left something here last time.'

'Aye, two of his fucking teeth.' Tasha cackled at the memory.

'I know he's been back since.' The woman's gaze settled on the kitchen cupboards long enough for him to notice. 'I want the gun.'

'What gun?'

'Don't mess with me, Tasha.'

'I don't know nuffin' about no fucking gun!' She was getting agitated and close to losing it.

'Okay. What about we do a trade?' He nodded. 'You scratch my back and I'll scratch yours.'

She watched him suspiciously. 'What do you mean?'

He was making progress at last. 'I'll give you something in return for what I want.'

Tasha dropped onto her knees in front of him and reached for his belt. 'It's always the fucking same with you coppers.'

He slapped her hand. 'Not that. The gun.'

She backed away. 'You still ain't told me what I get.'

'Fentanyl.' He reached beneath his shirt and took a small glass ampoule from a pouch on his belt. 'The gun. Where did Onion put it?'

Tasha grabbed for the ampoule and missed. '*All right!*' she screamed. 'He hid something in that cupboard under the sink. Thought I didn't see him, but I did.'

Ward took a strap of rubber from his pocket. 'Give me your arm. It's time for your goodies.'

Chapter 46

Onion made it to the housing estate unscathed and stopped in the dark alleyway to add to an assortment of urine samples. Something moved behind him.

'Who's that? Who's there?' He zipped up mid-flow, groaning while rearranging a damp patch at the front of his joggers. He'd been stupid to use such a place and knew he'd got himself into something that could well and truly ruin his evening. Keeping his back to the wall, he edged towards two kids riding bikes. They weren't looking in his direction and surely would have been if Denny Cartwright was waiting to batter him with an oversized shovel.

There it was again. Definitely movement behind him.

'I'm carrying,' he said, adding a layer of rasp to his voice. 'You come any closer and I'll stick you.' There was a high-pitched whine from the other end of the alley that, at first, he thought was a tomcat come to claim its territory. The sudden appearance of the silhouetted figure told him otherwise. The figure raised an arm and pointed what looked to be a gun in his direction.

Onion ran; the whining sound reverberating off the concrete walls as he burst into the street. The startled cyclists made off like a pair of sewer rats, leaving him alone with his assailant. His shoulder caught a lamp post and knocked him off balance. Spun him sideways. He stumbled and grabbed the post, avoiding the fall and propelling himself towards Tasha Volks's flat in one awkward movement. Up the steps he went, two at a time, banging at the door with both fists when he got there. It opened more quickly than was usually the case.

'Get in.' Ward pulled him by the wrist.

Onion broke free of the detective's grasp and rammed the bolts home in their slots. 'What are you doing here?' he asked, gasping for breath.

'Making sure you arrived in one piece.'

'You set me up.' Onion squatted to look through the letterbox.

'Nonsense.'

'He was waiting for me in the alley.' Onion went through to the kitchen and closed the blinds. 'Only you knew I was coming here.'

Ward stuck his head through the thin metal slats and saw nothing but darkness and broken streetlights. 'What are you talking about?'

'Denny Cartwright's outside with a gun.'

Ward checked for a second time. 'There's nobody there.'

'I'm telling you. I saw him.'

'You saw Denny?'

'Yeah. No. Well, not exactly.' Onion wiped his wet hair on a dirty tea towel while giving the situation more thought. 'I saw his shadow.'

'Waving a gun?'

'Aye.'

'So why didn't he shoot you when he had the chance?'

'I don't know.'

'And if it *was* Denny, don't you think he would have steam-rollered that door by now?'

Onion nodded slowly.

'It wasn't him. You hear me?'

Onion tossed the tea towel onto the floor. 'Yeah. Where's Tasha?'

'There's good and bad news on that front.' Ward led the way into the living room, where Tasha Volks was sprawled on the sofa with her chin resting on her shoulder. Her left arm was draped along the length of the armrest, a tight orange band digging into the skin above the elbow. She looked like she was at peace.

Onion shuffled towards her. 'Tash.' He prodded her with a finger. 'Tash, wake up, girl.' He turned to Ward. 'What happened? She knows her shit. There's no way she would have made a mistake like that.'

Ward skirted the chair and its deceased occupant. 'You screwed up her fentanyl dose.'

'Me?' Onion's face ran with a riot of confused features. 'Where would I get my hands on fentanyl?' The baseball bat slammed onto his collarbone with a loud snap, sending him to his knees, screaming.

'I found these in the kitchen cupboard.' Ward rolled six brass casings in the palm of his hand. 'Someone's been lying to me.' He aimed another blow.

Onion's protests came in short bursts, punctuated with gasps and high-pitched whining sounds whenever he moved. 'You didn't ask me about the bullets.'

'Stop fucking about. Where's the gun that goes with them?'

Onion lifted his good arm above his head. The other hung limply at his side. 'I don't have it.'

'Liar!'

'It's the truth. We lost it at the factory.'

'I'm giving you one last chance to tell me.'

'I don't know where it is.' Onion burst into tears and clawed at the threadbare carpet. 'You gotta believe me.'

The bat came down hard. More than once.

They bumped into one another on the doorstep of Tasha Volks's flat. Both grabbing the other's shoulders. Each startled and thrown momentarily off guard.

'You.' Ward wasn't entirely sure what drove him to such a rapid conclusion. The coat perhaps. The one he'd seen on the CCTV footage of the factory on the night of the murder.

Belle Gillighan struggled free of him, her hand going straight for her pocket.

'Oh, no you don't.' Ward caught hold of it and spun her around, forcing her tight against the wall.

'Let—me—go.' She spat the words and dragged the heel of her shoe down his shin.

'Fuck!' He yanked her hand up between her shoulder blades. 'I'll snap it off,' he warned through gritted teeth.

'You can't do this. Not now I'm so close.'

'Shut up and listen.' He tightened his grip when she protested. 'I said shut it.' He leaned closer and whispered in her ear. 'You and me might have more in common than you'd think.'

'I doubt that.'

'We both want Billy Creed dead.' He loosened his hold and let her turn to face him.

'How did you know?'

'It doesn't take a genius to work it out.' He watched her hands — a hot kiss from a Taser device, not on his bucket list right now. 'Let's say I've had good reason to find out as much as I can about Creed and his past.'

'And you came across me and the others in the case files?'

Ward nodded. 'I still don't know how you pulled off the disappearing act on the day out.'

'And you never will.'

A car went past but didn't stop. Ward waited until it had gone. 'I don't blame you for wanting to kill them. Creed especially.'

Belle stared at him. 'Have you shared what you know with anyone else in your team?'

'I'd be a fool if I did.'

'You know there's one more to die before I kill him?'

Ward shrugged. 'Shit happens. Wait,' he said when she descended the first of the concrete steps. He held out a clenched fist. 'I'm guessing you have the gun. These might be of use to you.'

Chapter 47

For a fleeting moment, Jenkins didn't know where she was. It was dark. Night-time still. She patted the space next to her and found it oddly cold and empty. Had she finally done it? Had she left Amy?

'Looking for someone?'

Startled, she rolled over in bed, her heart rate increasing as adrenaline flooded her system. 'What time is it?' Her mouth was dry and her voice croaky.

'Early still.' Amy was fully clothed and sat cross-legged in a velour tub chair on the other side of the room.

When the overhead light came on, it made Jenkins squint. 'Where have you been?'

'Here. Listening to you talk in your sleep.'

Jenkins sat upright and pulled the quilt tight to her waist. 'Did I say much?'

'You're a right little chatterbox once you get going.'

'Tell me what I said.' The nervous giggle sounded misplaced.

'As if you didn't already know.'

'Know what?'

Amy stood. 'You're insulting me again.'

Jenkins gripped the quilt, her stomach in her throat, almost. 'Stop looking at me like that.'

'You're nervous. Flighty. I've noticed that about you lately.'

'I'm no such thing.'

'*Liar!*'

Jenkins watched Morgan approach with two mugs of something hot. 'You were bang out of order, Ffion.' She'd promised herself she wouldn't cry, but was damn close. 'I confided in you, and didn't expect you to go shooting your mouth off. Especially to that wanker.'

'It wasn't like that.'

'Really?'

Morgan put the mugs down. 'No.'

'How was it, then? Come on, tell me, because I'd love to know.'

The door to the DI's office opened. He came across and stood next to them. 'The outfit is marginally better, I suppose. More feminine, for sure.' He circled Jenkins's desk like a helicopter pilot searching for a safe place to land. 'But those sunglasses – I think not.'

'I've a headache, sir. I'll be good to go soon enough.'

'You're going nowhere near a television camera wearing those.' He stopped to stare. 'Take them off.'

'I'd rather I didn't.'

'That's an order, Sergeant.'

Jenkins tossed the sunglasses onto her desk and offered up the best possible view of the cut along her eyebrow. 'Happy now?'

Morgan bent at the waist. 'Not again.'

'Piss off, Ffion.'

Adams smirked. 'Another catfight? Isn't that what your lot call it?' He gave Morgan a once-over. 'You'll do for today. Meet me in the press room in half an hour.' He tossed Jenkins a box of paper tissues. 'You can stay here and sort yourself out.'

Jenkins had never been good at doing as she was told. Especially when it was a knob in a suit giving the orders. She stood and watched the reporters wander into the press room and take their positions on plastic seats laid out in a dozen or more rows. There were cameramen and sound engineers fussing at the back of the room. Tens of metres of cabling ran in all directions.

Ken Ward sidled up alongside her and nodded at the cut eye. 'Amy?'

'Not now.' Jenkins slid a few feet further along the wall and toed an edge of raised carpet tile.

Ward followed. 'I meant nothing by it.'

'You never do. But that doesn't make you any less annoying at times.' She screwed her eyes closed and dropped her chin onto her chest. 'I'm sorry. That should've been for Adams, not you.'

Ward made a face she knew meant all was forgiven. 'This place is like a circus already.'

'And here comes the clown.'

Adams strolled in with a fistful of notes, Cable and Ffion Morgan next to take their seats behind a long table cluttered with microphones and bottled water. The room lit up with a battery of camera flashes; the media vying for the perfect image to accompany their fluffed-up stories.

'Ffion's doing all right for herself,' Ward said. 'I'm telling you, she's up to something, that one.'

Chief Superintendent Cable welcomed the audience and introduced Adams as the SIO for the case.

'Where's DCI Reece?' one of the reporters called before the chief super had the opportunity to finish. 'Any truth in the rumour he's been sacked for gross misconduct?'

Jenkins glared at the side of the man's head. She pressed her palms against the wall and watched a member of the admin staff hand out photofit images of the suspect.

Cable ignored the question, and with a well-practised smile, gave the floor to Adams.

'. . . and following a thorough review of CCTV footage gathered in the area,' he went on to say, 'I've every reason to believe that this woman is responsible for the murders of both Roxie May and Elizabeth Thorne.'

There was a rumble of voices. Chairs shifted position as reporters competed for an opportunity to ask the next question. Jenkins dared Adams to look at her.

Maggie Kavanagh raised her hand. 'And is the death of Paddy May in any way linked to the deaths of these women?'

It was Cable who replied: 'The fire service report concluded that Mr May died as the result of a tragic accident.'

'But he was missing six fingers?'

Cable did little to hide her surprise. 'I'm not at liberty to comment.'

'Hell of a day for the poor man, don't you think?' Kavanagh shook her head. 'To *accidentally* lose most of his fingers before *accidentally* setting himself ablaze.'

Jenkins whispered to herself. 'Yep, Maggie. Complete and utter codswallop to anyone with half a brain.'

Ginge caught her eye as he squeezed his way around the edge of the room towards her. 'I've got a note for DI Adams,' he said, holding it out in front of him.

'So why are you giving it to me?'

'Because I didn't think it should wait until he was finished with the press conference.'

Jenkins read, then folded the note in half. ‘Come on, Ken, we’re off.’

‘Where to this time?’

She kept her back to him. ‘Tasha Volks’s flat.’

Chapter 48

THEY ARRIVED AT TASHA'S place in a little over twenty minutes. The door was open, a uniform standing in the way. There were crowds of people on the street, held back by little more than a few lengths of flimsy crime scene tape. Some were jeering. Others making obscene hand gestures. A few drank cider from tins.

Once inside, Jenkins wished she had a splash of Forest Glade available. 'Makes my place look like a palace.'

'This lot don't know any other way,' Ward said. 'Scum, most of them.'

She glared at him. 'You don't know that. People like Tasha have history that would drive any of us to drink and drugs.'

'I stand corrected.'

'Don't touch it!' Jenkins couldn't believe what she was seeing. 'And where are your gloves, for God's sake?'

Ward put the baseball bat to one side. 'Sorry, I think the fumes must have affected my brain.'

'Something has. Let the CSIs know they're going to find your prints all over it.' She watched him leave to find the appropriate person. 'I'll put something in my report explaining how they got there.' She stepped around a corpse lying on the living room floor. She couldn't tell who the victim was yet and spoke to the back of someone wearing white coveralls. 'I'm DS Jenkins. You are?'

'Cara Frost.' The woman turned with a gloved hand extended in greeting. 'Home Office Forensic Pathologist.'

'Where's Twm Pryce?' Jenkins hoped the hot flush didn't show.

'Sick leave. A nasty chest infection has knocked him for six, by all accounts.'

Jenkins caught the scent of Marc Jacobs's Daisy. 'Oh.' Was that the best she could manage?

'Twm's not getting any younger,' Frost said. 'I didn't catch your first name.'

'Elan.' Jenkins cleared her throat. 'Friends call me Jenks.' She felt like a love-struck teenager, heady and suddenly breathless.

'That's a pretty name.'

'Thank you.'

'Be seeing you then.' Frost collected her case and turned to leave.

I hope so. 'Wait.' Was that too eager sounding? 'Cause of death?'

Frost began with Tasha Volks slumped dead on her sofa. 'A lethal dose of an opiate fix, by the look of things.'

Jenkins squinted at Onion's blood-soaked face. 'Shit, I've only just realised who that is.'

'He died from a blunt-force trauma to the top and back of the head. That's cerebrospinal fluid running out of his nose and ears – indicating the base of skull has been compromised. There's also a fractured collarbone. I'd say from the injuries sustained, this man was bent over and begging for his life.'

Ward reappeared from the kitchen, complete with blue latex-free gloves. 'A domestic assault, followed by suicide.'

'Looks that way.' Frost handed Jenkins a business card. 'Let me know when you find out . . . Jenks.'

Chapter 49

ADAMS PULLED OUT OF the station car park and skidded to a halt when a sizable chunk of concrete smashed through his windscreen and landed in his lap. The whole laminated panel of glass leaned inward; a basketball-sized hole punched through the centre of it. He was still struggling to lift the thing when the Volvo began rocking violently from side-to-side. 'Police,' he shouted, with no positive effect.

Aiden May appeared outside the right-hand window, his face contorted with a look of hate. His brother Brady came into sight only a few seconds later, swinging a boot at the Volvo's passenger-side door. Aiden went round the front of the car and took a length of steel to the headlights, while—it could only have been Seamus—danced a jig on the car's sinking roof.

Adams crouched in his seat, fighting for headroom, fumbling with his phone. 'Shit, no battery.' Tossing the handset onto the passenger seat, he made doubly sure the central locking was enabled. 'This won't help your parents.'

That only made matters worse. Brady ran out of lights to smash and started on the windows instead. He swung the steel until exhausted, and only then did he stop to catch his breath.

Adams drove his fist against the horn and kept it there. 'Fuck off, you inbreeds!'

'Coppers.' Aiden pulled Seamus down from the roof, Seamus caught Brady by the collar of his jacket, all three of them making off across the road with two unfit-looking uniforms '*sprinting*' after them.

'Where have you lot been?' The car door refused to open and let Adams out. 'They could have killed me.' He stuck his head through the missing side window and watched the trio disappear from sight. 'Get me out of here,' he growled, dabbing at a bleeding nose with the cuff of his shirt. 'Come on, hurry up.'

Belle Gilligan let a fistful of brass casings run free on the kitchen counter. She watched them roll and fan out on the granite surface.

Using a finger, she herded them back into an orderly pile before weighing one in her palm. It was surprisingly heavy for its size and would certainly wreak havoc on human flesh and bone.

She had no trust in the overweight copper. He was a slippery fish for sure. But then again, he had offered useful information regarding the piss-poor state of security in current use at the Midnight Club. Belle had seen a van parked outside while she'd been doing a recce of the place, and an engineer working with cameras and cabling. Maybe Ward was telling the truth after all. She'd have to give the matter more consideration when she had time.

The portable television called for her attention. The press was describing her work as 'Frenzied' and 'Barbaric'. A man wearing an expensive business suit claimed the murders were 'Attacks on innocent and defenceless women.'

They were anything but. And who the fuck was Elizabeth Thorne? 'Libby Barr!' Belle screamed the name at the pompous idiot. 'Her name is Libby Barr.'

Collecting the brass casings from the countertop, she went to a small dresser in the far corner of the dining room. She knew from experience that it was too heavy to shift without first removing the cutlery drawers. She heaved the bulky dresser to one side and lifted a loosened floorboard to expose a hole full of cobwebs, builder's rubble, and a handgun wrapped in an oily rag. She spread-open the stained folds of the material and put all six bullets inside for safekeeping. It was almost time. There was one more lying bitch to deal with and then—she still couldn't bring herself to use his real name—the tattooed man would die.

Chapter 50

Reece had returned to his house in Llandaff. He pushed on the front door and stepped over a pile of unopened mail. The heating was on its timer and he was glad it was. The plug-in diffusers had been Anwen's touch—one he'd never change—essence of vanilla filling the hallway and welcoming him home.

He ached to call her name. To hold her tight and share tales of his day. Instead, he stooped to sift through flyers for local pizzerias and double-glazing companies. There were credit card offers, quotes for home insurance renewals, and all manner of other stuff he put on the hall table along with his keys. He took the envelope carrying the postmark of the South Wales Police into the living room, where he sank into a comfy armchair nursing a glass of his favourite Sherrywood whisky.

Behind him, The Traveling Wilburys sang 'End of The Line' on an old Pioneer stereo, as though foretelling his future. He tapped the envelope on his knee to the beat of the song before putting it aside to ring Jenkins. 'You're out of breath,' he said when at last she answered.

'This isn't a good time, boss. The May brothers have just trashed Adams's car. He's going apeshit.'

Reece laughed. 'I'd have paid good money to see that.'

'Am I allowed to say it was sodding brilliant?'

'It's a green light from me.'

'Look, I'm sorry, but I meant what I said about being busy.'

'You weren't at the press conference earlier. Any reason why not?'

'Ken and I were called over to Tasha Volks's place. Can you believe it – she's killed Onion? As well as herself, this time. A lethal overdose of opiate.'

'That's depressing.' Reece meant it. He took no pleasure in hearing of loss of life, especially when it happened in such tragic circumstances.

'Boss—'

'I'm out of a job,' he said. The statement was short and to the point. 'My pension and everything else gone.'

'You're not serious?'

He took the unopened envelope and flipped it over in his hand. 'It's all here in front of me, in black and white. It even has the official frank mark on it.'

Jenkins whistled. 'Chief Superintendent Cable said no such thing when I spoke with her. What a two-faced . . .'

'You can't trust anyone in this game. I keep telling you that.' He heard Jenkins tell someone to give her a minute. He called her name. Called again when she didn't respond.

'It's Adams. I have to go.'

'Not yet. Please. Don't hang up—'

Adams took a black coffee, while Jenkins declined all, including a seat. She'd been made to take her own car and had snatched a radio from the hands of a bemused uniform on the way out of the station building.

Billy Creed got comfortable on the sofa. 'Shouldn't you two be out on the streets hunting for my sister's killer?' He looked more closely. 'You've got blood on your collar, Copper. What naughtiness have you been up to?'

'I'll need a full list of all the women you have working here,' Adams said, rubbing at the stain with a wet thumb.

'Past and present,' Jenkins added. 'One or more of them could be in danger.'

'Are you serious?' Creed almost spilled his drink as he shifted position. 'There's gonna be hundreds of them. They come and go like a dose of the clap.'

'Even with your charm and good looks to keep them entertained?' Jenkins tossed a notepad onto the table. 'Make a start on that.'

Creed ignored her. 'I'm told you've let the Flower Pot Men go.' His brow furrowed when neither police officer looked as though they had a clue of what he was talking about. 'I guess even Copper here is too young to remember the originals?'

Jenkins leaned over and shoved the pad towards the gangster. 'Put a star next to any employee who might have held a grudge against you or the known victims.'

'It keeps speaking.' Creed took a cigar from a black leather pouch and ran its full length under his nose. 'You should put her on a short leash.' He let his eyes travel over Jenkins's body, stopping to linger here and there. 'She's a pretty little thing.'

Jenkins pulled her jacket closed. 'Names. *There!*'

'Feisty too.' Creed turned to face Adams full on and spoke as though the two of them were alone. 'She's not a pedigree, though.' He shook his head. 'She's a mongrel.' It came as a whisper, but was fully intended for Jenkins to hear.

'Part Jamaican,' Adams said. 'On your father's side, right, Sergeant?'

'I'm not part anything!' She yanked the office door open with enough force for it to bang against the wall. She marched through with her head held high, speeding up on the stairs, all the while trying to keep it together.

Creed lit his cigar and spoke around a series of quick puffs. 'Hey, you didn't get to tell me what happened to your eye.' He jumped out of his seat and lurched towards the door, shouting down the steps after the fleeing detective. 'Billy likes the wild ones. Keeps a cage downstairs for taming them.'

Chapter 51

'I'M LEAVING YOU.' IT was a simple enough thing to say. Or was it? Jenkins was parked in a neighbouring street, rehearsing with the aid of the rear-view mirror. She was sick and tired of being played for a fool and was now more than ready to put an end to her abusive relationship. She turned the key in the ignition and selected first gear. Her foot slipped off the clutch, the car lurching several feet forward in a kangaroo stall when someone rapped on the side window with their knuckles. 'What the hell do you think you're doing?' she asked, getting out. 'You almost gave me a heart attack.'

Fishy grinned. 'You were talking to yourself. You're funny. Why were you talking to yourself?'

'I wasn't.' Jenkins shook her head. 'I wouldn't do such a thing.'

Fishy checked inside the car and pulled a face. 'Pound says you were.' He held his hand out in front of him and didn't take it away again until she'd crossed his palm with silver. 'Is that more than a pound?' he asked, poking his way through the coins.

'It's nearer three.'

'I can get chips now. You can't get chips for a pound. Do you like chips?'

'Sometimes. Look, there's something I need to be doing right now.'

'I can't find Onion.' Fishy looked worried and stared along the street. 'I've been all over the place looking and—' He stopped jabbering only when Jenkins lay a gentle hand on his shoulder.

'He was mean to you back at the police station.' She steered him onto the pavement and out of harm's way of passing traffic. 'He made up lies and tried to land you in trouble.'

Fishy looked lost, cold, and tired. 'I'll say sorry to him for losing the gun and then we'll be okay again.' He put his empty hand to his mouth and covered it over. 'Whoops. There wasn't a gun.'

'Darren? Tell me.'

He shook his head and looked away.

She checked her watch. Could spare another ten minutes. No more. 'Do you fancy a sausage to go with those chips?'

'I loves a sausage,' he said with a cheeky grin.

She shoved him towards her car. 'Get in and don't mess with anything that's not your own.'

Reece stood at the factory door. As far as he could tell, Ed and the fencing specialist had gone home for the evening. He ducked under the crime scene tape and took a crowbar to the new padlock, forcing it open with a loud *crack!* He waited a few moments to check no one was onto him and squeezed through the gap and went inside.

The place was colder than he remembered. A damp chill seeking him out and clinging to every inch of his shivering body. He pulled a thick woollen scarf close to his neck and a matching hat over his ears. There was a heady mix of machine oil and mould in the air. And something else. An odour that experience as a murder detective told him was the lingering presence of death. That wouldn't leave for months to come.

He swung a torch beam ninety degrees and followed its oval puddle of light to a floor stain marking Roxie May's final moments. Then stopped to examine an overhead pulley system, surprised at how freely the wheel travelled in its ageing mechanism. He'd fully expected the neglected machinery to be rusted and require a great deal of effort to get it going. But no such thing. He took one hand away and sniffed the fingers of his glove. The killer had doused the metalwork with a generous application of lubricating fluid. Definitely a premeditated act and not one of pure chance or whim.

His torch lit up the vaulted roof and a skeleton of steel girders, upon which were a pair of pigeons seeking shelter from the weather.

There were more birds further along the windowsill, several marching back and forth as though on a military parade.

Fishy had claimed the killer came along a balcony, chasing them across the factory floor and onto the concrete pad outside. He was adamant he'd seen or heard nothing that might be of more use.

Reece gripped a rusted handrail fixed to a brick wall and shook it. Satisfied the bolts held firm, he put his foot on the first tread and pressed. The structure objected little to the application of his full weight. It barely made a noise, every joint lubricated with the same oil applied to the overhead pulley system. Once safe on the upper balcony, he turned off the torch and let his eyes accommodate for the darkness. It was important that he experience the place exactly as the killer would have done. He hung his head over the side rail and tried to make out objects on the factory floor below. There wasn't much to see, even with slivers of moonlight peeking in through the broken windows. Moving in a hurry from one level to the next would have been a difficult feat under such circumstances.

He was almost at the very far end of the balcony when he stepped in something that scraped like sandpaper underfoot. Stopping to turn on the torch, he squatted and ran his fingers through it. He picked some up, like a pinch of salt, and let it fall again. It was grit, or mortar residue, to be more accurate. Given its dry consistency, it hadn't been there long. He straightened to his full height and swept the beam of light directly upwards. It took him no time at all to find the cause of the deposit. There were two neighbouring bricks missing their mortar joints, both sitting slightly deeper in the wall than they should have been. They'd been pushed into place and had he not been looking for them, would have gone unnoticed.

He tried but couldn't get hold of either brick using his fingers alone, and resorted to shoving the end of a pen into the widest joint until he'd worked one of them free. When he got enough of it shifted, he gripped its edges with the ends of his fingers and pulled. The brick gave and promptly fell from his grasp, crashing onto the metal flooring with an almighty bang. Its echo thundered through the old factory unit. Several pigeons took flight overhead. Loose feathers spiralled past him to land on the dusty ground floor below. He shone the torch into the cavity and reached inside.

Chapter 52

JENKINS WATCHED FISHY TUCK into his sausage, chips, and curry sauce. 'Those definitely hit the spot.'

'They're stonking.' He swept the tray high in the air, spilling a few chips onto the pavement in his childish excitement.

'Leave them where they are,' Jenkins said when he bent to pick them up. 'That floor is filthy.'

Fishy dropped a couple of plump ones back in the tray. 'Is Onion really dead? Like my nan's dead.' He licked his fingers and waited for an answer.

Jenkins thought it unnecessary to dwell on the gory details. 'Seems he and Tasha got into a bit of a fight.'

Fishy stopped chewing. 'He's dead for sure then.'

She watched him take three attempts to load another chip onto his fork and wondered what people like him and Mrs Pearce had done to deserve their shitty lot in life. 'The gun,' she said. 'And I don't want any of your bullshit.'

'Will I go to prison?'

'Not if you tell me the truth, you won't.'

'It was Billy's.' Fishy finished the last chunk of sausage, chewing noisily. 'Billy blew someone's brains out for dealing drugs on his patch. That's what Onion said. We were supposed to get rid of it. Proper get rid of it.'

Jenkins's train of thought was suddenly kicked into overdrive. Could this possibly be the missing weapon from the Midnight Club? The one Reece said could only have been removed by one of the team sent to find it.

'You're not list—en—ing.'

Jenkins let the thought go for the time being. 'What?'

'I was talking. You weren't listening.'

'I was. I promise.'

Fishy scrunched the empty chip carton and dropped it onto the floor. 'We were supposed to get rid of the thing for good.'

Jenkins collected the discarded wrapper from the pavement and looked for a bin. 'And?'

'Onion said I wasn't to say anything. It was our secret.'

'Who bought you sausage and chips?'

'He made me promise I wouldn't.'

'Onion's dead. He's never going to find out, no matter what you tell me.'

Once Fishy had told her everything he knew, she gave him twenty quid and advised him to lie low for a while. He waited on the white centre line, bowing at the waist, patting his belly in appreciation of the free meal.

'Get off the bloody road!' she shouted at him. 'You've lost one life already this week.'

And then he went. Waving as he limped off into the night to who-knows-where.

Jenkins made her way back to her car with the empty chip-carton in hand. She wondered how Fishy would cope now he was alone on the streets. The more she gave it thought, the more Onion's death troubled her. The crime scene had looked staged and not at all as though he and Tasha had been through a humdinger of a fight. And then there was Paddy May's death to throw into the mix. Coincidence? she wondered. Reece had always drummed into her that there was no such thing.

The lights were off at home, the place quiet and shut down for the night. Jenkins let herself in and went through to the kitchen. On the counter was a dinner plate with cling film spread across the top of it. A handwritten note alongside read:

Headache.
Gone to bed early.

Hope salad is okay?
Chicken and 7UP in fridge.
Hugs and kisses,
Amy.

Jenkins let the water run extra cold and held a glass under it until it spilled over. She quenched her thirst and put a wet hand to her throbbing forehead. So much for the big talk before bed. Tomorrow then. Trying Reece one more time, she hung up when he didn't answer. Did he know anything about the gun? He hadn't yet mentioned it.

She dumped the salad in the bin untouched; the note joining it in several ceremoniously torn pieces. 'And that's for starters.'

She went upstairs and inched open the bedroom door. Had contemplated sleeping on the sofa in the living room, telling Amy in the morning that she hadn't wanted to disturb her. But that would have suggested she still cared. She didn't. Bed it was. Stripped to her underwear, she didn't dare hunt for pyjamas before crawling beneath the duvet. 'You've no idea what's about to hit you,' she whispered into the darkness.

Chapter 53

JENKINS REACHED FOR HER phone and thumbed *decline* without properly opening her eyes. She plumped a pair of soft pillows against the sides of her head, using them as makeshift earmuffs. The phone rang again, chirping like an annoying dawn chorus. 'Leave me alone,' she said, unable to focus on the culprit's name. 'Do you have any idea what time it is?'

'It's Ffion.'

Jenkins groaned. 'Nope. It's *fuck-off-and-leave-me-alone* time.'

Morgan paused. 'I thought you and I were all right again, after our talk?'

'Not if you keep this up, we're not.'

'Jenks, I'm ringing—'

'To piss me off.'

'Will you please be quiet and listen. It's Amy. There's a problem.'

Jenkins shook herself awake and rolled into the empty space next to her. 'Tell me what's happened. What's she done?' She sat up and listened to every word.

The journey to the police station was completed with total disregard for the local speed limits; her car near-enough abandoned with its driver-side front wheel resting on the raised kerb. She didn't stop to lock it, and flew up the steps, bursting through the automatic doors at the top. 'Where is she?' The desk sergeant was caught off guard. 'Where's Amy?'

George ushered her through an open door. 'DI Adams wants to see you in his office right away.'

Jenkins followed along the corridor. 'Is Amy with him?'

'Best let the DI explain.'

'George, you're scaring me.'

'Close the door and sit down,' Adams said when she got there.

Jenkins leaned heavily on his desk. 'Don't take any notice of her. She's unwell.'

'I'm afraid it's not that simple. Not now she's confessed to the murders of two women.'

Jenkins pushed off the desk and paced within the confines of the room. 'She's needy. Doing it for the attention it'll bring her.'

'Not this time.'

'It's all in her head.'

Adams handed over Amy's statement. 'Only the killer would know such details of the case.'

Jenkins read the first few lines, her legs buckling beneath her. She took a seat and buried her face in her hands. 'I told her all this.'

Adams came about slowly. 'You?' His tone had changed to one of simmering suspicion.

Jenkins lay the statement on the desk, partly read. 'I told her just about everything she's put in there.'

Adams went to the window, speaking over his shoulder. 'Walking out on me in front of Billy Creed was one thing, but this is a career-ending offence.'

Jenkins got to her feet, her hand resting on the edge of the desk for balance. 'I left because you did nothing to defend me. Those comments were . . .' She fought to cling on to what little composure remained. Failing miserably, she gritted her teeth and said: 'They were fucking unacceptable.'

Adams spun. 'And what you've done trumps Creed's antics by a country mile.'

'I wasn't only talking about Billy Creed.'

'Oh, stop being a snowflake.'

Jenkins closed her eyes. Was the job worth this level of shit? She considered hurling something heavy at him and be done with it. 'What happens now?' she asked.

'There'll be an investigation, obviously.'

'Professional Standards?'

'At the very least.' Adams took the paperwork from the desk. 'I've every justification to arrest you here and now.'

'You can't be serious? I brought this to you voluntarily.'

'Like hell you did.' He waved the statement under her nose. 'If it wasn't for this, I'd have been none the wiser.'

That was true. Jenkins lowered her voice. 'Give me a chance to put this right.'

'No can do. You've pretty much ruined any possibility we have of a successful prosecution.' Adams put the statement away in a drawer of a filing cabinet. 'I hope you're able to look Martin Thorne in the eye when you tell him.'

Jenkins edged towards the door. 'Amy's got nothing to do with this. I'd know if she did.'

'Always so sure of yourself. Your level of arrogance is nothing short of astounding.'

There was nothing to be gained by holding back. Her brief career would be in tatters just as soon as Chief Superintendent Cable got wind of what had been going on. 'You're a fine one to talk. You've got your head stuck up your own arse most of the time – sir.'

'Get out. *Out!*'

Jenkins stopped in the doorway. 'I'll find this killer, not you.'

'You're off the case. Suspended as of this minute.'

'Not yet, I'm not. You don't have the authority to do that.'

Chapter 54

ADAMS HAD GONE STRAIGHT after Jenkins, following her down to the custody suite, demanding that he be the one to run things.

The man in control of the computer was someone not involved in the case, and sounded as though he was in no particular hurry to get past the explanation phase. 'It's called VIPER: Video Identification Parade Electronic Recording,' he said. 'It does away with the old-style ID parades. There are thousands of images stored in its database. The trick is to find those bearing the most resemblance to the suspect.'

'Get on with it,' Adams said.

The man clicked the return key and reclined in his chair, looking pleased with himself. 'I've chosen nine others to give us a nice round ten in total.' The two patrol car officers were ushered into the room and given front row seats by the screen. 'Take your time,' the keyboard detective told them.

The pair studied each recording in turn, keeping quiet when the women read out a paragraph from a card held in front of them. The uniforms glanced at one another and shook their heads in unison. 'She's not there, sir,' one of them said.

Adams's face creased. 'Are you sure? Look again.'

'You mustn't,' the keyboard operator told him. 'Any interference on your part could jeopardise a successful prosecution.'

'We're well beyond that point already,' Adams said, glaring at Jenkins. 'Go back to number three.'

'I'm not allowed to do that, sir.'

'That's an order.' Adams turned to the uniforms. 'Are you sure this isn't the woman you spoke to outside the factory?'

'Definitely not,' Beard said. 'Her accent was Scouse, not Irish.'

His colleague agreed. 'And her hair's all wrong.'

'Yeah, the other woman's was much shorter. And dark, not blonde.'

Jenkins breathed a sigh of relief. *Thank fuck for that.*

The keyboard operator shut down the program and looked up from his screen. 'That's it, sir. All done.'

Jenkins had an idea of what an acute psychotic episode was—had seen plenty of addicts kick-off in the custody cells—but this was

Amy they were talking about and not some jacked-up junky dragged in off the city streets. 'Did you have to section her?'

'It didn't come to that thankfully.' The medical practitioner was from the South Wales Liaison and Diversion Team, there to safeguard Amy's mental wellbeing.

Jenkins was sitting opposite him, tearing the lip from a paper cup. 'Why the hell would Amy confess to the murders of two women?'

'Because delusions are one of four main symptoms associated with such an episode. Hallucinations, disturbed thoughts, and a lack of insight or self-awareness are the others.' The practitioner paused to take a gulp of his coffee. 'Amy couldn't make sense of much of what you'd told her, and at the time of her confession, really did believe that she was the killer.'

Jenkins doubted it, but had no idea of what to say in response.

'Anything like this ever happen before?'

'Amy isn't big on sharing her past.' Jenkins only then realised how little she knew about her partner. 'There are moments, but not like this. Not that I've seen, anyway.'

'And is Amy ever violent towards you?'

Jenkins balled a fragment of paper, pill-rolling it between finger and thumb. 'Sometimes.'

'More so recently?'

'Over the past month. Yes.'

'And the episodes of self-harming – what triggers those?'

'She's absolving herself of all blame, I guess.'

'Blame?'

'For hurting me.'

'I see.'

Jenkins doubted the man did and wasn't at all sure she fared any better in that respect.

'And what makes you stay in such an abusive relationship?'

She gave the question a good deal of thought, and when her answer came, even she was surprised. 'Because I'm all Amy has.'

Jenkins was shown to a holding cell that smelled of stale urine and strong disinfectant. 'Why would you do such a thing?' The two of them were perched either end of a thin blue mattress, Jenkins with both feet planted firmly on the floor, Amy with her knees drawn tight under her chin. 'I have to work with those people out there.'

Amy didn't look up. 'Here we go again. It's always you, you, you.'

'That's unfair, given the circumstances, don't you think?'

'The doctor said I could go home now that you've promised to take proper care of me.'

'I had little choice. It was either that or let them admit you to hospital.'

Amy raised her head. 'You do still love me, Elan?'

Jenkins stared at the demarcation line between the linoleum floor and the tiled wall. Wrong time, wrong place. The goodbye speech would have to wait. 'Yes.'

'You're a liar.'

'I'm warning you, Amy. Enough of your shit, okay?'

'You were careless thinking I was asleep last night.'

Jenkins swallowed. 'Pardon?'

'Maybe it's you who's in for the bigger shock.'

There was a rattle of keys outside the cell, the custody sergeant calling for both occupants to stand clear of the door.

'What the fuck are you up to, Amy?' Jenkins raised a hand when the door swung open to reveal DI Adams. 'Could you give us a moment, sir?'

'This isn't a knocking shop,' Adams said. 'It's time for you love-birds to go home and play happy families together.'

Chapter 55

ADAMS LOOKED UP FROM what he was doing with dawning comprehension. 'Say that again.'

Morgan stuck her head through the office doorway but went no further. 'DCI Reece says he's found something of interest, sir. At the factory.'

'At, or in?' Adams closed the file and rested his pen on top of it. 'For all our sakes, he'd better not have put a foot inside that building.'

'He didn't say much more than that, sir.'

Adams got up and marched towards the open door, Morgan getting out of his way in the nick of time.

'Can I ask where you're going?' She followed only part-way across the incident room.

'To see the chief super. I've never before come across such an unprofessional department.'

Morgan stayed where she was. 'What do I do with the May brothers now we have them in custody?'

Adams was already out of sight.

Reece marched through the busy foyer, not stopping to chat. 'I thought I told you to go easy on those mince pies?'

George, the desk sergeant, stuck his neck out of the hatch and called after him, 'Hey Brân, you back already?'

'We'll have to wait and see what the old witch decides.' Reece thrust his cupped hands out in front of him and made off down the corridor, broomstick-fashion. 'The woman is a complete and utter—'

'Do go on.' Chief Superintendent Cable leaned against the corridor wall, her arms folded, her leading foot resting next to the toe of a highly polished shoe. 'Don't hold back on my account.'

'Ma'am.' Reece pulled up in the nick of time. 'I could have knocked you over.'

'That would make it twice in one week. Quite a farewell you bid me last time we met.'

He put his hands away. 'I was pissed off with you.'

'I'll take that as an apology, shall I?' Cable stepped off the wall and blocked his way when he went to pass. 'Dr Beven tells me you've not yet responded to her letter.'

Reece's eyebrows morphed into one. 'Beven? Letter?' He shook his head slowly.

'Dr Miranda Beven.'

'Am I supposed to know this woman?' He didn't care either way and tried to get past for a second time.

Cable was having none of it and stood her ground. 'You haven't opened the bloody thing, have you?'

'I've been busy.' He waved an evidence bag at her. 'I found this at the factory. It's the one Jenkins's mystery woman was carrying. All scrunched up and—'

Cable grabbed his elbow and steered him clear of someone pushing a shopping trolley full of office supplies. 'We'll get back to the tampering with evidence bit in a moment.'

'Tampering? I wasn't—'

'Listen to me, Reece. You're not returning to active duty until I've had the all clear from Miranda. You got that?'

'You're sending me to see a shrink?' He raised his head to the ceiling and belly-laughed until he realised it wasn't a joke. 'You can sod that for a game of soldiers.'

'You think you've any choice in this?' Cable poked his chest with her finger. 'You've one last chance to save your career. Don't balls it up for the sake of pride.'

Jenkins placed a steaming dish of lasagne on the kitchen table and watched Amy help herself to a generous measure of Chianti. 'Do you think you should mix alcohol with all that medication they gave you?' She looked away again when the glass was close to full. 'Never mind. Do what you want.'

Amy took a sip of wine. Some of it ran down the side of the glass, marking her blouse when it dripped free of the stem. 'Thank you for bringing me home, Elan. You're so very thoughtful.'

'It was hard to say no, what with them suspending me from duty pending a Professional Standards investigation. 'Amy I'm—'

'Ssh. Let's eat first. Then we'll snuggle up on the sofa and chat.'

Jenkins couldn't think of much else she'd rather do less.

'That's settled then.' Amy served the salad while Jenkins watched her. 'It's such a shame you don't drink,' she said, reaching for the bottle again. 'You really don't know what you're missing.'

'Is that why you spiked my drink the other night?'

'Is that what you think? That I'd stoop so low?'

Jenkins shoved her plate away; the meal untouched. 'I know you did.' The air was suddenly charged. A powder keg awaiting a spark. She raised her glass of lemonade and sniffed it. 'Is this safe to drink? *Well* . . . is it?'

'Safe — such an overrated word, don't you think?'

Jenkins had no idea what that meant. 'Why me? What was it you were looking for?'

'You still don't know?'

'Coming here like some love-struck teenager. All giggles and blushes.'

'You're not saying you didn't reciprocate? Because we both know you did.'

Jenkins had been drawn to the sweet-talking stranger on first sight. Just as she was now attracted to the forensic pathologist, Dr Cara Frost.

'I was star-struck,' Amy said. 'What more can I say?'

'Like hell you were.'

'It's true. That local newspaper article about women detectives and the dangers of the job had me drooling after you.'

'Piss off.'

'You needn't worry, Elan. You'll be safe as long as I'm here to protect you.' Amy got to her feet and edged closer. 'There's that word again – *safe*.'

Jenkins reached for the bread knife. 'No more bullshit. I want to know what's going on.'

'It's better you don't.'

Jenkins pushed her chair away from the table. 'For you or me?'

'He wouldn't like it if I told you.'

Jenkins glanced over her shoulder. There was no one else there but the two of them. 'He. Who's he?'

'My secret friend is coming to stay.' Amy was almost within touching distance. 'And he's not nearly as forgiving as I am.'

Jenkins stood, knocking her chair against the glass door of the cooker. She gripped the knife's wooden handle and pointed the serrated blade in self-defence. 'Touch me again and I swear to God I'll bury this thing in the middle of your fucking chest.'

Chapter 56

'A PSYCH REPORT.' REECE was sitting at what used to be his desk, rearranging things while awaiting Adams's arrival. He had his phone wedged under his chin. 'Are you listening to anything I'm saying?'

'I'm trying to,' Jenkins said.

'What's that noise? It sounds like there's a war going on.'

'That'll be Amy. Things got a bit tense earlier. She's taking it out on the bedroom.'

Reece lay a framed photograph of Adams's kids face down on the desk. *Ugly sods.* 'You've told her you're leaving?'

'Yep. No bullshitting this time. I came straight out with it. Quite surprised myself, actually.'

'Any more bruises to show for your troubles?'

'Let's say I'm carrying an insurance policy about my person at all times.'

Reece groaned. 'That's a dangerous game you're playing there. Get out if you're scared.'

'Not a chance. I've given her until the end of the week to shift herself and everything she owns.'

'Why risk staying there when you know how volatile she can be?'

'Because it's my house and I'm not having her drive me away.'

'I'll come round and spend the night on the couch.'

'No can do,' Jenkins said. 'The sofa's all mine. The other bedrooms are too close to hers for my liking.'

'So, you *are* scared. Give me the armchair. I've had plenty of practice sleeping in those.'

'I appreciate the offer, but it would only inflame things, and I want this week to pass as trouble-free as possible.'

'Do you think she'll go when the time comes?'

'I'll get a court order if she doesn't.'

Reece reclined in the swivel chair and rested his feet on the desk. 'I heard Amy confessed to both murders. What was that about?'

'Delusional is what the doctor said. An exacerbation of her underlying issues – whatever those might be.'

'You don't sound convinced?'

'What if . . . ?'

'If what?' Reece asked when he got fed up of waiting.

'It doesn't matter.'

'Tell me.'

'What I was going to say was: these mental health people don't always get it right.'

'Quacks, most of them.'

'I didn't mean that.'

'*I* did. And if this Miranda Beven starts any of her psychoanalysis nonsense with me, then . . .'

'Good luck to her if she tries.'

'What's that supposed to mean?'

'Nothing. I shouldn't have mentioned it.'

'Mentioned what?'

'I said it was nothing.'

'Don't give me that. What are you not saying?'

There was a long, silent pause. Then: 'You have PTSD. And burying your head in the sand isn't going to make it go away.' She couldn't take it back now that she'd put it out there.

Reece took his feet off the desk and sat up straight. 'What did you say?'

'What you went through last year with Anwen would have brought anybody down.'

'Now you listen to me—'

'We're all trying to help you. The chief super included. But if you won't let us, then—'

Reece didn't hear the rest. He hurled the phone against the glass wall of his office without hanging up.

'Do you know how many rules you've broken?' Adams tried to shoo him from behind the desk. 'Not to mention that window.'

Reece stayed put. It was his chair, after all. 'Come on then, genius, let's hear what you can remember from class.'

'It's all too much for you, isn't it?'

'What is?'

'Modernisation and new ways of policing.'

Reece glared at the man. 'How many murder cases have you investigated before this one? That's right. A big fat zero.' He formed the number using his finger and thumb. 'There are traffic wardens walking the streets with more experience of violent crime.'

Adams slammed the office door and made a beeline for the chair. 'Did you do this?' he asked, standing the family photographs upright.

You're lucky I didn't chuck 'em in the bin. Them and their horse-faced mother. 'They must have toppled over when I got up.'

'You should've called your find in and let us collect it. *Jesus*, you shouldn't have been there in the first place.'

'Then you should have made sure your team found it. That mortar residue on the balcony would have been easy enough to see with all the lighting you had in there.'

'I'll speak to Sioned Williams about her CSIs. One of them needs their arse kicked.'

'Five to ten minutes is all it took me. In the pitch-black and all on my own.'

'Bully for you.'

'But not for you on this occasion.'

Adams slumped into the vacant chair. 'What's that supposed to mean?'

'You have to take full responsibility for the cock-up,' Reece said. 'Your team, your fault.'

Chapter 57

Reece paced outside the three-story building on Cathedral Road, checking and double-checking its address against the one on the letterhead. Built for the city's wealthiest a little over a decade before the onset of the First World War, most, if not all, the properties along the stretch of prime real estate were now home to law firms, dentists, and psychotherapy practices. He reached for a small stainless-steel box on the wall next to the front door, and choosing from a list of five business occupants, pressed the buzzer corresponding with Dr Beven's name.

'Push.' It was a woman's voice. 'Second floor. First door on your right at the top of the stairs.'

'Hello to you too.' He let himself in when the door beeped and clicked open. He stopped to give way to a man wearing a beige cardigan and matching shirt. They nodded at one another. Nothing more.

There was no birdcage-style lift, as Reece might have expected of such a grand property. Only a staircase laid with a functional grey office carpet. He took the steps one at a time, slowing when only halfway up, contemplating turning back and calling it quits.

'You must be DCI Reece.' The woman appeared at the top of the stairs. She was younger than he'd expected—early forties maybe—and wore a black trouser suit with a white blouse. 'Too late for that,' she said when he looked behind him. 'You're all mine for the next forty-five minutes.' They shook hands. She smelled good. Looked good.

'What happens now?' he asked, entering the office and taking in his surroundings.

'Were you expecting an ashtray and a threadbare couch?'

'No,' he lied. 'I don't want to sound rude, but I can't see either of us getting anything out of this.'

Jenkins sheltered in the doorway of the Norwegian Church, waiting for a meeting she'd arranged not an hour earlier. The place was deserted save for a few hardy dog walkers and maintenance crews wandering the dock in blue boiler suits. She lowered her face into the thick woollen fabric of a brightly striped scarf, hunching her shoulders in a failed attempt to keep warm. Just as she was ready to give up waiting, a silver Mercedes trundled past, its sole occupant having no difficulty finding an empty parking space on such an inclement day.

Maggie Kavanagh slammed the car door and tossed a half-smoked cigarette onto the pavement. 'Let's get inside before we both freeze our tits off.'

Jenkins invited the journalist to enter the café area ahead of her and waited while she draped a camel hair jacket over the back of a chair. 'It *was* black, no sugar, wasn't it?'

'Well remembered,' Kavanagh said. 'It must be a full six months since we did that interview with you.'

'Nearer twelve.' Jenkins removed her scarf and gloves and took a seat opposite.

'Is it really? Well, well.' Kavanagh blew on her coffee and returned the steaming mug to the table without taking a sip. 'So, what's this about? I hear your boss has been up to his usual tricks again. He even put a window through at the station this time, didn't he?'

'How do you know about that?' Police stations leaked information like sieves. She'd be a fool to think Cardiff Bay was any different. 'Never mind.' She wondered how best to begin.

'Come on,' Kavanagh said, her loud voice drawing the attention of the customers sitting at the table next to them. 'Like the bishop told the choirboy — spit it out.' She waved her hand dismissively. 'You'll get used to me in time.'

Jenkins knew she wouldn't. 'I brought you here under false pretences.' She waited for a reaction but got none. Considered apologising and didn't. 'This isn't about the case. Not directly anyway.'

'Go on.'

'You have influence over the Assistant Chief Constable, and I thought—'

'*Ah*, I see where this is going.'

'You do?'

Kavanagh reached under her chair and took a battered pack of Lambert and Butler from her bag. She removed a cigarette and popped it in her mouth. 'You want Brân Reece back at work?'

'If anyone can manage it, that person is you.'

'Don't you be brown-nosing me, girl.' Kavanagh stood and collected her bag and coat. 'Let's go talk outside.'

Chapter 58

REECE WAITED FOR HIS *interrogation* to begin. The silence was close to freaking him out.

Dr Miranda Beven was seated opposite. On a matching armchair. In a room furnished with expensive fixtures and fixings. 'It's not at all uncommon for the sufferer to be in denial,' she said. 'Or to be completely unaware of their illness, even.'

The session was only five minutes old, but already Reece was feeling tetchy. 'PTSD is for soldiers and disaster survivors. Not for ordinary people like me.'

'Not true. It can affect anyone who experiences a traumatic or life-changing event. But the good news is, two in every three sufferers get better within a few weeks, even without treatment.' Beven paused to hand him a coffee. 'And so we often employ something known as Watchful Waiting.'

'That's what we'll do then,' he said, rising from the armchair. 'Watch and wait.'

Beven had him sit down again. 'Your wife passed away in the autumn of last year.'

Reece gripped both armrests, his fingertips digging into their leather edges. 'Anwen didn't pass away. She was murdered. Stabbed by some street thief in Rome.'

'My point being, we're now well past the watchful waiting phase.'

Reece rolled his eyes. 'We would be.'

For a long while they sat listening to a clock tick on a mantelpiece at the other end of the room, Beven staring like a cat waiting to pounce. When Reece thought he could take no more of the silence, she smiled and said, 'You're not a fan of roleplay, I'd hazard a guess?'

He looked away, not trusting himself to answer without offending the woman.

Beven lay her coffee cup on a table and gave the matter more thought. 'There's a new treatment called EMDR – Eye Movement Desensitisation and Reprocessing.'

'For the love of God.' He was up on his feet again, but only momentarily, Beven telling him to sit for a second time.

'Okay, let's try something else,' she said.

'Like what?'

'We could talk about a case from early in your police career. One that almost had you leave the force.' She checked her copy of his personnel file. 'It was in nineteen-ninety and quite obviously had a profound effect on you. I've chosen it for that very reason.'

Reece's eyes narrowed. 'What case?'

'The brutal rape of a seventeen-year-old girl.' Beven thumbed the paperwork until she found what she was looking for. 'Her name was Belle Gillighan.'

Reece felt a knot twist in the pit of his stomach. 'That was a long time ago.'

'Billy Creed.' Beven sat back and monitored his response.

'What's with the names? These people aren't relevant to why I'm here.'

'I've a theory that says they are.' The counsellor stood and took their cups to a table near the far wall, their first session together almost complete. 'You never fully got over what happened to that poor girl,' she said, returning empty-handed. 'No justice for her. And Billy Creed getting off Scot free.'

Reece put an elbow on the arm of the chair and leaned his chin on a fist. 'And Anwen's death . . . ? Where does that fit into your theory?'

'Doesn't her killer also remain unpunished?'

Reece shifted position, his heart rate suddenly doing a gallop. 'For now.'

'There's the similarity, Chief Inspector. The link if you wish. I'd say that what happened to your wife last year reopened old wounds that made it impossible for you to properly grieve.'

Reece got up and left, regardless.

He walked along Cathedral Road with thoughts of his dead wife and the young Belle Gillighan pressing heavily on his mind. He had no idea what happened to the girl following her discharge from hospital. Only that her mother and a catholic priest had arrived one day to take her back to Ireland. He hoped with all his heart she'd found some peace in life, now that she was with people who would care for her.

That's something likely to give a person PTSD. He turned up the short path into the Cricketers and ordered coffee and a ham salad roll.

'Crisps to go with it?' the barmaid asked. 'We've Brussels sprouts flavour selling half price if you're interested?'

'Go on then. I'll be over there.' Pocketing the change, he headed for the far corner of the room.

'I'll bring it across,' she called after him.

Reece took his phone from his coat pocket and hit the contact number for Idris Roberts. There were things he could no longer remember about the Belle Gillighan case. Facts that nagged and gnawed at him like an itch he couldn't reach. Idris would know. The man never forgot a thing. After several failed attempts, he gave up trying; an uneasy sensation settling in the pit of his stomach. He finished his coffee, and for the time being at least, put the feeling down to the Brussels sprouts crisps.

Chapter 59

JENKINS HELD HER BREATH and crept across the landing, not knowing what she'd do if Amy exited the bathroom and caught her. What she was up to was beyond risky. Tantamount to suicide, some might say. But Amy was leaving in a day or two, allowing her no further opportunity to rummage through the case she kept hidden at the foot of the wardrobe.

She paused. Startled by a noise coming from the master bedroom. One foot only making contact with the soft carpet. She put an ear to the bathroom door and heard water playing against the glass shower screen, Amy singing along with Celine Dion on a waterproof radio.

She came away and gripped the handle of the bedroom door. Threw it wide open, half expecting to come face-to-face with a burglar, or worse. She ducked instinctively as the pigeon flew overhead. The bird hit the light shade, knocking it against the ceiling with a loud thud. Next was the turn of the dressing table. A wayward wing wreaking havoc among the forest of lipsticks and eyeliner pens kept there. She'd wring its scrawny neck if she could only get a hold of it. 'Go on. Sod off,' she said, shooing the bird towards the open window.

Celine Dion had since given up the stage to Whitney Houston. Amy speeding through her set like she was auditioning for a spot on a Saturday evening talent show. Climbing onto the bed armed only with a pillow, Jenkins blocked the bird's frenzied attempts to get past her. 'It's behind you, you stupid sod.' The pigeon took to the air and flew another tight circuit of the room before settling on the windowsill. It perched there, cluelessly staring at her, the open window not more than six inches from where it was. 'Go,' Jenkins said, with one final swing at it.

The case was on Amy's side of the double wardrobe, lying beneath a bag of winter hats and scarfs. Jenkins took it over to the bed and thumbed both brass clasps, thankful of there being no combination lock to pick. Inside was a diary, a single photograph, and a few drawings.

She examined the first of them. It was the work of a young child. There were dark clouds drawn in thick crayon, and long grass scribbled with a heavy hand. A hangman's noose dangled from a horizontal strut. A large crucifix dripping with the crude depiction of blood. At the bottom right-hand corner of the drawing was the name and age of the artist: ***Belle, aged 8.***

Who was Belle? Jenkins had never heard Amy mention the name. Could she be a friend or sister, perhaps?

The next drawing was no less alarming. There were two headless stick figures standing beneath the same bleeding cross. An entry along the top edge of the page read: ***No head means dead.***

The radio went quiet all of a sudden, and from experience, Jenkins knew there were a little over five minutes to be had before Amy entered the bedroom.

The artwork was disturbing in and of itself, but Jenkins was looking for something else. Anything that might shed a light on Amy's secretive past. She returned the drawings to the case and busied herself with the diary. ***Belle's. Keep Out or Die,*** it said in the front matter. The writing style suggested it belonged to an older child—early teens at a glance—and used the same religious symbology to deliver its message.

The toilet flushed. Jenkins read more quickly, and with Wednesday's entry came across a second unfamiliar name. *Father Quinn.* He was there again on the next page. Wednesday, always Wednesday. On the inside of the back cover was a stickman hanging from a noose, and alongside the gallows was the name Father Quinn. She was about to give the photograph more attention when the bathroom door opened. 'Shit, shit, shit.' She hurled herself towards the wardrobe with the case in hand, and with no time to put any of it back as it was, she tossed the case inside and piled the hats and scarfs on top of it. That would have to do for now.

'Elan?' Amy entered the bedroom wrapped in a bath towel, a blonde wig trailing from her hand. She looked surprised. 'What are you doing up here?'

'I heard a noise from downstairs. I knew it wasn't you. It couldn't have been because you were taking a shower.' She was well aware that she was rambling, but couldn't stop. 'You must have left the window open. A bird. There was a pigeon flying about in here. Can you believe that?' Still rambling.

'Is it gone now?' Amy asked, unwilling to advance any further into the bedroom until certain it was.

Jenkins got up off the floor. She leaned against the wardrobe and pushed it closed. 'Yes, it's gone. There's still the odd feather here and there,' she said, bending to collect one from the carpet.

'Good. I'll go to bed now. I'm tired.'

Jenkins let her breath out slowly. She'd been lucky. Had almost got caught in the act. Then she saw it: the photograph lying in open view next to her pillow.

Chapter 60

Reece burst into the waiting room of the respiratory ward, fidgeting like an expectant father. 'Can I see him?'

Maldwyn Roberts put a magazine to one side and got to his feet with a groan. 'The nurses are giving him a quick freshen up before I go back in.' He offered a hand in greeting. 'Good to see you, Brân.'

'You too, Mal. Thanks for letting me know. I rang earlier, but it kept going to voice mail.'

Maldwyn produced his brother's phone from a pocket. 'I couldn't work the bloody thing.'

Reece told him it didn't matter. 'What happened? Idris was okay at Stokes's funeral the other day.'

'He's been coughing up blood since midnight. And more than usual.'

Reece sat down, massaging his knees. He wasn't ready for this. Not yet. 'What happens next?'

Maldwyn rested a hand on the detective's shoulder. 'The doctors came in earlier—a whole bunch of them—and said he wasn't a candidate for intensive care given the advanced lung cancer. Keeping him comfortable is all they can do now.'

When Reece entered the cramped cubicle, he wasn't sure that Idris could hear him. 'This place could do with a lick of paint.' They had Idris on an intravenous infusion of morphine, and a humidified breathing mask that spewed aerosol and was intolerably loud. 'You and me will give it a good makeover when you're better.' He knew his words sounded misplaced, but there wasn't much else to say or do. Perched on the edge of the bed, he took his old boss's hand in his and looked away. 'Come on, Idris. It's just a bad cold. You'll be up on your feet again soon enough.'

Maldwyn listened to Reece utter anything that came to mind, while his brother coughed and rattled his last. 'Why don't you talk to him about the job? He always liked it when the two of you did that.'

'That's why I was ringing earlier,' Reece said with a deep nod. 'To talk about a case we both investigated only months after I joined CID. Nineteen-ninety it was. The rape of Belle Gilligan.'

Maldwyn smacked his lips at the memory. 'That was a nasty one. I remember it being the only thing Idris spoke about at the time.'

Reece turned to the bed. 'What was that, Idris? It's Brân. I've come to visit. Maldwyn's here as well.' He put his ear closer to the face mask. 'Bin men. Yeah, that's right. They found the girl dumped in the alley like garbage.' The bouts of coughing were becoming more frequent, the old man's speech less audible by the second. Reece dipped a gauze swab into a glass of water. He reached under the face mask and wiped fresh blood from Idris's lips. 'Rest now,' he said, giving Maldwyn a worried look. 'I think we should call a nurse.'

Jenkins flew onto the bed and slid the photograph up and under the pillow in one swift move.

Amy went round to the other side and lay her wig on its polystyrene head, fussing with the hairpiece until fully satisfied it rested just right. 'Staying or going?' she asked, folding back the duvet. 'I don't give a fuck either way.'

'Are you reading before you go to sleep?'

'Which bit of tired did you not understand?' Amy switched off the lights without warning. 'You're not getting undressed?' she asked when Jenkins rolled onto her side fully clothed.

Jenkins faked a yawn and pushed the photograph under the waistband of her jeans. 'I'm too knackered.'

'Shoes. Off.'

'They're clean. I only wear them around the house and never outside.'

'Take them off or I'll have you sleep on the floor like a dog.'

Jenkins threw her legs over the side of the bed and pushed herself into a sitting position. 'I'll go sleep on the sofa downstairs.'

'Suit yourself.'

She was only halfway across the bedroom when Amy called her name. She tugged her sweatshirt over the waistband of her jeans before turning around. 'What do you want now?'

Amy was grinning. 'I thought you'd best know—my secret friend has arrived—it's no longer safe.'

Chapter 61

THE HOSPITAL CAR PARK looked like a graveyard for unwanted vehicles. Everything except the blue lights of a passing ambulance was painted in dull shades of grey. 'I still can't believe he's gone,' Reece said, helping Maldwyn load Idris's things into the boot of the Peugeot.

Maldwyn climbed into the passenger side and fastened his seat-belt. 'He'd fought hard and for long enough. You could see it in his eyes these past few weeks.'

'It's just like him to bow out on New Year's Eve.' Reece managed something of a smile and looked towards the heavens. 'Say good-night to Anwen and tell her I miss her every day.' Drying his eyes before getting in, he started the engine with a single turn of the key.

'Thanks for letting me stay over,' Maldwyn said as they got going. 'I'll fetch my car in the morning and be gone from under your feet.'

'It's no trouble at all. Stay for as long as you want.' Reece knew how it felt to grieve alone.

'You're a good man. My brother always spoke very highly of you.'

Reece pulled out of the car park without passing comment for fear of breaking down completely.

Jenkins woke up on the sofa and checked her phone: 2.30am. The house was uncomfortably cold. And quiet, except for the occasional click and creak of water pipes contracting under the floorboards upstairs. When she sat up, she felt something pinch at her groin. The photograph. She rescued it from her waistband and used the torch function of her phone to get a better look.

It was an old Polaroid. Slightly out of focus and yellowed with age. There were two girls as subjects: both smiling into the camera; neither more than eight to ten years old. She recognised one of them as a younger Amy. She had a full head of hair back then – long before repeated cycles of chemotherapy had robbed her of it.

Jenkins turned the photograph over and read from the reverse side. Belle Gillighan and Amelia Hosty, 1981. 'Amelia – Amy. Amy – Amelia.' Jenkins played with the names, repeating them in a whisper. 'You never told me you'd shortened your name.' There was something forced and unnatural about the girls' smiles. They looked as though they were frightened of whoever was hidden behind the camera. She had seen that same look a thousand times before, and mostly while working vice. 'Were you and Belle Gilligham friends?' She tapped the photograph against her other hand, knowing she needed to find out.

Reece sat with the Blueridge guitar on his lap, noodling at the kitchen table, not wanting to go to bed and give in to the nightmares that lurked in the shadows. He'd brought the instrument back from Rome only because Anwen had already purchased it without him knowing. Most days he couldn't face looking at the thing, and wanted to smash it into a million pieces for the part it had played in his wife's death. But tonight, it seemed appropriate. Comforting, even.

'That's nice.' Maldwyn sat back and listened to Reece finger-pick a sweet melody. 'Anwen played piano.' He spoke as though he was the only one who knew. 'Pretty well too, if the last time I heard her was anything to go by.'

Reece's noodling slowed while his conscious thought drifted elsewhere. 'Grade seven.'

'But the two of you never bought one? A piano, I mean.'

Reece rested his strumming hand on a knee. 'We talked about it a few times, but this place isn't big enough, and she didn't want one of those foldaway keyboards.'

Maldwyn pulled a face. 'I'm not surprised. They're nothing like the real thing.'

Reece's fingers returned to the strings. 'We'd seen one in Gardner's on the Gabalfa roundabout. An old upright from Berlin.'

'A German piano?'

'Over a hundred years old, with a honky-tonk groove Anwen loved.' The memory brought a smile. 'We put a deposit down, asking the owner to keep it at the shop until the place in Brecon was finished.'

'And you cancelled after . . .'

Reece propped the guitar against a chair. 'I never got round to it.' He reached across the kitchen counter and banged an unopened bottle of Penderyn Sherrywood onto the wooden table. 'Pass us those glasses, Mal. What say you and me do this whisky some serious damage?'

Maldwyn got up and returned with three. 'Pour one for Idris as well.'

Reece did, then raised his glass. 'To absent friends and loved ones.'

The Yale lock engaged with a loud click. Jenkins froze, waiting for the landing light to come on. When it didn't, she made a break for it, checking the upstairs window as she hurried towards her parked car further up the street. There was a chink in the curtains that hadn't been there a moment earlier. Or was it her mind playing tricks? That wasn't important. Not now she'd put some distance between the two of them.

Her car unlocked with a single peep of its after-market security system. She got inside and took a moment to calm her nerves. Scribbled on a notepad on her lap was a telephone number and a woman's name. Both had been taken from the back cover of Belle Gillighan's diary. A hushed phone call made in the early hours had earned her answers to the many questions she had, but only if she was willing to make the journey in person.

She started the car and took one more look at the bedroom window before pulling away. She was definitely being watched.

Next stop, the airport.

Chapter 62

ERYL GOUGH KNEW SOMEONE was watching her. From a vantage point midway along the car park and next to a high-sided panel van. It would have been innocent enough, by most people's reckoning. Instinct and experience told her otherwise.

She'd become accomplished at noticing such things. Ever since changing her name and moving to the other side of the city.

Had they let him out of prison early? That was her first thought. If so, then she should have been given due notice beforehand.

When she pulled out onto the main road, a white Ford Fiesta turned left with her. Several other cars came the same way, but it was the Fiesta that had her keep one eye fixed on the rear-view mirror for the entire journey home. When at last she came to a stop, it went past with its driver paying her no attention.

Gough relaxed and opened the boot. Collected her shopping bags while mocking herself for being so silly. They'd have told her before releasing that violent scumbag. Those were the rules.

But there it was—the white Ford Fiesta—now parked at the top end of the street with its engine running. The driver's upper body was turned to face her. Something wasn't right.

Earlier that day, she'd sat and watched a news broadcast. The one in which police had circulated CCTV footage of a woman they were trying to trace. A woman they suspected of being involved in the recent violent murders that had shocked the city. There was a warning not to approach the suspect. And a telephone number to call with information, should there be any. Though the images were lacking any real clarity of detail, the woman's profile picture bore an uncanny resemblance to the driver of the white car. Gough hurried inside her flat and reported the sighting without a moment's delay.

Eryl Gough waited with a second glass of chilled Pinot Grigio on the breakfast bar in front of her. The police had promised to come and take a statement when they could. But they'd have received dozens of crank calls by now. Mostly from people with nothing better to do with their time. But unlike the crank callers, she hadn't pretended to know the woman's identity, only that she drove a white Fiesta on a '68 plate.

The clock showed 5.35pm, over an hour since she'd made the third call to the incident line. Where were they? They'd better not have put her down as yet another time-waster. She could help them solve this case, but only if they arrived before she'd opened another bottle of wine.

The microwave pinged three times. 'Dinner's ready,' she told Arnie. The film lid came away in several ragged pieces, steam spewing forth before she could move her hand. She blew on her fingers and ran the cold water tap. 'How difficult can it be to design one that comes off whole?' The cat had little in answer and went back to licking its own arse.

Gough forked the watery cottage pie and took another gulp of wine while waiting for the meal to cool enough to eat. 'There they are now,' she said, sliding off the barstool in response to the ringing doorbell. 'It's just as well you got here before the killer, because if you hadn't—'

When the door opened, her body went rigid as a burst of electricity surged through the two barbs nibbling her skin. She collapsed onto the floor. Someone stepped over her, shutting the door behind them with the sole of their shoe.

Before she died, Libby Barr—Elizabeth Thorne to use her married name—had told Belle everything she wanted to know about Roxie May's movements and whereabouts. But Libby had claimed that Sasha Ingram had dropped off her radar some years earlier. Libby had earned herself a few more minutes of agony for playing that game. It had taken Belle an age of trawling through public records, and umpteen telephone calls to discover that the woman she sought had been calling herself Eryl Gough, and not Sasha Ingram, for the best part of a decade. Belle made a mental note-to-self to offer Libby an apology if ever their paths crossed in hell.

'Did you ring the police?' Belle slapped Gough's cheeks. 'Did you?'

Gough worked her jaw with the help of a shaky hand. 'They're on their way. I told them I saw you at the supermarket.'

Belle shook her head. 'They'll have gone over there to look at the CCTV footage before responding. Far too many time-wasters for them to act on everything they're given.'

Another pulse of the Taser had Gough pass out and miss the bit when she was dragged by the ankles along the wooden floor to the kitchen. Belle knelt and tore open the buttons of the cheap dress, exposing the woman's pelvic region. 'An eye for an eye,' she said, unrolling a black cloth wrap. 'Or in our case, a womb for a womb.'

Survival instinct kicked in just then. Gough came to and went to sit up, but couldn't. Her hands and feet were bound to the breakfast bar's shiny chrome legs. She tried to scream, but was unable – a length of tight duct tape saw to that.

Belle loomed over her. 'All you had to do was speak up and tell them what you saw that night. That's all I asked of any of you.'

Gough groaned under the tape when the scalpel travelled across her lower abdomen. Her eyes bulged in their lidless sockets – two folds of bloodied skin lying next to her thrashing head. The wound pinked along a thin and straight line, beads of dark blood mixing with small squirters of a brighter kind. Where were the police? The skin edges were forced apart, the scalpel making a second pass. This time, it cut deeper. Through the yellow fatty layer and down to the muscle beneath.

The doorbell rang. A tacky model pre-programmed with a dozen or more ghastly ringtones. Then a knock. And a voice.

'Mrs Gough? It's the police.'

Chapter 63

THAT GAVE ERYL GOUGH a new lease of life. She pulled at the leg of the breakfast bar for all she was worth, heaving and growling at the same time.

Belle forced her free hand against the other woman's chest, pinning her flat to the floor. 'No, you don't,' she said, checking over her shoulder. 'You're not getting out of this one alive.'

The letter box flapped open. 'Mrs Gough, it's the police.'

Gough pulled on the chrome leg. It gave, but only a little. She pulled some more, not letting up until it was free of its holding point. She did the same with the one anchored to her feet, giving it a hefty kick. The horizontal counter of the breakfast bar broke away from its wall-fixings with a snapping sound and fell against the tiled surface only inches from her head.

'Mrs Gough, open the door!' The man's voice was more insistent.

'Don't you dare think this is over.' Belle pressed the scalpel against Gough's straining neck. 'Time to die, bitch.' She leaned out of the way and drew the blade in a wide arc. The police officer was banging against the door with a shoulder, and not a battering ram, which would have finished the job a lot quicker. Belle ran for the rear exit of the flat, abandoning her tools in what was fast becoming an expanding puddle of blood on the kitchen floor.

The uniform burst through the front door and went straight to the writhing body, slipping and sliding on his knees in the warm puddle. He pressed a folded tea towel tight to the gash in Gough's neck. She was already paler than anyone he'd ever before seen. 'You're going to be okay,' he said, knowing she'd be dead before he could finish a count of ten.

Gough opened her eyes and tried to pull him closer, but didn't have the strength. 'Belle.' She barely got it out.

'Is that your daughter's name?' the uniform asked. 'Is there someone else here in the flat with you?'

Gough's pupils dilated as she stared at him.

'Mrs Gough, stay with me. The ambulance is on its way.'

It took the others more than twenty minutes to get there. 'Who's Belle?' Adams asked, walking blood around the kitchen floor. 'Come on, people. Anyone.'

Ken Ward stayed well clear of the mess. 'There's no one else here except for the cat.' He stroked the frightened animal and tried the name Belle on it. 'It doesn't seem to answer to that, sir.'

Adams turned to Ginge and almost fell over the dead woman's body. He quickly righted himself. 'Are you sure that's what she said?'

'No doubt about it, sir.'

'That's all she had to say before she died. Nothing else?'

'She was practically dead when I found her.'

'And the killer - you get anything of them?'

Ginge shook his head. 'I was a bit caught up here, to be honest with you.'

'You should've gone after them instead of messing about with a lost cause,' Adams said.

'With all due respect, sir, I disagree.' Ginge wiped his hands on a wet cloth. 'Can I get out of this uniform now?'

Adams grunted something and told him to hand it over to the CSIs.

'I will, sir.'

'And get yourself back to the station to write up your notes.'

'First thing, sir.' Ginge turned and left.

'You're here at last,' Adams said when Twm Pryce entered the kitchen carrying his doctors' bag. 'Better late than never, I suppose.'

'I got caught in traffic.' Pryce donned a pair of surgical gloves and made a brief examination of the victim. 'The killer was disturbed before the peritoneum was opened.'

Adams tutted. 'Tell me something I don't already know.'

'I'd be reasonably confident to say the assault was carried out by the same killer.' Pryce checked the head-end of the body. 'Yep, no eyelids.'

'Coins?' Adams made no attempt to hide his irritation.

'Not that I've seen.' Pryce removed his gloves and leaned into the shrinking DI. 'Anyone I know?' he asked, referring to the bridge of Adams's nose.

'I doubt the May brothers frequent your gentleman's club, Doctor.'

'Shame that. I'd have bought the boys a drink.'

Ward reappeared in the doorway—this time, minus the cat—before Adams was able to reply. 'It got away,' he said, producing an armful of scram marks as evidence he'd put up something of a fight. 'There's a communal garden leading onto a busy road, sir. The bus stops on both sides.' He shrugged. 'The killer could have gone in either direction.'

'If she got on a bus after making this mess, then she'd stick out like a sore thumb.'

Ward didn't disagree. 'I've got uniform onto all companies serving those stops, sir.'

Adams circled Eryl Gough's exsanguinated body. 'Have traffic pull over any bus that would have gone past here within the last hour. I want their CCTV images downloaded pronto. Do you hear me?'

'Yes, sir.' Ward went outside and stood under cover of a bush at the bottom of the garden. He dialled a number on his phone. Denny Cartwright answered. 'Get Billy on the line,' Ward said, keeping out of sight. 'I don't give a fuck what he told you. I need to speak to him.'

There was a brief silence, followed by the sound of a door opening. Then Cartwright's wheezy breathing. Knocking next. Knuckles on metal. Then raised voices and a door slamming shut.

'This had better be worth my time, Copper.' It was Creed. 'I was on for a hole-in-one just then, and you're messing with my swing, if you get my drift?'

'There's been another murder.' Ward told it like it was.

'What's that got to do with me?'

'A woman called Eryl Gough this time.'

'Never heard of her.' There was a brief pause. 'Should I have?'

'She worked at the Midnight Club a good few years back. Danced with Roxie and Libby. You might remember her as Sasha Ingram?' Ward let Creed ponder the depths of his memory. 'She started a new life for herself while her husband was doing time for knocking her about.'

'Same question, Copper. What's it got to do with me?'

'I know about the rape case,' Ward said. 'The one where the teenage girl nearly died.' There was silence except for the sound of breathing. 'That's Roxie, Libby, and now Sasha. Three witnesses who refused to give evidence against you. It's like they've been punished for keeping quiet.'

'Who told you about the girl?'

'Jack Stokes did. Years back. It was quite a case, by all accounts.' The man was dead and buried and therefore in no position to deny it.

The gangster's voice was raspy. 'He always did have a big mouth.'

Ward hoped the wide grin didn't show in his voice. 'You're next, Billy. I'm sure of it. The killer's coming for you.'

Chapter 64

'*They're talking about you.*'

The news channel reported the death of Eryl Gough as its main feature. And how the police had come so close to catching the killer journalists had dubbed 'Santa Claws'. The television reporter droned on about the latest victim for what must have been a full four minutes. Unnecessary, in Belle's opinion, given the fucked-up state of the world.

The woman was dead. Sprawled across her own kitchen floor, bleeding from a slit throat like a pig in an abattoir. Get over it. But her uterus was intact, and that wasn't how it was supposed to be.

The police had spoiled things. They always spoiled things.

'*I said they're talking about you.*'

Belle turned towards the voice. 'You're back.'

'*Because you need me.*'

She paced the room in search of her secret friend, but couldn't find him anywhere. 'I've killed three of the bitches so far,' she said, giving up the hunt.

'*The last one was rushed.*'

It wasn't like her secret friend to criticise her. That's what others did. Not him. 'They almost caught me this time.'

'*Then you should have killed the policeman for interrupting you.*' Her secret friend knew about that? He must have been watching the whole time.

Belle put a hand to her mouth. 'Killing a police officer would be so wrong.'

'*You do still want to punish the tattooed man?*'

'More than anything I've ever longed for.'

'*Then it might come to that if someone tries to stop you.*'

'Someone?'

'*You know who I mean.*'

Belle chewed on freshly scrubbed nails. 'Elan?'

'*Exactly.*'

'Elan has to die?'

'*If she gets in our way, then yes.*'

Chapter 65

Chief Superintendent Cable rested the telephone on its stand and looked skywards for help. When none was forthcoming, she went in search of DI Adams and found him pacing in front of the evidence board, talking to himself. 'Tell me you've got our killer in custody,' she said. 'The Police and Crime Commissioner is throwing his toys out of the pram and that's got the Assistant Chief Constable snapping at my arse.'

Adams looked surprised to see her. 'Ma'am. I thought you'd be well gone by now.' He checked his watch. 'You'll be late.'

Cable took a seat opposite. 'I can't go to a Divisional New Year's Eve dinner party with this shit storm going on.' She crossed her legs in an ankle-length black dress and heels. 'Brief me, and be quick about it.'

'We got a call around three-fifteen from a woman named Eryl Gough. Claiming she was being followed from the Western Avenue Tesco store.'

'Followed by whom?'

'That's the thing. She rang back a bit later.' Adams checked his notes. 'At four-thirty, saying the person who'd followed her had been on one of the recorded news channels earlier in the day. I'm guessing that was the CCTV footage we put out.'

'And you sent someone to look at the store recordings?'

Adams nodded. 'We'd received so many crank calls that we had to be sure we weren't wasting our time.'

Cable did some quick mental arithmetic. 'Let me get this right. The first phone call came in somewhere around three, and time of death was just before six.' She closed her eyes. 'What took you so long to realise you were onto something?'

'Uniform were stretched, ma'am. The city is like a madhouse at this time of year. We got a car over there as soon as we could.'

'But by then it was already too late.'

'Only marginally.'

Cable shot out of her seat. All five-feet-three inches of her. 'A woman lost her life. Margins was all it took.'

'Ma'am.' Adams came away from the evidence board. 'Eryl Gough gave us a name before she died.'

'And?' Cable asked with a glimmer of hope. 'What was it?'

'Belle.'

'And do you know who she is? Does anyone know?'

Adams puffed his cheeks and sunk both hands into his trouser pockets. 'Not exactly, ma'am.'

Chapter 66

JENKINS TOUCHED DOWN IN Dublin, feeling tired and more than a little grubby. She'd got a seat on the aircraft only because of a late no-show and the fact she was travelling alone. After that, her good fortune took a sudden nosedive when the car hire company screwed her over - something to do with bank holiday rates and a last-minute booking fee.

'It would be cheaper to go by taxi,' she'd told the unhelpful agent, and had received an open invitation to do just that. So much for Irish charm and hospitality. New Year too. And to trump things, the vehicle hadn't been adequately fuelled for her onward journey. Luckily, there was a petrol station nearby.

She pulled onto the garage forecourt and dialled Ken Ward's number. 'Happy New Year and all that bullshit,' she said. 'You're still awake and not pissed. I'm impressed.' She let Ward ask the expected stuff. 'I'd rather not say where I am at the minute. Can't get you in trouble if you don't know what I'm up to. No, nothing to be concerned about, just something I needed to check for myself.'

Someone behind her hooted their horn. Jenkins waved an apology at the driver and got out of the hire car. 'I'll be back the day after tomorrow,' she said, lifting the nozzle of the fuel line from its holder. 'I've heard nothing from Professional Standards as yet.'

Ward said something she didn't catch over the noise of the tannoy telling her not to use a mobile phone near the pumps. She nodded at the woman through the glass of the shopfront and indicated that she was close to ending the call. 'I can't hear you, Ken,' she said when the hooter behind her hit his horn again. 'None of this to Adams. Promise me.' She hung up, not knowing if Ward had heard, and put her phone on the pump while she finished filling the tank.

Amy rummaged through the case from the wardrobe, pleased that things were progressing even better than planned. She ticked the items off in her head: Diary and drawings – yes. Photograph – gone. The list of victims' initials – still there. She took the case over to the bed and congratulated herself on having provided Niamh

MacBride's name and telephone number on the inside of the diary's back cover.

'Well done, Elan. You're getting close now. Very close indeed. Joining the dots, but what do you see? Not yet the vicious killer they've described on the news. Even you can't be that good. Just enough of the picture to have your inquisitive mind needing to know more.' She clapped her hands in triumph.

A quick check inside the top drawer of the bedside table confirmed that Jenkins's passport was missing. 'You've certainly lived up to all expectations, which is why I insisted we let you live. That's right, we watched you sleep tonight for a full ten minutes. My secret friend wanted to kill you, but I said no, and now he's pissed at me. I did that for you, Elan. For us. I still love you.'

Amy knew she could no longer stay at home. One telephone call from Jenkins could bring the whole thing crashing down around her. She knew exactly what to do. The fat detective had given her everything she needed, including details on how to get into the Midnight Club when ready.

She closed the front door behind her and headed for the white Ford Fiesta.

Billy Creed stood in the doorway of the Games Room, fastening the belt of a black-silk dressing gown. 'You told me already; Belle Gillighan killed Roxie. What else is there to talk about?'

Ward looked past the gangster, at four or five naked women wandering the room unashamedly collecting underwear. 'Jesus, that one looks young enough to still be in school.' The redhead shook her chest at him and squealed when Jimmy Chin threw her over his shoulder and slapped her bare buttocks.

Creed shut the door and shoved the detective towards the steps leading from the basement to the ground floor. 'Phones and nice clobber costs them money they don't have.'

'Even so, Billy, you're sailing close to the wind there.'

Creed pressed his forehead against Ward's, a noxious cocktail of cigars, brandy, and women, heavy on his breath. 'You want to make it any of your concern?'

'I'm just saying.'

'Good, because Denny's always happy to give his shovel an outing.'

Ward knew that wasn't an idle threat.

Creed propelled him up the last few steps. 'When's it going down, Copper? When do you reckon this Gillighan bitch is gonna try her luck?'

'She won't.' Ward kept his back to the gangster as they walked. 'I reckon she'll lie low now she knows we're onto her. We'll have her under lock and key in no time. Don't you worry about that.'

'Who says I'm worried?' Creed gritted his teeth. 'Belle Gillighan's mine. You make sure none of your lot go anywhere near her.'

Chapter 67

It was almost fully light when Jenkins pulled up in front of *Glenway Guesthouse* in the county of Waterford, southeast Ireland. She'd booked a room while waiting in the departures lounge of Cardiff airport, the proprietor sounding positively gleeful to be receiving a booking.

After driving for more than two and a half hours from Dublin, she was tired and in need of a hot shower and sleep. The route had hugged the beautiful coastline—not that the night had offered any sight of it—before cutting inland somewhere northwest of Ardamine. She reached into her jacket pocket, suddenly needing to know if Amy had tried to contact her, screaming threats of violent retribution. The phone wasn't there. Nor was it in the glovebox or on the passenger seat next to her. She groaned with the realisation that she'd left it on the petrol pump in Dublin.

She screwed her eyes shut and sighed before getting out of the car. Then swung a kick at the front tyre on her way past. Almost gave it a second helping, but didn't. She'd have to work the old-fashioned way. Use legwork, and telephone boxes if such things still existed.

The guesthouse resembled its online image, minus the summer sunshine and tubs of bright red geraniums. It was a base nonetheless for a day or two's detective work. With a swipe of her credit card, she signed in at the front desk and opened a tab for her brief stay. 'I'm sorry for the early arrival,' she told the man fussing behind the counter, 'but Niamh MacBride recommended you.'

Mr O'Leary pressed a hand to his mouth and stifled a yawn. 'Niamh's a good woman, so she is.'

Jenkins hoped he was right and put the credit card away in her wallet. 'She was very helpful.'

'Will you be wanting breakfast?' O'Leary was a short man in his late fifties and wore a knitted tank top that caught on the buckle of his trouser belt. 'We do a full English. Or, if you'd prefer, a continental buffet. There's cereal, obviously. And a selection of yogurts.'

'Shower and sleep before anything else,' Jenkins said, mirroring the owner's yawn. 'It's been a long night.'

'What about dinner with a table next to the garden window?' The poor sod was trying to eke out a living and working bloody hard at it.

'Put me down for something light. I'm not a big eater, mind you.'

O'Leary's mood brightened. 'Dinner it is,' he said, clicking a mouse before turning his back on her to take a room key from a box on the wall behind him.

Jenkins took it and produced the creased Polaroid of the two young girls. 'Do you know anything about Niamh's sister, Amelia – or Amy, as she prefers to call herself?'

The hotelier regarded her with a look of deep suspicion, ignoring her outstretched hand and its contents. 'Who are you?' he asked. 'And what are you doing here?'

Jenkins saw no need to tell the man the complete truth. She still didn't know what that was, in any case. 'I was passing through on my way back from New York and thought I'd look up an old college friend.'

O'Leary's face crumpled. 'College friend?'

Before Jenkins could mastermind an appropriate explanation, a woman appeared in the doorway on the other side of the counter, and said something in Gaeilge. O'Leary answered his wife in the same Irish Gaelic and nodded towards the new arrival.

Chapter 68

Jenkins put the need for sleep to one side, her head now crammed with more important things. She walked past houses painted in pastel blues and rich clotted creams, and boat masts that rattled in the wind, all the while searching for the waterside home of Niamh MacBride.

When she got there, the sign in the coffee shop window read: **CLOSED.** She tapped on the wood surround of the half-glazed door and waved enthusiastically when someone appeared at the back of the room. 'Hello,' she called through the glass. 'It's me, Elan Jenkins. We spoke on the telephone last night.'

In a little under five minutes, they were seated at a wooden table with mugs of hot chocolate warming their cold hands. Jenkins gave an approving nod. The chocolate was very good and hit the spot. 'If you don't mind me saying, you and Amy don't look at all alike.'

Niamh MacBride leaned on an elbow and squinted. 'And how could you possibly know that?'

The table wobbled with the added weight. Jenkins lifted her mug before it spilled. 'It's just an observation.'

MacBride disappeared momentarily to wedge a folded napkin under the offending table leg. 'Of what exactly?'

Jenkins let out a nervous giggle. 'I'm saying I don't see the family resemblance between the two of you. Have I said something I shouldn't?' she asked when the woman responded with a look of anger.

MacBride got to her feet. 'I think you should go.'

'I've only just arrived.'

'You said you were searching for the truth. That's the only reason I agreed to meet with you. Do you know how many journalists and authors have been here over the years?'

Jenkins wondered what had provoked such a reaction. 'I thought you'd help me make sense of the things I'm still struggling with.' She shrugged. 'I'm here for no other reason. That's what you asked, wasn't it? That I come here in person?'

'Because I needed to see who I was talking with. Those journalists have played every dirty trick in the book just to get themselves a story. Any story. Deceitful is what they are.'

Jenkins went to produce her warrant card, then remembered Chief Superintendent Cable had confiscated it as part of the suspension process. 'I'm not a journalist. I'm a serving police officer, and until yesterday, was Amy's partner.'

Niamh MacBride was in floods of tears, the knuckles of both her hands pressed against the table top for support. 'This is so cruel. You should be ashamed of yourself for what you're doing.' She slumped onto her chair. 'My sister has been dead for just short of forty years.'

Several minutes passed before they spoke again, neither of them keeping track of exactly how many.

'I'm sorry,' Jenkins said, the silence between them finally broken. She had absolutely no clue what was going on. 'You'll have to explain.'

MacBride went and stood against a radiator. One of those grey chunky types found mostly in old schools and churches. 'Belle Gillighan's father died at sea before she was born.' She looked out of the window, towards the harbour that couldn't be seen from their current position. 'The storm of seventy-two took the lives of three good local men, and several more in the seas of Northern Europe.'

As the conversation ebbed and flowed, Jenkins slowly came to terms with the fact she'd been living with an impostor for the last nine months. The girl in the photograph; the one in the yellow blouse; the one who was without a doubt her ex-partner, wasn't Amy—or Amelia Hosty, to use her real name—she was Belle Gillighan.

More silence.

'What was Belle like as a girl?' Jenkins decided she might as well know.

'Poison is how many described her. Father Quinn said he saw the devil himself in her eyes, and that man's word was gospel in these parts.'

Quinn. The name from the diary. 'But she was only a child. They all go through a rebellious phase.' Jenkins knew she certainly had.

'With a foul mouth and a wicked will to match.'

Jenkins thought it best not to argue the point. 'This priest—'

'Said vile things about him, so she did. And spread terrible rumours.' MacBride crossed herself. 'No one would dare believe a word of it, mind you. Father Quinn was a man of God.'

In Jenkins's experience as a murder squad detective, God didn't give a flying fuck who did what to whom. 'And was he moved to another diocese by the bishop?' Unlikely, she knew. The church had a habit of dealing with such things in their own way.

'I think I've said too much already.' MacBride cleared their mugs from the table, returning them to the serving counter with a solid thump. 'I'm sorry your trip turned out to be a wasted one, Detective Sergeant.'

O'Leary hovered; a bowl of hot soup clamped between his trembling fingers. Jenkins leaned out of harm's way and waited until supper landed safely on the table. 'Was Mrs MacBride of any help to you?' he asked.

'There are still a few gaps here and there.'

O'Leary undid the strings of his apron. 'That's a shame. She's been dragged through an awful lot, so she has.'

Jenkins used her foot to push a chair towards him. 'The summer of eighty-one, for instance, when Amelia Hosty fell from the tree and broke her neck.'

'Mrs MacBride told you about that?'

'Bits and pieces. But what I don't understand is why people automatically thought it was anything more than a tragic accident?' Jenkins had a point. Kids climbed, swam, and crossed roads all the time. And some got themselves killed in the process.

'Amelia's death was no accident.' O'Leary sounded sure of himself.

'There was no proof of foul play. Only hearsay,' Jenkins said. 'As a serving police officer, I'd need a lot more than that.'

O'Leary sat down and balled the apron in his lap. 'What if I told you there was an eyewitness to what happened in that tree? Would that make you take more notice?'

Chapter 69

Cable massaged her temples. She used the other hand to pick specks of fluff from the sleeve of her uniform jacket. 'Yes, sir, I *have* seen this morning's newspapers.' How could she not have done? They were everywhere, including the front desk of the foyer downstairs. 'No, sir, I'm not trying to turn the Force into a laughing stock.'

She disconnected the speakerphone. No one else in the building needed to hear the ACC exhaust his full repertoire of well-polished expletives.

'With all due respect, sir, DCI Reece isn't in any fit state to return to work. I have the preliminary assessment report right here in front of me.' She flicked through to the summary page. 'Dr Beven says—'

Cable stopped for another interruption. Another rant.

'No, sir, I didn't think you would. I will, sir. And you too. Goodbye.' She slunk into the chair and mouthed a string of well-chosen adjectives of her own. For a while she sat there digesting Harris's words of warning. She pressed '1' on her desk-phone's keypad and spoke to her PA. 'Kathy, did you tell DI Adams I wanted to see him?'

'I did, ma'am. More than twenty minutes ago.'

Cable screwed both eyes shut, and against all better judgement, uttered the words she'd not expected to hear herself speak for a long while to come. 'Ring DCI Reece and tell him to get over here. And get me a multipack of aspirin while you're at it.'

Adams threw himself into his office swivel chair, spilling a pot of multicoloured Biros when he banged against the desk in temper. 'How dare she,' he said, slapping the folded newspaper against the mess of wandering pens. 'How fucking dare she.' Maggie Kavanagh's evaluation of events was scathing.

Cardiff gripped by unprecedented crime wave . . . South Wales Police no closer to solving the Santa Claws case as body count rises . . . Senior detective and deputy both serving suspension while inexperienced ex-bank manager flounders

alone . . . Utter chaos at the Bay station . . . The people of our city deserve better.'

And so it continued. 'Get me the South Wales Herald,' Adams said when the woman downstairs answered. 'No, not another bloody newspaper. I meant the editor or whoever.' He thumped the handset into its cradle and stared at an invisible spot on the ceiling.

Ffion Morgan appeared in the doorway with a sheet of A4 paper hanging limply from her hand. 'Sir, we might have something.'

'This had better be good news for once.'

'It looks like our killer used an Edwins bus, but got off again only one stop after getting on.'

'Looks like, or did?'

'Did.'

'Only one stop, you say.' He got to his feet. The newspaper article temporarily forgotten. 'And you're sure it was her?'

Morgan waved the grainy printout. 'As far as I can tell.'

'Give.' Adams snatched the document as he went past. 'But why only one stop?'

Morgan followed. 'Someone on the bus might have recognised her from the images we put out. Then there's the blood. She wouldn't have had time to clean it all off.'

'Do we have any calls to support a sighting?'

'None that were put through to the briefing room.'

'But you're checking for any that weren't?'

'Ken is onto it.'

Adams scratched his head. 'One stop.' It was a whisper.

'It might mean she's a local.'

'We'll talk later. I'm wanted upstairs.'

'And if the press call back?'

He wasn't listening, his curiosity leading the way to the third floor.

Chapter 70

Reece balked at the chief super's suggestion.

Adams had heard it all a short time earlier, and sat with his arms folded, staring at the wall like a moping kid.

'You're winding me up?' Reece looked from one to the other of them, neither responding quickly enough for his liking? 'Well?'

Cable opened the window and took a few deep breaths before returning to her desk. 'Those are the conditions of your return.' She sat down again. 'Are you in or out?'

'With him in charge? I'd rather have my scrotum nailed to that door.'

Cable's eyes widened. 'Don't tempt me, Detective Chief Inspector.'

'Give me a couple more days and I'll have this woman banged up,' Adams said.

'Like hell you will.' Reece shook his head. 'You're only where you are now because Jenkins refused to listen to your bullshit. Clutching at straws and going round in circles is all you're doing.' He used three fingers to count off the points he was making. 'You've got no idea as to identity, whereabouts, or motive.' He turned to Cable. 'You called me, remember? So the way I see it, you must be thinking the same.'

The chief super went to the door and opened it. She spoke to Adams: 'Give us a moment, Robert.'

'Ma'am?'

'Go get three coffees,' she said, ushering him out.

'Two sugars in mine.' Reece winked. 'And see if you can rustle up some Hobnobs while you're at it.'

Adams glared, but left all the same.

'Doesn't know his arse from his elbow, that one.'

Cable didn't reply and went back to her seat.

'What?' Reece frowned. 'Why are you looking at me like that?'

Cable removed a file from her desk drawer. 'We haven't exactly hit it off since I arrived in Cardiff.'

Reece sniffed. 'Can't say I've noticed.'

'You've something of a reputation on the Force. A local folk hero from what I gather.'

'I get the job done, if that's what you mean.'

Cable opened the file. 'But often with something of an unconventional approach, if what's in here is anything to go by.'

'I don't wine and dine them first, if that's what you mean?'

'Policing is changing.'

Christ, not this again. 'In my day you got an apprenticeship on the beat, not in the classroom. From the likes of Jack Stokes or Idris Roberts. These days it's all university degrees and fast-track programs. There's nothing to be learnt from a PowerPoint presentation that can't be done a whole lot better out on the streets.'

Cable straightened. 'There's more to Police College than that, and you know it.'

'Really? Take Adams, for example: a pound to a penny he hasn't found the kitchen yet.' Reece thought he saw Cable hide a grin behind a hand. He pounced when her guard was down. 'I want Elan Jenkins back. She's the best copper we have here.'

'Not possible. Not before Professional Standards are done with her.'

'This is bollocks. *They* are bollocks.'

'And that's your professional opinion, is it? Listen to me, Reece. If it was left to my judgement alone, you'd still be off along with your sergeant. Shut up,' Cable said when he protested. 'I put you on leave for your own good. Before you could ruin your career and lose everything you've worked so bloody hard to achieve. We're on the same side here — only you can't see through the fog you've been living in lately.'

Reece drummed his fists on the desk. 'What is it with everyone? I'm fine.'

'No, you're not.' Cable leafed through the file until she found the bit she was looking for. 'Dr Beven's preliminary assessment,' she said, adjusting her readers. 'Here we go, and I'm only skimming the surface, you understand. "DCI Reece reports experiencing frequent nightmares, and sudden, often vivid, flashback memories of his wife's death. He admits to lapses in concentration, together with episodes of intense irritability and overwhelming anger . . . He could not fully rule out the possibility of taking his own life".' Cable removed her glasses and looked up. 'You have Post-Traumatic Stress Disorder, and why the hell wouldn't you given the circumstances?'

'I told you—'

'Yes, I know, you're fine.'

'Well, then.' Reece knew his voice was louder than it should have been. He needed to be careful. He'd only just got back to work.

'This here says you're not.' Cable dropped the file into the desk drawer and shut it away. 'ACC Harris wants you back on the case, and there's nothing I can do or say to stop that. *But*, and it's a big but – I won't have you risking your own safety or that of anyone else on this team, do you understand?'

'You really need me to answer?'

'Just say yes, for Christ's sake.'

'I'm in charge and Jenkins rides shotgun. Take it or leave it.'

Cable helped herself to two aspirin, swallowing them dry. 'And DI Adams. What do you expect me to do with him?'

'Here's the tea boy now,' Reece said, getting up. Adams used a foot to open the office door, three coffees in hand and a half-eaten packet of biscuits hanging from his clenched teeth. Reece snatched them from him and nodded at the coffee. 'You're going to need something a fair bit stronger than that, sunshine. The chief super's about to ruin your day.'

Chapter 71

JENKINS PARKED THE HIRE car opposite the red-brick structure of the now defunct prison and stared in disbelief. 'Scary would be my first impression of the place.'

Mary Doyle watched the stationary hands of the white clock face high above the imposing archway. 'You get used to it after a while. Numb to it, I suppose.'

Jenkins took the nurse's word for it. 'And you worked here for how long?'

'Three years, four months, and six days. I hated every minute of being there.'

'But I thought you said . . . ?'

'I lied.' Doyle glanced at her. 'How can anyone be expected to get their head straight while cooped up in a place as drab and depressing as that?' Beyond the wrought-iron railings was a narrow rectangle of overgrown grass, bordered by a few winter shrubs. A short pavement with a curve led to the front entrance and whatever horrors lay behind the stout metal doors.

'Mr O'Leary said you'd be willing to tell me more about Belle Gillighan.'

'And he'll have also warned that I can sniff a troublemaker like hogs do truffles.'

'He did. Said you'd be out of the car in a flash if I tried it on.'

'And he wasn't wrong.' Doyle was clearly happier now she'd set some basic ground rules.

Jenkins fought to get comfortable, twisting side-on behind the steering wheel. 'I'm a serving police detective back in Cardiff, and until yesterday, thought I'd been sharing my home with a woman named Amelia Hosty. Amy, as I knew her.'

'And I'd imagine Niamh MacBride telling you her sister has been dead all these years has come as something of a shock?'

'It's a lot more than that. But what I don't understand is why Belle would come into my life and lie about her true identity?'

'Belle.' Doyle frowned. 'Belle *Gillighan?*'

Jenkins nodded. 'We've been living together for the best part of nine months.'

'I thought we were clear on there being no bullshit?'

'Pardon?' Jenkins had no idea what the woman meant by the comment.

Doyle frowned more deeply. 'Are you saying you really don't know?'

Jenkins took her hands off the steering wheel and rested them in her lap. 'I'm afraid you're going to have to spell it out for me.'

'Belle Gillighan is dead.' It was said matter-of-factly. 'And has been for a couple of years.'

'Whoa. Wait now.' Jenkins opened the car door and swung both feet onto the road. She had her back turned to the passenger seat. 'First, I'm told it's not Amelia Hosty I've been living with, and now you say it wasn't Belle Gillighan, either.' She twisted slowly to look over her shoulder. 'What the hell is going on?'

'Would it help if I started right back at the beginning?'

Jenkins took a deep breath and let it out slowly. 'I think you'd better.'

Doyle put her window down. 'It was for Father Quinn's murder they got her. But there were plenty who said she was just as guilty of her mother's death.'

Jenkins groaned. 'Just when I thought it couldn't get any worse. I've been shacked up with a mass murderer. Professional Standards are going to throw the sodding book at me.'

'It does get worse, I'm afraid,' Doyle said with a dry cough. 'A neighbour called the guards when he found Belle wandering the garden covered in blood and gibbering incoherently.'

'Where are we time-wise?' Jenkins asked. 'I'm trying to keep up.'

'She'd have been about eighteen at the time. When the guards entered the house, the mother was sitting in an armchair downstairs, her wrists slit and already dead.'

'Oh, my God.' Jenkins put a hand to her mouth, a wave of cold nausea washing over her.

'And that brings us to the old priest. Belle had hanged him from an overhead beam on the stairs. Castrated, with his you-know-what resting in the mother's lap.'

Jenkins vomited onto the greying tarmac and raised her feet out of the way of it.

'I didn't have you down as the squeamish type.' Doyle handed her a tissue from her bag.

Jenkins took a moment to wipe her mouth and blow her nose. 'It's the shock of realising what I was into without knowing.'

'It all came out in court. The poor girl had endured a lifetime's abuse from the priest, with the mother doing precious little to stop it. Belle's defence lawyers argued that the impulse to return home and kill them was likely triggered by the trauma of the rape in Cardiff, as well as the emergency hysterectomy.'

'*My* Amy, or Belle, or whoever the hell she is, has an abdominal wound. But the surgery was for ovarian cancer. She lost her hair after repeated cycles of chemotherapy.'

'Belle didn't have cancer,' Doyle said. 'The hysterectomy was to stop internal bleeding caused during the rape.'

Jenkins threw up again. 'Can we walk?' she asked when able. There was a lot for her to take in.

'Belle was bound for London. Had it in her head that she'd become a top performer in the West End.' Doyle smiled at the memory. 'She could sing, you know? Did a great Cilla Black.'

Jenkins knew that to be true. And Celine and Whitney to keep Cilla company. Even a bit of Pink after a few too many glasses of chianti.

'She took it a step too far, though,' Doyle said. 'Insisted on speaking like Cilla for the last eighteen months she was here. Even wore redhead wigs.'

The patrol car officers had been adamant the woman they'd spoken to outside the factory was from the Merseyside area. Jenkins watched a crisp packet somersault its way towards them. She bent and picked it up. 'It's something I do,' she said, looking for a bin to put it in. 'What about London?'

'She got nowhere close. The rape put paid to all her hopes and dreams.' Doyle swept her arm towards the building. 'She ended up here instead of the Lyceum.'

'And her death?' Jenkins still couldn't square that one in her head.

'Belle kept her nose clean while inside. Attended therapy and earned herself privileges in the process. Then, with more than fifteen years on the clock—and thought to pose no danger to anyone else—she and two other inmates were taken out on a day-trip.'

Jenkins lowered herself onto a park-style bench. 'No prizes for guessing where this is going.'

Doyle nodded. 'Only two of them returned. One minute Belle was there, and the next, she was gone.'

'Gone. How?'

'Witnesses on the beach claim to have seen her wade into the water fully clothed.'

'Did no one try to stop her?'

'It all happened too fast. And there was panic, obviously. The Coastguard came across her jacket a few days later.'

'And her body?'

'That was never found,' Doyle said. 'Still feeding the fish somewhere in the Celtic Sea is my best guess.'

Chapter 72

REECE HAD THE TEAM huddled near the evidence board in the briefing room. 'Is Jenkins here yet?' He checked, but couldn't see her anywhere.

Morgan waved enthusiastically. 'Welcome back, boss.' She blushed and moved quickly on when Adams glowered at her. 'Elan's not answering her mobile.'

'What about the land line?' Reece asked.

'Tried that twice already.'

It wasn't like her to go silent. 'I'll pop round there in the morning,' he said, wondering if she might be having more problems with Amy.

'You're not worried something's happened to her?' Chief Superintendent Cable was seated in the front row. 'The last thing I need now is an officer-gone-missing situation.'

'She's probably too embarrassed to show her face,' Adams said. 'And rightfully so.'

'I'm happy to send a car if you think there's a need?' Cable looked to Reece for an answer.

'That won't be necessary, ma'am.' He pointed to a photograph on the board and directed his question at Sioned Williams, crime scene manager: 'Anything yet on my factory find?' Behind the loose bricks on the balcony was a rolled-up shopping bag that Jenkins's mystery woman had been carrying in the CCTV footage. She must have made a hurried attempt at hiding it when disturbed during the act, initially thinking that Onion and Fishy were from a security company. With the arrival of police, she presumably hadn't been able to go back and retrieve it. Inside the bag was a black cloth wrap, complete with a limited set of surgical instruments smeared with dried blood.

'The blood was a match for Roxie May,' Williams said. 'No prints on the instruments, unfortunately. The killer wore gloves I'd imagine.'

Reece looked disappointed. 'I was hoping for better news.'

'There is,' Williams said, making her way towards the evidence board. 'An identical cloth wrap was found at Eryl Gough's crime scene. The killer made off in a hurry and left it there when Ginge gained forced access.'

'Can we trace them to a particular hospital or clinic?' Reece asked hopefully.

'Unfortunately not. You can buy sets of surgical instruments on eBay these days.'

'You're kidding me?'

'I only wish I was. Most are shipped to the UK from Pakistan. You need a medical licence to use them, obviously, but they're easy enough for the general public to get their hands on.'

'Brilliant. So, any Tom, Dick, or Harry could be responsible for this?'

'Probably not,' Williams said. 'The types you find on the auction sites are non-branded versions. The ones used by our killer were manufactured by a German company called Shultz. They specialise in mini-kits.'

'So they'd have proper records, right?' Reece asked. 'Orders with invoices?'

'We're already on it,' Morgan said. 'But they're not the quickest to reply.'

'You told them we're investigating a series of murders here?'

'I did, boss.'

'Let me know as soon as you hear anything.' He scratched his head. 'And these coins – all minted in nineteen-ninety. What's that about?'

'The killer's leaving us clues?' Morgan suggested. 'Jenks says they do that sometimes. Gives them a buzz thinking they've got the upper hand.'

'Stringing us along is what she's doing,' Adams said authoritatively. 'Leaving a smokescreen to get us chasing our tails.'

'It certainly worked in your case.' Reece stared until Adams looked away. He asked Morgan to check the HOLMES 2 database, cross referencing the date on the coins with any attacks on women resulting in missing body parts, or artefacts left near or on the deceased.'

'Any objection to me adding Billy Creed's name to the search criteria?' she asked.

Adams turned away. 'Will it never end?'

'It's just a hunch at the minute,' Morgan said. 'I'll need Ginge to give me a hand. He's a wiz with computers, apparently.'

Cable stood. 'You're not going anywhere near Creed. Not with an allegation of harassment still hanging over you.'

Reece stood with his hands on his hips. 'Tell his lawyer he can go and take a—'

'Two of the victims had injuries consistent with being hit by a Taser device,' Sioned Williams said, playing peace envoy. 'Thorne's body was badly decomposed, but it did have marks that might once have been similar in appearance.'

'A Taser?' Reece looked dumbfounded. 'Don't tell me you can pick up one of those on eBay as well?'

'No. I've checked.'

Cable almost buckled. 'Someone tell me it didn't come from an officer working at this station?'

'The dark web, ma'am.' Ward nodded slowly. He smacked his lips. 'You can find yourself just about anything on that.'

Chapter 73

'You got here before me.' Reece shut the car door and crossed the road in a jog to beat the minibus coming round the bend towards him.

Morgan was sitting on a dwarf wall in front of Jenkins's house, fiddling with her phone. 'Elan's still not answering.' She waved the handset at him, stood and brushed grit off her trousers. 'This really isn't like her.'

Reece stepped onto the pavement and checked the bedroom windows. The curtains were open. 'Did you ever meet this Amy character?'

'Just the once, and then only from across the road where you're parked now. She's a bit stand-offish if you ask me. Wouldn't come out any further than the doorway.'

The garden gate was in urgent need of a repaint. New hinges wouldn't have gone amiss. Reece pushed on it, making it squeak, and started up a short path of black-and-white tiles. He went to the front door and tapped on a frosted glass panel, called Jenkins's name through a tarnished brass letterbox, and knocked again when she didn't answer. 'Have you given the place a proper once over yet?'

'I thought I'd wait for you to get here.' Morgan peered through the front window. 'There's nothing out of place that I can see.' They both came away and looked in opposite directions - at neighbouring houses and the general locale. 'What about trying round the back?' she asked.

'Who are you?' The stranger stood with his head and shoulders poking over the top of a featherboard fence.

'Police.' Reece showed his warrant card. 'And yourself?'

'I live here.' The neighbour inhaled on a multi-coloured vape stick and disappeared behind a cloud of rising aerosol. 'You looking for that pair?'

Reece stood on an upturned bucket and clung to the splintered fence like his life depended on it. 'Have you seen either of them these last few days?'

'Hear, not see. All they've done is argue and scream blue murder lately.' The neighbour went to take another drag on his vape-stick, stopping before it reached his mouth. He lowered his hand. 'Is one of them dead in there?'

'Who's dead?' A woman appeared in the vaper's back doorway; all vest-top and tattoos.

'The missus,' he told Reece. 'It's the police, love. Come to sort out that pair next door.'

'When did you last see either of them?' Reece asked.

The woman folded a pair of flabby arms and made her way across a cracked patio wearing pink fluffy slippers and bulging leggings. 'Not since New Year's Eve.' She glanced at her husband. 'Must have been two or three days ago.'

'Aye, that'll be about right.'

'Boss, you should see this.'

'Don't go anywhere,' Reece told the pair and got off the bucket with an awkward wobble.

Morgan was leaning with her forehead pressed against the kitchen window. She pointed inside and moved out of his way. 'Over in the corner. There.'

Reece used a hand to shield the glass from a brief appearance of sunshine and peered inside. 'You two still there?' A puff of vapour said they were. 'Fetch me something to get this door open.' It took the man less than five minutes, coming round the front way with a chisel from his shed. Reece forced the end of it between the uPVC door and its frame and heaved.

'That's a five-point lock,' the neighbour said, getting much too close for Reece's liking. 'You'll do well to shift it.'

Morgan put a hand on Reece's shoulder. 'You're breaking it, boss. Look, the thingy's warping.'

'I'm trying to do more than warp the sod. Get out of my way. Both of you.'

Morgan gave the neighbour a look of warning and moved him to one side. 'Why don't we smash the glass?' she asked.

'Because . . .' It wasn't such a bad idea. Reece got up and used the sleeve of his jacket to dry his forehead. 'Close your eyes,' he said only a millisecond before hurling the chisel through the window.

'Not like that!' Morgan stared in disbelief. 'Jenks will go apeshit when she sees what you've done.'

'You told me to do it,' he protested.

'I thought you'd give it a tap.'

'*Smash*, is what you said.'

'There's glass everywhere.'

'Not you,' Reece told the neighbour when he tried to follow them inside. 'I'll get someone over to take a full statement later.'

They made their way into the kitchen, broken glass plinking underfoot like plates of thin ice. Reece put a hand to the bowl of the coffee pot – cold. And pressed his toe against the lever of the pedal bin – empty.

Morgan leaned on a cabinet that had been pulled away from its corner position. Next to it, and resting on its end against the wall, was a leg-length section of varnished floorboard. 'What do you think was in there?'

Reece knelt and pushed his arm into the hole, up to the elbow. 'Rats?'

'Are you for real?' She tugged on his sleeve.

He got to his feet, gripping a piece of cloth in a clenched fist. He put it to his nose and sniffed. 'Rangoon oil.'

'What's that?'

'It stops guns rusting in storage and lubricates them at the same time.'

Morgan stared. Her forehead creased. 'Why would Jenks have a gun?'

'I hope this doesn't turn out to be what I think it is.' Reece sniffed the cloth for a second time.

'No.' Morgan shook her head. 'You can't think it's the missing firearm from the raid on the Midnight Club?'

'Bag it, and get it checked over.'

'Jenks would never be involved in anything like that. No way, boss.'

'I said bag it.'

Morgan completed the label with identifiers unique to her. 'I can't believe we're doing this. This is Jenks we're talking about.'

Chapter 74

'SHE'S INNOCENT UNTIL PROVEN otherwise,' Reece said, preoccupied with several superficial scuffs on the wood flooring. 'Someone moved this piece of furniture only recently.' He had no idea what was going on, and would have been a lot happier had Jenkins answered her phone and explained her actions and whereabouts.

Morgan followed him into the living room and trailed a hand along the back of the sofa. 'The tree's dropped its needles. No one's watered it in days.'

'It should have been taken down by now.'

'Not before the day after Epiphany. You're asking for bad luck if you do.'

Reece checked the date on his watch. 'The fourth is plenty close enough for me.'

'What exactly are we searching for?' Morgan asked. 'Apart from the gun, that is.'

'Anything that'll give us a clue to what's happened, or where they've gone. You start down here and I'll go upstairs.'

On reaching the landing, he called Jenkins's name. Amy's too. He pushed on the bathroom door and moved on when he found it empty. The first bedroom was little more than a box-room-cum-study. The second wasn't much bigger than the first. Leaving only the master to try. It was untidy and smelled of pot-pourri and a mix of female scents. On one bedside table were two polystyrene heads, the nearest bare, the other draped with a long blonde wig. Next to those was a metal case - its lid left open and positioned to reveal something written on the underside in red lipstick. He took the case in both hands and angled it to get a better look.

You're almost there!

He had no way of knowing what that meant and emptied the contents of the case onto the duvet. In the diary were scribblings of dark clouds and tall grass; the hangman's noose; and the bleeding cross.

When he read Belle Gillighan's name, his fingers lost their grip, the diary falling next to a sheet of folded paper. He spread it open with trembling hands, revealing a short list of initials: ***LB, RM, SI.***

And a final one circled in a thicker ink: ***TM.*** 'Tattooed Man,' he said aloud.

During the initial police investigation, Belle Gillighan had refused to speak of Creed by name, referring to him only by the appearance of his skin. Her method of coping had been to make the gangster less of a real person.

'Did you say something?' Morgan waited in the bedroom doorway.

He hadn't heard her climb the stairs and cross the landing. He didn't look up and sat with the list held in his lap. 'Give me a minute.'

She handed him a photo frame: 'I thought this might be useful.'

Reece took it and couldn't believe what he was seeing.

'Incident Room. Detective Constable Ken Ward speaking.'

'Ken, the landline's rubbish. Listen, I've just landed in Cardiff and needed to speak with someone I knew I could trust.'

'Hey, where have you been?' His manner was annoyingly jovial. 'I've been worried about you.'

'I know who the killer is. There isn't time for me to explain the ins and outs,' she said when he asked for more detail. 'Just get yourself and backup over to the Midnight Club, pronto. I'll tell you more when we get there.'

When the line went dead, Ward dialled a number he'd committed to memory. 'Where are you?'

'Nice try.' The voice was female. Her accent broad Scouse. 'Not thinking of turning me in, are you?'

'You need to move,' he said with a nervous glance over his shoulder. 'Time's running out.' He told Belle what little Jenkins had given him.

'How long do I have?'

'An hour. Maybe less.'

'I need more.'

Ward gripped the handset and swore. 'And the week I already gave you wasn't enough?'

Chapter 75

REECE TOSSED HIS JACKET over the back of a chair. 'Round up the troops for a briefing. That includes the chief super.'

Morgan followed him into the incident room, waving the photo frame of Belle Gilligan like a flag of celebration. 'We've got our killer. Where's Ken?' she asked, seeing he wasn't at his desk.

One of the other detectives answered. 'He went out a short while ago. Didn't say where he was going.'

'What time's the next race?' someone else said. 'You won't set eyes on him again until that's over.'

Reece got Ginge's attention by clicking his fingers. 'I want you to dig up everything you can on Belle Gilligan. Where she went and what she's been doing in the years following her return to Ireland.'

'We know she's been working as a sales representative for Schultz Medical Supplies,' Morgan said. 'Under an alias, obviously. The company just confirmed that. I can't believe I didn't put two and two together and say something when we came across those instrument wraps. Jenks told me months ago what Amy did for a living. I just don't remember her mentioning the company's name.'

'Don't beat yourself up,' Reece said. 'We know now.'

'Chief super's on her way,' someone called from the back of the room. 'She says you're not to start without her.'

Cable didn't miss a second of it. Although she probably wished she had. 'A serial killer shacked up with one of the lead detectives on the case.' She found somewhere to sit down and groaned. 'What's Maggie Kavanagh going to print when she hears that?'

'I don't give a flying—' Reece stopped himself in time. He prowled; his hackles raised. 'Jenkins could be dead for all we know.'

'I doubt it,' Adams said. 'She and the Gillighan woman are in this together. You mark my words.'

'What makes you say that?' Cable's voice was raised a good octave higher than its usual pitch. 'Richard?'

Adams called a uniform from where she was waiting on the other side of the room and handed the fax to the chief super after reading it himself. 'Jenkins went through passport control not more than an hour ago.'

'On the run?' Cable asked.

'She flew into the UK. Not out of it, ma'am.' Adams turned to Reece. 'Didn't you say Ireland was home to our killer?'

'Coincidence. Nothing more.'

'I thought there was no such thing in your book? That's what you keep telling your team.'

Cable got to her feet. 'I have to act, Brân. We can't take any more risks. Not with three women already dead.' To Adams, she said: 'I want an *all persons* put out on them both. Get their faces on every news outlet you can, and make damn sure the public are warned to go nowhere near them.'

Reece closed his eyes. 'Tell me this is another wind up.'

'Boss.' Ginge was standing out of sight of the others, a sheet of paper rolled like a baton in his hand.

'What are you doing back?' Reece asked. 'You can't have finished already.'

Ginge waited for Morgan to join them. 'I did something else first.' He didn't look at Reece. 'You're going to like this,' he said excitedly. 'I've been on to the mobile phone companies using DS Jenkins's address and personal details. The phone registered to her is in Dublin and hasn't been used in two days. But there's a second device registered to the same property in Rhiwbina—in the name of Amy Hosty—and that got a call from a mobile in this building about forty-five minutes ago.'

Reece stared at Ken Ward's empty seat. 'No prizes for guessing who made it.'

Chapter 76

JENKINS SPED THROUGH THE Cardiff traffic, the Principality Stadium whizzing by on her right-hand side, the castle coming up fast on her left. Braking hard for a red light, she reached into the glove box for the radio left there when she and Adams had gone to see Billy Creed. The battery indicator suggested it wouldn't be of much use for long. Enough to check that help was on its way was all she needed.

Fine-tuning the frequency one-handed, she earned herself a middle finger from a cyclist in a camouflage jacket, and a loud blast from an angry coach driver when she swerved to a halt in the castle lay-by. 'You're kidding me?' She couldn't believe what she was hearing and sat listening to the rest of the transmission in utter disbelief.

'What the hell did you tell them, Ken?' And now there were several reported sightings of her red Fiat 500 travelling city-bound on Castle Road. That wasn't too much of a surprise. Not with Cardiff having over a thousand CCTV cameras in operation the last time she'd enquired.

Sitting tight and trying to explain where she'd been for the past few days, and why, wasn't a realistic option, she quickly decided. Belle would surely know by now that she was on to her. And by the time she'd get done arguing the toss with Adams back at the station, Billy Creed would already be dead.

She got out of the idling car, her grip on reality fading fast. 'This isn't happening to me. It's a bad dream, that's all.' The wailing of an approaching siren was ample evidence of it being no dream. A pedestrian flagged down the patrol car and pointed towards the woman who'd almost run over the cyclist. For a moment Jenkins thought she recognised the driver. Then, when he raised his head, she remembered recently kicking his arse in the staff canteen. She crossed the road in a slow jog, quickening her pace when Beard did the same.

Elan Jenkins was on the run. An accessory to murder.

Ken Ward turned his newly cut key in the lock of the side door and made his way into the Midnight Club. There was no blinking red dot on the domed camera. No click or beep. The security system was still not fixed. A few overhead strip lights did their best to illuminate the space. The cleaning lady looked up from her mop and bucket, saw who it was, and went back to pushing and pulling a soapy puddle without challenging him.

Ward knew he'd have to find some way of preoccupying Billy Creed and Denny Cartwright. He couldn't have Belle walking straight into their clutches, even though she'd be armed better than most inner-city riot squads. His phone vibrated against his thigh for the third or fourth time. The caller: Ffion Morgan. He let it ring off unanswered. It had been foolish of him to use his own phone for his dodgy dealings—he should have got himself a burner instead—but if everything went to plan, there'd be no reason for anyone to ever find out.

He dialled Cartwright's number. 'Denny, I'm on the ground floor. Where are you?'

'How did you get in?' The doorman's gruff reply was unwelcoming, to say the least.

'The cleaner was round the side emptying her bucket.' Ward let it hang there. He was nervous and didn't risk his explanation sounding too contrived. 'I need to see Billy right away.'

There was a delay on the line. Then: 'He already told you he isn't worried about that Irish piece.'

Ward gritted his teeth and tried to calm himself. 'If he's there, he'll want to hear this.'

The line went dead. Ward heard someone rattling empties behind the bar and recognised the heavily made-up face on the other side of a half-shut metal grille. 'Chantelle, what are you doing here?'

The bubble burst on a pair of plump red lips. 'Mr Creed's been giving me a few shifts, cash in hand. And you?'

Ward knew Creed had likely given the curvy blonde a damn sight more than that. 'Police business,' he said, tapping his nose.

'You're bullshitting me. I *knows* you are,' she said, reverting to local dialect.

'Have you seen Billy?'

Chantelle stared at him. Chew, chew, chew. Bubble. Pop. Chew, chew, chew.

Ward forced his head beneath the grille, his friendly smile now gone. 'Where's Billy?'

'How the fuck am I supposed to know? You tried his office yet?'

'He's not there.'

'I'll call Denny,' she said, strutting towards the phone at the other end of the bar. Ward let her get all the way there, his eyes glued to a pair of legs that were as good as any he'd previously seen.

'Leave it,' he said when she reached for the receiver. 'I'll go check downstairs.'

Chantelle came back and rested her ample cleavage on the edge of the bar. 'You'll get a right good kicking if he catches you snooping about down there.'

Ward winked. 'Don't forget what I told you the other day. My luck's about to change for the better.'

Chapter 77

JENKINS SPRINTED DOWN HIGH Street; a mostly pedestrianised area that put her on a level pegging with her pursuers. She pushed through a crowd of people stood talking outside the Goat Major pub, whacking her knee on a steel bollard and almost falling over. Someone reached to steady her, pulling away again when she slapped their outstretched hand.

There were sirens everywhere.

All getting louder.

The bearded uniform who'd followed from the castle lay-by was nowhere to be seen. Two other uniforms were heading in her direction. A third exited the doorway of a shopfront over to her left.

She cut down a narrower street on the right-hand side of the road, not daring to take her eyes off what might be in front of her. The police helicopter lurked somewhere behind the city skyline, systematically following the track of all reported sightings of her. She'd asked for backup, not bullshit. This fiasco had DI Adams's name written all over it. But Adams couldn't possibly know where she was headed. She had that over him for the time being.

She stopped to catch her breath in what was little more than a hole in the wall when the helicopter made another pass overhead. When it was gone, she made a break for it, hurtling to the other side of the alleyway to push on the door of the Midnight Club. It was ajar, a cleaner's bucket waiting next to the drain cover. That couldn't have gone any better.

But what should she do now that she'd arrived? Warn Creed about Belle Gillighan, of course. Then sit it out and wait for backup. After that she'd have to wait and see. A sudden movement startled her. 'Ken. Thank God. Where's everyone else?' She nodded towards the door. 'And what the hell's going on out there?'

He looked edgy. 'Just the troops arriving.'

She retreated a step when he came closer, not knowing why. 'I asked you what's going on?'

'Well, lookey-lookey.' Creed came through a doorway in the far wall, Denny Cartwright lumbering close behind. 'This ain't Belle Gillighan.' The gangster's eyes narrowed. 'Not trying to set me up, are you, Copper?'

Jenkins shifted. 'Ken, what have you done? How did you know about Belle?'

He silenced her with a backhand across the face. 'The stupid bitch must have scared Gillighan off just as I was closing in on her.'

Creed scowled. 'She got away?'

'For the time being,' Ward lied.

The gangster clenched his fists. 'And I was looking forward to saying hello.'

Jenkins put a hand to her hot cheek. 'Ken—?'

'Shut it!' He shoved her to her knees with his hand raised in warning. 'We've got to kill her, Billy. She knows way too much about what's been going on here.'

Creed laughed. 'And they say there's no honour among thieves.'

Ward took a length of wire ligature from his pocket and dangled it in front of Denny Cartwright. 'You or me?'

Chapter 78

Belle Gillighan stood with a foot planted on either side of the writhing blonde. 'Where's the tattooed man?'

Chantelle lay in a puddle of pink gin, shards of broken glass nibbling at the bare skin of her legs and buttocks. She stretched every objecting muscle in her body, her eyes fixed on the blue and yellow Taser device held in her attacker's hand. 'What is that thing?' she asked when able.

Belle's hand came up and aimed. 'Don't make me kill you.'

The barmaid used a shaky arm to point in the general direction of the stairs leading to the basement. 'There's other people down there with him.'

'Who, and how many?'

Chantelle spat the bubble gum to one side and shifted position, crying out as the broken glass took another bite of her. 'His doorman, Denny Cartwright.'

'And?'

'Coppers. Kenny and a mixed race woman I've not seen before.'

Belle grabbed a handful of her short black wig and hurled it at the wall opposite. It caught on a row of optics and hung there like an intoxicated cat. 'Damn you, Elan. You weren't supposed to be here yet. Not until it was over.'

'*You'll have to kill her*,' said her secret friend. '*I warned you might*.'

Belle clawed at her bare scalp. 'Not Elan. I can't.'

'*You must*.'

'No!' She stamped her foot.

Chantelle squirmed on the wet tiles. 'I told you everything I know.'

'Give me your phone.' Belle tossed the blinged up handset onto the floor and pressed her heel against the screen until it shattered.

'I'm on contract. *Shit!*' Chantelle was still complaining when a second bolt of electricity hit her.

A woman screamed downstairs, the shrill echoes stirring memories that had been locked away for so long.

A door slammed.

Men shouted.

This was it. Her time had come. Gun in hand, Belle headed for the steps and her final meeting with the tattooed man.

Chapter 79

Reece, Morgan and Ginge arrived at the Midnight Club without the use of sirens. They'd left the station via the back door, Reece choosing not to wait for the chief super and her entourage. 'Here goes.'

'You're not going in there,' Morgan said when he got out of the car. 'Not until armed backup arrives.'

Ginge squeezed his head through the gap between the two front seats. 'And we're supposed to have done a safety brief by now, boss.'

Reece glared at the young uniform. 'Fuck off, Ginge. This is the real world.'

'He's right,' Morgan shouted after him. 'We should have done it on the way over.'

There were police officers stringing lengths of blue and white tape wherever they could, and cars with flashing lights blocking all exits. A couple of ambulances were squeezed into the alleyway, and behind those, the first of the reporters were setting up their stalls. A uniform approached Reece.

'There are five people inside, sir. Possibly one more.'

Reece pointed to an older woman talking to a female officer. 'Who's she?'

'The cleaner from the club, sir. She left when it got ugly in there.'

'So why are you lot still out here?'

'We've been given orders to hold off and wait for armed backup.'

Authorised Firearms Officers – AFOs. Reece had heard as much over the radio. 'More guns is all we need.' He thanked the uniform and went over to speak with the cleaner. 'What's your name?'

'Beata. Beata Domanski.' The woman looked worried. 'I legal this country,' she said almost immediately.

'Not my department,' Reece told her. 'What's happening in there?'

'Fighting.' Domanski ducked with her hands pressed to the sides of her head when a single gunshot rang out from deep within the building.

Reece ducked with her. It seemed a reasonable enough thing to do. 'I want the key to that door,' he said, straightening.

'Not locked. I leave open,' the woman said.

He was on his way, flashing his warrant card and running towards the side entrance of the club.

'No, boss,' Morgan shouted after him. 'You promised, you stubborn sod.'

He took no notice and slammed the door to the Midnight Club behind him.

Denny Cartwright slumped against the bars of the cage, a bright red stain spreading across his broad chest. Before he died, he looked from Belle Gillighan, to the gun in her hand, to Billy Creed, and then back again.

Jenkins fell onto her face, gasping for breath as she clawed the ligature free of her neck. Her brain flooded with oxygen-rich blood, abstract smudges of colour morphing slowly into people she knew. She coughed and spat, and by using the bars for support, got up onto her knees. When Belle pointed the smoking weapon at her, she dropped onto her buttocks and doubted she'd hear the noise of the discharge before the bullet struck and shattered her skull.

'Shoot her.' Ward edged away from Creed's side. 'Shoot both of them.'

'What is this?' Creed asked.

Ward grinned. 'You know how it is, Billy. It's just business.'

'You fat fuck!' When Creed lunged, his right kneecap exploded in a shower of blood and bits of bone, the deafening blast of the gunshot bouncing off all four walls of the Games Room.

Chief Superintendent Cable's black Jag screeched to a halt almost twenty metres away from the entrance to the Midnight Club.

Adams was out of the car before her. He approached Morgan. 'What the hell do you think you were doing leaving the station without us? And where's Ward?'

She leaned against her pool car. 'We were acting on orders given by a senior officer.'

'Reece?'

'Yes, sir.'

Cable rounded the Jag and joined them. 'Where's the DCI now?'

'Inside ma'am.'

The chief super surveyed the cluster of buildings, her attention settling on the closed door of the Midnight Club. 'If this becomes a hostage situation . . .' She shook her head and didn't finish. 'Could neither of you stop him before he went in there?'

Morgan looked away. 'DCI Reece isn't the listening type, ma'am.'

Cable removed her service hat, and with a deep sigh lay her leather gloves inside. 'And don't I bloody-well know it.'

Chapter 80

Reece had been helping a groggy Chantelle to her feet when the second shot sounded from the basement. He sent her on her way, tottering towards the exit wearing a single high-heeled shoe. She pushed on the handle and left the door ajar when she disappeared from sight.

Reece made for the stairs, descending at a fast pace, his nose picking up on the pungent scents of patchouli oil and cordite. When he entered the Games Room, no one looked more surprised to see him than Belle Gilligan.

She raised the gun but didn't point it in his direction with any genuine conviction. 'Stay where you are. I've no reason to harm you.'

He squatted in front of Cartwright and put a finger to the side of the big man's neck. 'I don't remember seeing Denny's initials on your list of targets.'

Belle shifted position. 'He was hurting Elan.'

'You okay, Jenks?' There were red-raw lines on the skin of her neck. One end of the ligature was still gripped in the dead man's hand.

'I've had better days, boss.' She sounded hoarse.

Reece regarded Ward with a look of utter contempt. 'Billy not paying you enough to keep your little partnership going?'

'It was nothing like that.'

'Save it for the judge and jury.'

Creed was hunched on the floor, using a leather belt as a tourniquet to stem the flow of blood from a missing knee. 'You won't last a day inside,' he growled at Ward.

'It won't come to that. Belle and me have plans of our own.' Ward nudged her. 'Get on with it. We're running out of time.'

She turned the gun on him. 'You hurt my Elan.'

'*Your* Elan?'

Jenkins rubbed her neck and winced when she swallowed. 'Ken, meet Amy. Amy, meet Ken.'

'Need me to spell it out for you?' Reece asked when Ward failed to respond. 'I've had my eye on you for a couple of months. How could you ever have thought you'd get away with it?'

There was loud footfall trouping along the dance floor above them. Lots of it. 'Armed police!' someone shouted. 'Put down your weapons,' was the clear command.

Reece kept his eyes on Ward. 'In my experience, it's best not to piss this lot off.'

Belle came towards Jenkins. 'There's something I need to explain. You have a right to know what this was about.'

A door opened not far away, followed by the sound of boots descending steps at speed.

Belle spoke of the rape and the three older women who had refused to support her by giving evidence against Billy Creed. 'They told lies about me,' she said, wiping tears from her cheeks. 'Told the police I was a whore like my mother. For that reason, they had to die.'

'Shove it.' Jenkins raised a hand. 'I don't want to hear any more of your lies.'

'I left those clues for you to find. The diary. Drawings. Even Niamh MacBride's contact details. You were meant to work this out. A just reward for all the deceit and hurt I caused you.' Belle clawed at her bald head, drawing blood, and stamped a foot in temper. 'But you were supposed to be here alone.' Another stamp of the foot. 'I'd get to kill the tattooed man. You'd take me in and be hailed as the true heroine you are.'

Jenkins was crying. 'I was a pawn in a game? A plaything.'

'Only in the beginning.' Belle reached her free hand. 'I grew to love you, Elan. I still love you.'

Ward took his chance and lunged at Belle, snatching the gun from her hand and knocking her towards Creed in one swift move. 'Get over here,' he told Jenkins, as a pair of AFOs burst into the room. He pulled her against him, using her as a human shield.

'It's over,' Reece said. 'Whatever happens next, you're coming out of this smelling of shit.'

'Take the shot.' Jenkins struggled in Ward's grip, trying to give the AFOs a clear target.

'Shut it.' Ward was panicking, his movements more erratic as two red beads of light from the AFO's gunsights danced on his upper chest. 'Move,' he screamed at Belle, and swung the handgun in Creed's direction.

Reece leapt, knocking Belle and Jenkins away from the line of fire as three loud shots rang out in quick succession. Ward jerked and fell, his head slamming against the hard floor with a sickening crack.

Jenkins grabbed for the spilled gun when Belle came for it. 'Back off or I'll—'

'Put the gun down and lie on your front with your hands behind your head,' the nearest AFO told her.

'I'm a police officer.'

The AFO repeated his order, this time with added authority. 'You too,' he told Belle.

From her position low on the floor, Jenkins saw Reece lying in a puddle of blood. At first she thought it was coming from Billy Creed's knee. 'Get a paramedic in here,' she called when it became obvious it was the DCI's.

They brought Reece out first. Flanked by a team of AFOs dressed in black body armour and visored helmets. A medic squeezed on a bag of fluid connected to a drip in the back of Reece's hand, another hand-ventilating him through a tube placed in his windpipe.

'You're going to be okay,' Jenkins kept saying. She was running alongside the stretcher.

Morgan sprinted towards them. 'Don't you die on us. Don't you bloody dare!'

Belle came next, head down and handcuffed. She looked across to Jenkins and mouthed the word 'sorry.' She got no reply for her efforts.

'What did they say?' ACC Harris asked when Cable was back from speaking with the medical team.

'They're going to airlift him. The bullet is still lodged somewhere inside his chest.'

Chapter 81

THERE WASN'T A SAFE enough spot for the regional air ambulance to land on the city street. By the time they'd have transported Reece to its holding position in a nearby field, precious time would have been lost. And so he was taken the short distance to hospital by road.

'Carefully,' someone said as they pulled up outside the busy Emergency Department. 'We don't know where that bullet is lodged.'

They took him through a doorway into the main hospital building. Corridors were negotiated at speed. People getting out of the way by pressing themselves against the walls. In *Resus*, they worked on him with all the efficiency of a Formula-1 pit-stop team; every member knowing exactly what they had to do. There were x-rays.

More x-rays. Scans and trauma surveys checking for impending threats to life.

Reece had a deflated left lung, which pressed against his heart, lowering his blood pressure to dangerous levels. 'I did a needle thoracocentesis,' said the accompanying doctor. 'He was tensioning.' Meaning the medic had inserted a small cannula between the upper ribs at the front of the chest, allowing air to escape and the lung to re-expand.

But that was a temporary measure only. The cannula would now be swapped for a more substantial underwater-seal chest drain before it became useless and Reece's condition deteriorated further. The *Major Haemorrhage Protocol* had already been initiated, portering staff racing through the hospital with boxes of stored blood and other clotting products. A brief phone call upstairs confirmed that the cardiothoracic operating theatre and a new team of experts were ready for receipt of their VIP.

Reece was on his way and fighting for his life.

They were blue-lighted across the city in high-performance pursuit cars, Jenkins refusing to get her own injuries looked at beforehand. 'If he dies because of some fuck-up of mine.' She slammed her hand against the seat.

He won't.' Ginge said. 'The boss is as hard as nails.'

'There's a bullet in his chest. It doesn't matter how tough he is.'

'He's in good hands,' Morgan said, putting an arm around Jenkins's shoulder. 'They got to him straight away.'

'That's got to make a difference.' Ginge again.

'It does. It will.' Morgan attempted a smile. 'You know the boss can't do a thing without making a fuss.' She broke down, clinging to Jenkins for comfort.

The pursuit car dropped them off at the back of the hospital. They took the lifts once inside the building, wishing almost immediately they hadn't. When they got out on the third floor, they were wondering what to do now they'd arrived.

'Are you colleagues of the police officer in theatre?' Behind them was a staff nurse waiting next to a set of swing doors marked Cardiac Intensive Care.

'Is he alive?' was Jenkins's first question. She was breathing hard even though they hadn't used the stairs.

'They've started the operation,' the staff nurse explained. 'We won't know any more until he's on his way out to us.'

'But he got here alive?'

'Yes.'

'There you go,' Ginge said. 'I told you. Indestructible.'

The staff nurse held the door open. 'You're welcome to come in and wait, but I'd imagine it's going to take a while.'

'Is there somewhere we can go to get a coffee?' Jenkins asked.

The nurse let go of the door and came closer. 'That neck needs seeing to,' she said, reaching towards it. 'Come on, I'll get someone to rustle up some tea and toast while I give it a clean.'

The police officers followed like children.

Chapter 82

IT WAS NEARLY FOUR hours later when they were let in to see him. Two at a time.

'I'm scared,' Morgan said. 'These places give me the creeps.'

Jenkins took her by the hand. 'It beats the mortuary any day of the week.'

'You're not wrong there.'

The unit was busy. All beds occupied on both sides of a large rectangular room. Several patients were connected to breathing machines via tubes in their airways. Most had tubes going just about everywhere. The noise was almost as bad as the sight of it: a cacophony of alarms, beeps, and clicking sounds bombarding them from all directions. A radio was playing music. Another close by was tuned to a different channel.

They were led to the far end of the unit, to a solitary cubicle, where a white-haired doctor sat on a high chair reading through observation charts and blood test results. There was a small team of other people with him, all with stethoscopes draped round their necks. The consultant got up and introduced himself as John. He was Irish, jovial, and doing his best to put them at ease.

'It isn't as bad as we initially thought,' he said before they could ask. 'The bullet deflected off a rib, collapsed the underlying lung and got lodged in the joint of the shoulder, just here.' He spun one of his juniors without warning, poking them in the back to demonstrate.

'Is he okay?' Morgan asked, nervously peering through the cubicle door.

'He lost a lot of blood at the scene, and there's always the risk of infection and other complications. But all being well, we'll wake him in a couple of hours and see how he does.'

'He's on a breathing machine.' Morgan gripped Jenkins's arm so tightly that she pulled away and gave it a rub.

'Only temporarily,' the consultant said. 'Would you like to go in and see him?'

They next saw Reece the following day. He was sitting in a chair alongside his bed, wearing an ill-fitting patient gown and a complexion to match the grey sky outside. There was a physiotherapist knelt in front of him, going through breathing exercises, asking the nursing staff if more painkillers were due.

'We've renamed you Lazarus,' Jenkins said from her position in the open doorway. She had a bottle of Lucozade and a punnet of strawberries with her. 'There's a card coming once everyone's had a chance to sign it.'

Reece groaned as he caught his breath. 'It's these things,' he said, tapping a pair of tubes disappearing into his upper and lower chest. 'It's like being run through with a pitchfork.'

Jenkins followed the course of the tubes back to a pair of containers that were half-full of blood. 'Looks painful.'

Reece shifted position with what sounded like a battle cry. 'And my sodding arse is killing me.'

'Too much information.'

'It's this chair.' He moved again. 'How is everyone? From the club, I mean.'

Jenkins explained that the AFOs had shot Ken Ward dead. Reece hadn't remembered. He wouldn't lose sleep over it in any case. Billy Creed had lost most of his knee according to initial reports. That brought a smile to Reece's face, regardless of the pain he was in.

'What happened to Belle?' he asked, wetting his mouth with some water. His hand was shaking, and it took a great deal of effort to lift it.

'She survived and was arrested.' Jenkins lowered her head. 'It'll be prison or a secure hospital for her now.'

'Whichever it turns out to be, she'll never be able to hurt you again.'

'True. But it'll all get raked up in court and that won't be pleasant.'

Reece raised an arm and groaned. 'I'd forgotten about your neck. It looks sore.'

Jenkins put a hand to the purple crease in the skin. 'I got off lightly.'

'Me too, all things considered.'

Chapter 83

TWO MONTHS HAD PASSED since the shooting at the Midnight Club.

Reece stood out of harm's way and let the lorry come to a full stop with a squeal of its front axle and a hiss of its air brakes. When the driver dropped from the bright red cab, Reece went round to the other side to meet him, tapping his watch and making a point. 'What time do you call this?'

His friend Yanto wagged a finger in warning. 'Don't you start on me, Brân. I'm having a bastard of a day.'

Reece fell about laughing. 'What's happened now?'

'Sheep.' Yanto climbed onto the back of the low-loader and offered no further explanation.

'Sheep?'

'Aye, they don't listen to a fucking word I tell 'em.'

Reece gripped his aching shoulder. 'Don't. Please. You're killing me.'

'I'm glad one of us finds this funny.'

'You're spreading yourself too thin—running a farm and a builders' yard—something's got to give.'

Yanto rooted about under a blue tarpaulin. 'Without both on the go, I'd be bankrupt within a matter of months.' He caught hold of the first of four straps and fastened it to the nearest pallet of Welsh slate. 'Who's doing that roof?'

'Me.'

'*You!*' It was Yanto's turn to laugh. He doubled over, coughing.

'Go on. Take the piss,' Reece said. 'The new boiler's done, even with a hole in my shoulder.'

Yanto pointed to the roof. 'But it wasn't up there, was it? Scared shitless of heights you are.'

'Only because I got stuck halfway up a quarry as a kid.'

'Here we go. How many times are you gonna use that one as an excuse?'

'It's true. You were up there with me. Don't you remember?'

'How can I ever forget when you're always banging on about it.'

'It was your stupid idea in the first place.'

'Get over it. We were only ten at the time.' Yanto nodded at an aluminium urn resting on the back doorstep. 'That Idris, is it?'

'It used to be.' Reece gazed towards the mountains and the clouds rolling off them to gather in the valley below. He collected the urn and made it safe in his rucksack.

'You taking him up there with you?'

'It's the first decent day we've had in a long while.' Reece swung the bag over his good shoulder and was almost ready to leave. 'It's what he wanted ever since I lay Anwen to rest at the summit.'

Yanto jumped off the back of the lorry and wiped his dirty hands on the thighs of his jeans. 'How are you managing, Brân?'

Reece toed the gravel. 'One day at a time.'

'Hey, did you see the look on that vicar's face when Elvis walked in during the service?' Yanto said, filling the awkward silence. Reece played air guitar, the two of them descending into a loud chorus of *Return to Sender.*

Chief Superintendent Cable and Assistant Chief Constable Harris waited impatiently for Jenkins to finish the telephone call. They were sheltering beneath the front archway of the City Hall building, sidestepping dignitaries and guests filing inside for the presentation and dinner.

'*Um . . .*' Jenkins said once the call was over.

'What does that mean?' Cable asked. 'What did he have to say for himself?'

Jenkins did well not to fall about laughing. 'DCI Reece sends his apologies, ma'am. Says he can't make it today.'

Harris removed his hat and patted a Brylcreem'd comb-over. 'What did you say?'

'Just that, sir. DCI Reece says he's too busy to attend.'

For a moment, the ACC stood open-mouthed. Then, as disbelief turned to anger, he balled his fists and spoke through gritted teeth. 'This is for him. We've even got the Lord Mayor of Cardiff to present him with a bravery award.'

Cable nodded. 'And it's costing the Force a bloody fortune.'

'Find him and get him here,' Harris told her.

'Where is he?' Cable asked Jenkins. 'I'll drag him kicking and screaming if he gives me any of his bullshit.'

'I don't think you will, ma'am.'

Cable glared. 'You just watch me, Sergeant.'

'What I mean is - he's up a mountain.'

'What in God's name is he doing there?' Harris asked. 'Today of all days.'

'He said it was the first nice one we've had in a long while, sir.'

'For what exactly?' The ACC was practically apoplectic. '*This* was supposed to be a nice day.'

'For reuniting a father and daughter.' Jenkins excused herself and pushed through the crowd, making her way towards a car that sat idling not more than twenty metres away.

'You kept my number.' Cara Frost held open the passenger-side door. 'So, what happens next?'

Jenkins got in and fastened her seatbelt. 'Drive,' she said, closing her eyes. 'We'll take it from there.'

About the Author

Liam Hanson is the crime and thriller pen name of author Andy Roberts. Andy lives in a small rural village in South Wales and is married with two grown-up children. Now the proud owners of a camper van nicknamed 'Griff', Andy and his wife spend most days on the road, searching for new locations to walk Walter, their New Zealand Huntaway.

If you enjoy Andy's work and would like to support him, then please leave a review in the usual places.

To learn of new releases and special offers, you can sign up for his no-spam newsletter, found on his Facebook page: www.facebook.com/liamhansonauthor

Printed in Great Britain
by Amazon